I0891396

The Killer's Protégé

Center Point
Large Print

Also by Robert J. Horton and available from Center Point Large Print:

Rider of the Stars

The Killer's Protégé

Robert J. Horton

CENTER POINT LARGE PRINT
THORNDIKE, MAINE

This Center Point Large Print edition
is published in the year 2024 by arrangement with
Golden West Inc.

Copyright © 1928 by A. C. McClurg & Co.

All rights reserved.

First US edition: A. C. McClurg & Co.
First UK edition: Hodder and Stoughton

The text of this Large Print edition is unabridged.
In other aspects, this book may vary
from the original edition.
Printed in the United States of America
on permanent paper sourced using
environmentally responsible foresting methods.
Set in 16-point Times New Roman type.

ISBN 979-8-89164-209-6 (hardcover)
ISBN 979-8-89164-213-3 (paperback)

The Library of Congress has cataloged this record
under Library of Congress Control Number: 2024933837

TO MY FATHER

Chapter I

Courage

Everyone in Morning Glory knew that Sneed was in the camp before he had been there an hour. The news, as it filtered through the bustling mining town, was jubilantly received by ne'er-do-wells and parasites, and a certain class of miners, as well as by those who were unemployed, whether by choice or through circumstances beyond their control. For the adventurers who trailed with this man were known to be notorious spenders, and, ordinarily, those who partook of their hospitality were not prone to ruminate on how the money which flowed so freely was obtained. Indeed, it was policy to accept bounty at the whim of Sneed and his companions without asking any questions.

But the law-abiding element of Morning Glory took a more dubious view of his advent. This amounted to actual concern on the part of mining officials, clerks who had to do with payrolls, the staff of the local bank, business men, and labourers who had snug stakes hidden in their cabins. It also annoyed certain individuals of questionable reputation who were accustomed to have things pretty much their own way when there was trouble.

For Sneed was nothing less than a bandit, and he was known throughout those hills, and in the stock country in the great basin below, as The Killer. His gun was said to be notched from butt to barrel. They called him Killer Sneed—but not to his face. Such was the ominous portent of his name.

Sneed rode into the camp at the head of some half-dozen members of his band as the twilight of the longest day of the year was filling the gulch. This appeared propitious to those who had heard the rumours whispered in the hills. He was said never to enter a town in broad daylight unless he came on business; which business might involve the robbing of a bank or store, or the hold-up of an emporium of chance. Thus his arrival in the late evening indicated that he came bent on pleasure.

It was Sneed's very boldness which was his best protection. Seldom could a sheriff get a victim to swear that he had actually *seen* this outlaw during a raid; for Sneed was noted for swift reprisals. Men feared him, respected him, secretly hated him; but most of all they feared him. His lightning draw and uncanny accuracy with his gun was a tradition in that rough country. He played with posses as a cat plays with a mouse, and it was reported that he had made a deal with the authorities of the three northern counties not to operate in their territory. In return for this promise, he was not to be molested in his ranch rendezvous somewhere in the foothills.

The new arrivals put up their horses in the stage barn, and proceeded to the hotel, where they invaded the dining-room, although it was two hours past supper-time. They were supplied with food, however, and waited upon by a smiling waitress who reaped an apronful of silver. It was dark, with a new moon silvering the pines on the jagged ridges, when they went out and moved down the short street to the Mother Lode resort. Here they found that for which they were seeking: a bar where the white moonshine of the mountain stills was served, gaming tables where poker and blackjack were played, and a throng of revellers and gamesters.

As they came in room was made for them at the bar, and they lined up before a nervous but smiling proprietor who chose to honour them by serving them himself. Sneed, a great towering monster of a man, looming fully a head above his tallest follower, growled to one of those with him.

"See the bunch gets what it wants, Snark," he said, his grey eyes roving over the crowd in the place.

Snark Levant, his lieutenant, scowled upon the "Mother Lode's" proprietor and signalled for bottle and glasses. A miner, standing near them, raised his glass. With a quick step and a flip of his arm, Snark dashed the glass from the man's hand.

"Keep your glasses bottom down on the board till we've had our welcome drink!" he exclaimed as silence fell. The miner gulped and stood motionless, looking at his empty hand.

Thus was the authority of the Sneed contingent established, and Sneed turned away with a short laugh, leaving his men to amuse themselves after their own manner.

He took possession of the extreme lower end of the bar, where he was soon joined by the proprietor and the special deputy who suffered the handicap of trying to keep law and order in the camp, and deliver the vote of the residents. The resort-keeper and the deputy did most of the talking, selecting casual and commonplace subjects concerning the mining outlook and the prospects for luring a big company to invest in the district. Sneed listened and grunted, and noted the surreptitious glances of awe directed at him. Even to Snark Levant, who was closest to him, to say nothing of Lucy Ware, his housekeeper at his ranch, Sneed was more or less of an enigma. He kept his thoughts to himself, disclosed such of his plans as he *had* to disclose at the last possible moment before he put them into execution, and held his followers at arm's length, so to say. But one thing all knew: Sneed kept his word, and once he started anything, he finished.

Snark was buying for the house now, and other members of the band were doing likewise. The proprietor and the deputy were taking small, complimentary drinks, the former, who had served the first libation gratis, carefully estimating when, for the sake of policy, it would be his turn again. But Sneed drank nothing. He ordered the resort-keeper to bring a box of his best cigars, took a handful and thrust one between his teeth. The others he crammed into his vest pockets. As he snapped a match into flame its fire seemed reflected in his eyes. Sneed was annoyed for somc reason. The proprietor vaguely wondered if he had done anything to irritate this formidable visitor, and he hurriedly ordered a drink for the house to go with the cigars.

Sneed strolled away from the bar and paused at a table where a man was dealing blackjack. He reached leisurely into a pocket, deposited a little pile of gold on the table where several others were playing, and called for cards. As he received them and looked at them, he slipped them, face downward, under the gold.

"Good," he grunted.

"The limit's twenty dollars," said the dealer monotonously.

"There are no limits with me!" Sneed's voice cut through the room.

The dealer, evidently a new man in the place, looked up to see the proprietor motioning to him frantically. He made out that it was all right with his boss for this big stranger to boost the limit as he pleased.

"All right," he said, turned his cards over, showing twelve, drew a ten—which made his count one more than the twenty-one on which he could collect—and signalled for more money with which to pay all the bets.

Snark's mean laugh shivered metallically in the place. "First blood!" he roared. "*Every*body step up! I'm burnin' up with money that's too heavy to carry!"

As the men in the place crowded four deep about the bar, Sneed looked at the reflection of his lieutenant's face in the mirror narrowly. Already Snark Levant's eyes were becoming inflamed with the fiery liquor, which had the potent strength of a mule's kick. Someday Sneed would tell this Snark to quit drinking. And he would quit, Sneed decided grimly.

At this moment Snark pushed through the crowd and stared angrily past Sneed. The latter looked around and saw a small, grizzled man, dressed in neat but much-laundered overalls and jumper, sitting quietly in a chair, where he had doubtless been watching the play.

"You coming?" barked Snark.

"I don't drink," was the astonishing reply of this lone absentee—saving for Sneed.

"I didn't ask you if you drank," said Snark

loudly, taking a step toward the man in the chair. "I asked you if you was coming."

"Why should I come if I don't want anything?"

This audacious question, put in a mild voice and accompanied by a steady look that was in itself a reproof and a defiance, seemed to stagger Snark. His brow wrinkled in perplexity and astonishment, and then darkened in swift anger.

"Maybe you're just naturally a fool hillbilly," he sneered. "Now listen hard." He took two more steps. "Hard, I say," he snarled. "For the third time—*are you coming?*"

"You'll have to excuse me," came the calm retort.

Snark grasped the table that was in his way, and flung it crashing among the chairs. Then he leaped toward the man who had defied him, refused his invitation and therefore, in his own opinion, vilely insulted him.

But Sneed had his own devices for dealing with emergencies of this kind. He didn't mind his men fighting; it relieved the monotony of periods of inactivity from which they, as well as he, were suffering at this time. But the attacking of an unarmed man—he could see no weapon upon this stranger—was apt to involve public sentiment in favour of the victim. Moreover, he found it necessary to curb Snark's bullying tendencies early during every visit to a town, lest they become embroiled in a free-for-all mêlée which would certainly end in bloodshed. And Sneed had no desire to lose any men, or have any laid up, except it should happen during the carrying out of one of his profitable enterprises.

He caught Snark as he was hurling himself upon the stranger, and threw him to one side as if he were a child instead of a man.

"Let me 'tend to this fellow," he said sharply.

Snark recovered his balance and glared at his chief. "You heard what he said," he snarled. "It's *my* money I'm spendin', an' this rat—"

"I'm not deaf," Sneed interrupted, his eyes narrowing. "Did you hear what *I* said?"

"You goin' to let him get away with it?" yelled Snark.

Sneed raised an arm and pointed to the bar, where the throng was staring breathlessly. "Go back to that bar!" he thundered.

Snark hesitated. The fingers of his right hand quivered above his gun. But Sneed's word was law. He knew it; the men with him knew it; the people of the camp knew it; and, more than anyone else, Sneed himself knew it. To dispute his leadership before a crowd could result in only one thing. And Sneed wouldn't hesitate the fraction of a split-second!

Snark turned on his heel, and a path opened like magic to his place at the bar.

The little grizzled man looked up at Sneed with his eyes twinkling. But this only served to anger the outlaw.

"What you tryin' to do?" Sneed demanded; "get yourself broken in two an' the pieces trampled."

"I'm not armed," said the stranger calmly. "Except with one thing." He looked at Sneed fixedly.

"A knife, I suppose," sneered the outlaw.

"No; with—courage!" came the cool retort.

Sneed snorted. "What you think is courage is a fool empty head!" he exploded. The small man's confident manner enraged him. He, too, was suffering the tedium of prolonged inactivity.

"Then why did you interfere?" the other asked brazenly.

"To keep you from gettin' your neck twisted," said Sneed savagely. "I don't want to start this holiday with a killin'! Do you think I care anything about *you?* If you *had* been heeled you'd be ridin' a cloud now. Listen to *me,* now. You see that front door yonder? You beat it. You beat it like your shoes were greased. I might give you time to get started an' I might throw you the length of this room an' through the window. *You goin'?*"

The stranger got up from his chair. He could almost *feel* the menace in Killer Sneed's eyes. He walked rapidly to the door and went out.

“Second blood!” cried Snark Levant, bringing his fist down in a mighty blow upon the bar.

The spectators drew in a long breath.

Sneed advanced to the bar and gruffly ordered his first drink.

Chapter II

The Brave One

During the rest of that night, Sneed remained at his chosen post at the lower end of the bar, drinking steadily. But the white fire he consumed appeared to have no effect upon him; at least, any effect it might have had was not visible. His grey eyes remained cold and clear, watching the doors, keeping vigil on his men and the others in the place. He spoke rarely, although the resort-keeper hovered near, anxious to please or entertain. It would not do at all to appear to slight The Killer, or to ignore him.

"Who *was* that old snipe in the chair?" Sneed asked finally.

The proprietor had expected this, and hastened to answer. "Name's Albert Ryder," he said, frowning. "Got a prospect, or a mine or something, a little north of here near the up road, I hear. Comes in here an' warms himself in the winter, cools himself in the summer, wears out the chairs an' never spends a cent."

"Huh," grunted Sneed. "Not much of a customer."

"If they were all like him I'd be running a

charitable institution," the proprietor complained.

"An' as it is, you've got a mint," said Sneed, looking at him.

The man shifted on his feet uneasily and forced a thin smile.

"I don't make as much as a lot of people think," he said lamely.

"You make plenty," Sneed growled. It might have been that he was thinking that here would be a place to make a rich haul. This conjecture gave the resort-keeper a bad night, or morning; for he never went to bed until dawn.

The Sneed gang disported themselves under the watchful eye of their chief until daylight. They patronised the games and played havoc with the house limits. Some lost, some won—all drank to excess with the exception of one. This one was called Buck. He was a young fellow, good-looking, well set up, blond, and of good disposition. He took one drink to the others' three or four, and devoted himself to poker, at which pastime he was lucky.

All of the men seemed well supplied with money. In fact, they displayed gold by the handful, and large, thick rolls of yellow bills. A prosperous outfit this, and one which made the deputy uncomfortable. He knew that money which had been gained unlawfully was being spent before his eyes.

The resort-keeper took advantage of an

unexpected opportunity about dawn to speak to the deputy.

"Is there anything in this report that Sneed's supposed to lay off the north counties?" he asked anxiously. "You know I carry a lot of cash in my safe."

"I haven't any information one way or the other," replied the deputy, frowning. "But I've had a hint or two to let Sneed have his fun." He laughed scornfully. "I'd have a fat chance to stop him from having it, now, wouldn't I?" he added.

The proprietor left him thoughtfully. The deputy had given him an intimation that his surmise was correct. Well, it was a good deal for the authorities. It gave Sneed a sanctuary, to an extent; but it also stopped his depredations in that district. If they couldn't catch the wily outlaw, they could protect themselves. But, just the same, the Mother Lode resort *was* a mint, as Sneed had said, and the proprietor decided he wouldn't feel safe until the outlaw and his men had shaken the dust of Morning Glory's street from their feet and ridden away. And this was to be sooner than anyone had expected.

Members of Sneed's band drifted in pairs to the stage barn, where they turned in in the hay in the loft and sank into slumber. It was characteristic of these men that they always slept near their horses and that at least one of them was always on the alert. This morning it was the young fellow, Buck, who loitered in the barn entrance. Sneed had taken a room in the hotel, which was nearby.

Soon after breakfast the man Ryder came hurrying to the barn and ordered his horses. The barn was a livery, although the care of the stage horses furnished its principal income. Ryder waited while his animals were being saddled. He looked closely at Buck, who stared at him curiously. Finally he spoke to the youth.

"You look like too clean a chap to be associating with those ruffians," he said.

The young fellow bristled and looked him up and down. "For a small man you've got a longer nose than anybody I ever *did* see," he drawled. "You're a lot older'n me, but I'm tellin' you straight if you don't keep yore nose out of other people's business you won't have no more use for it soon."

Ryder shrugged as though he saw it was no use, and turned away. A short time afterward he rode away on a fairly good mount, trailing a pack horse. Buck asked the barnman about him, and learned that he was packing supplies to his mining prospect several miles north.

It was Buck who first saw Sneed along about noon. As the young fellow had done very little drinking, and had had plenty of sleep in the past month, he was still fresh despite the loss of a night's rest. He liked Sneed, in a way, regardless of the man's sinister character. After all, Sneed had saved him a term behind prison walls when he had rescued him from a posse of cattlemen and given him refuge after he had made the one big mistake of his life—horse stealing. It had linked him with Sneed's band, of course, and he had hung on. And Sneed treated him decently enough.

Sneed nodded to him as he came up.

"Bunch is asleep, I suppose," grunted the chief. "You look pert enough."

"Aye, an' that old duffer you gave the walkin' papers to last night was just tellin' me I was a clean-lookin' chap," said Buck with a grin. "Was goin' to read me a lecture, I reckon; but I shut his trap quick enough."

"What's that?" said Sneed, showing interest. "Tell me."

Buck related the remarks which had passed between himself and Ryder, and he saw Sneed's face darken with anger. Sneed *was* mad. If there was one thing he would not under any circumstances countenance it was interference with his men. Here was a promising young recruit, whom Sneed rather liked, and whom he kept away from the more dangerous of his enterprises to protect him, and this prospector was trying to turn him against him. It might have been that Sneed hadn't got out of bed in any too good a humour. It was trying for such a man to see evidences of cash prosperity on all sides of him, to be taken—as Sneed certainly could take it—for the asking. The miners were paid in cash; they gambled, drank and bought what they needed with cash; the safes in the town were full of cash. Yes, Morning Glory was like a great, golden nugget lying far from the nearest town of importance. Yet Sneed was bound by his pledge to hold this territory inviolate, and he had to keep his word.

"Get the men out," he ordered. "An' saddle my horse."

Buck moved briskly. This meant action. In a few minutes the men were up, grumbling at the news, and being sworn at by Snark Levant, who was in a terrible temper.

They got their horses ready and crowded into the hotel bar for eye-openers. When they returned to the barn they carried sundry bottles which were stowed away in slicker packs, and were munching sandwiches from the lunch counter in the bar.

Sneed came and mounted the splendid black that Buck led out. The barnman gazed with undisguised admiration at the horses of these men. He smiled, too, in friendly fashion, for he had been well paid. Sneed always left a trail of gold behind him, which was one reason why there were those in all sections who had a good word to say for him, bits of timely information to give him, warnings of hostile moves against him to send him. In a way, Sneed *did* deal squarely with poor men. And his raids were most often directed against those who could afford their losses or had insurance of some kind to protect them. But his heart was said to be hard as flint. The mention of his name was always followed by an interval of silence.

Riding at the head of his men, Sneed led the way down the dusty street and out of town by the lower road. The deputy saw them go, his face dark with a frown; the resort-keeper didn't know whether to feel sorry over the loss of such excellent customers or glad to be rid of the menace of Sneed's presence; and the derelicts were openly sorrowful, while the conservative element was greatly relieved.

Of these things Sneed knew nothing and cared less. At the fork in the road, where the main road, well tracked by the ore wagons, stages and other traffic, led down toward the basin, he turned off on the up road, as it was called, and followed this less-travelled trail northward. The tracks of two horses showed plainly in the dust as they wound about the hills through the wide aisle between towering pines and firs.

It was mid-afternoon when they turned a bend and saw the saffron-coloured sides of a dump on a slope just above them. At the same moment Sneed caught sight of horses up there. He reined in his mount and gave a curt order to

Snark Levant to the effect that they were to wait for him. Then he spurred his horse up the trail to the dump, and found Albert Ryder standing on the little platform about the top of a shaft he was sinking.

"I want to talk to *you,*" said Sneed roughly as he dismounted. "What was you tellin' that man of mine at the barn down there this morning?"

Ryder's eyes narrowed and he looked far more belligerent here on his own claim than he had appeared in town the night before. Moreover, a rifle was leaning against one of the uprights of the windlass.

"You followed me up here?" he said, his mild eyes taking on a stern look.

"I didn't come here to have you ask *me* questions," Sneed said angrily. "What was you tellin' my man down there about him lookin' too good to be trailin' with a crew of ruffians?"

"You seem to know what I said," was the cool retort. "Why ask me something you already know?"

Sneed's eyes narrowed dangerously. "You think we're ruffians?" he said grimly. "We're worse than that. Ruffian is a tame word, my brave one. I won't have anyone insulting me to one of my men." He surveyed the other coldly. "I'm goin' to make an example of you," he continued in a hard voice, his great form seeming to tower to a monstrous height. He pulled up his coat sleeves, baring a mighty pair of forearms which were as matted with hair as those of a gorilla.

"No man will put much stock in what a man says if he's laughed at that man," he went on with a cruel smile. "I'm goin' to teach that man of mine something, an' you too, for that part, by takin' you out on the edge of that dump in plain sight, an' *spanking* you!"

He reached for the prospector, but Ryder displayed an agility no one would have suspected he possessed. He leaped for the rifle. But even as he felt its cold barrel in his hand he tripped and fell forward. A wild, piercing cry shot through the hills as Ryder plunged headlong down the shaft.

Sneed stood rooted to the spot for a few moments, thunderstruck by the suddenness of it; then he ran to the edge of the dump and beckoned to his men, who came riding up the steep trail, startled by that fearful cry.

"He fell down the shaft," said Sneed, showing some excitement in the presence of a death which was not accompanied by the crack of pistols and the pungent smoke of burnt powder.

Snark Levant looked at Sneed's bare forearms, at the rifle lying on the planks, and grinned. But his face froze when he met the look Sneed gave him. Sneed realised that his henchman thought he had thrown the prospector down the shaft. His eyes blazed with fury.

"You hear me?" he cried hoarsely. "I say he fell down the shaft." He grasped Snark Levant and whirled him about.

"All right. Then he must be dead," was Snark's comment.

He stepped to the yawning mouth of the shaft bore and looked down into utter darkness. No sound came up from below. He turned with a shrug.

"I reckon it served him right," he said with a leer. He had heard about the incident of the morning from the youth, Buck. Sneed had been angered; he had come up to take the prospector to task. Well, he had his revenge. It was all clear to Snark. Sneed had been about to administer a good licking to Ryder; the prospector had tried to shoot him with the rifle; Sneed had picked him up like a baby and thrown him down the shaft. It was none of Snark's business. In a way, he felt himself vindicated for the prospector's defi of the night before.

Sneed made a move indicating that he thought of going down into the shaft. Buck stopped him with a hand on his arm.

"I wouldn't try it, if I was you," he cautioned. "That ladder probably wasn't made to carry a man of your weight. I'm the lightest man in the outfit, I reckon. I'll go down."

But before he could start to carry out this enterprise there was a pound of hoofs, a shower of fine shale, and a boy riding the bare back of a big, roan horse appeared on a trail from the right.

He pulled up on top of the dump and stared at them. He was a fine-looking boy, about fourteen, his chestnut hair gleaming in the sun for the lack of a hat, his brown eyes regarding them gravely with concern, his clear skin bronzed, tall and slender, with the promise of a fine pair of shoulders to come, and the thin waistline of the natural-born rider.

"Where's—where's pa?" he asked.

It was Sneed who answered. "He's—we heard a cry an' came up," he said, glaring about in warning to his men. "I thought I heard something down the shaft, an' I was goin' down. Maybe, he fell—whoever it was. Was it your dad?"

The boy was off his horse in a twinkling. He ran to where a candle-holder was sticking in the side of the tool shack. "A—*match!*" he cried, and Buck hastened to supply it.

With the candle lighted and the holder in one hand, the boy disappeared down the shaft. Buck, at a nod from Sneed, followed him.

Sneed paced the little platform in a dark mood. He seemed strangely upset. His men, including Snark Levant, seeing the humour he was in, drew away. They wondered if Sneed *had* thrown the prospector down the shaft. They wouldn't put it past him. As for Snark Levant—he was sure this had been the way of it. What of it? He would have done the same thing himself!

It seemed an eternity before the pair came back up the shaft. The boy came out first. His eyes were wide and frightened. Buck shook his head at Sneed significantly.

"Was it your dad?" Sneed asked in a milder voice than his men had ever heard him use. He looked at the boy closely. "Is he—hurt?"

"He's—dead," said the boy slowly, with a gathering mist in his eyes.

Sneed turned abruptly on Snark Levant. "You an' the men go back to the ranch," he ordered sharply. "I'll keep Buck here."

They saw him shaking down his coat sleeves as they rode away.

Chapter III

Ted Ryder

The boy stood straight upon the platform, looking up at the towering peaks, their silver minarets flashing in the sunlight. His hands were clenched, and he struggled manfully to keep back the tears. He looked like a young god of the forest, his fine face lifted to the breeze that ruffled his hair and played with the open collar of his shirt.

"What's your name, son?" Sneed asked, not unkindly.

"Ted Ryder," came the answer, clear though his lips trembled.

"Where do you live?"

The boy waved an arm toward the pines beyond the north edge of the dump. "In the clearing," he said.

"I guess we better go over there," Sneed decided aloud.

The boy walked at once to his horse, took up the halter rope, and they started along the trail with him in the lead, Sneed following, and Buck bringing up the rear. Sneed was wondering just what he would say to the boy's mother. Had not the boy arrived when he did, it was highly probable Sneed would have gone his way and that would have ended the matter so far as he was concerned.

They came into a large meadow nestling in a bowl in the hills. The boy turned his horse loose and led the way across a little trickle of stream to the log cabin at the farther end of the meadow. He stopped before the doorway and looked about vacantly.

"Is—your mother here?" asked Sneed.

"Mother?" The boy looked up at him surprised. "I have no mother," he said gravely.

"You lived here alone with your dad?" asked Sneed.

The boy nodded. "Pa always said there was only the two of us left," he murmured, and went into the cabin.

Sneed followed, his lips pressed queerly together. The front room of the cabin was neat and homelike. There was a table with a red and white checked cover in the centre, a fire-place at one side and a couch at the other, easy chairs, a bookcase and a small box-phonograph. Doors led into sleeping rooms and the kitchen.

Ted Ryder stood at the table and the first tears came into his eyes. But he shook them away bravely.

"I expect, mister, I'll have to ask you to help—bury—my pa," he said slowly.

Sneed was plainly ill at ease and troubled. "You

want to bury him here?" he asked. "Without a minister or—or anything?"

"I'll read something from the book," said the boy. "Pa always said he wanted to be buried in the meadow, an' that when we sold the mine to a big company they couldn't have this place in here. An' he said he didn't have to have a preacher to tell him what was right an' what wasn't."

This remark left Sneed staring strangely at Buck, who had taken off his hat, and was looking uncomfortable.

"We'll help you," said Sneed, rousing. "Ah—well, you wait here, son, while we go over to the mine. We won't be long."

He motioned to Buck to go out and followed him.

"The kid wants to be alone for a spell, I reckon," said Sneed, as they walked across the fragrant meadow. "Best for him, too. Seems a decent sort of youngster. Do you think you could get that—the body up out of there?"

"We can tie our ropes together," said Buck, "an' you let the end down if I need help, or should slip. He fell on some rock down there, an' never knew what hit him."

"He stumbled an' fell," said Sneed, as if to himself. "Went in head-first. His yell brought the kid. You know, Levant thinks I *threw* him in!" He looked at the younger man closely. "I was goin' to—but no matter. I had my sleeves up, but

I wasn't goin' to hurt him. I didn't care a hang about his rifle." He snorted at the thought of being afraid of a gun.

They reached the dump and took their ropes from their saddles. Buck looked at the ore bucket on the platform, and shook his head. "That ain't big enough an' it would be more trouble," he said. "I'll go down. I don't believe the ladder would hold you, an' if it breaks with me you'll have to haul up the two of us."

Sneed nodded, and Buck went down the shaft. Sneed let down the rope, and soon he was keeping a tight hold on it as Buck came up. He took the body of Albert Ryder from Buck and lifted it to his own saddle. Then they walked back, Buck leading his horse, and Sneed walking by his mount, holding the burden across the saddle.

They put the dead man down on his bunk, as the boy requested. Ted drew a cover over his father. His eyes were clear, Ted's were; and there was no sign that he had given up to the tears which strove to break through.

They went into the front room, and Sneed spoke again.

"I reckon we'd best stay here with you to-night, son." It was unthinkable, even to Sneed, to leave the boy alone with his dead. "If you'll show my man Buck, here, where things are, he'll make us some coffee."

"I'll get supper," said the boy stoutly. "I've—

I've got Johnny cake. Pa liked it. Do you like it, mister?"

Sneed appeared confused and taken aback for a few moments. "Yes, I like it," he said finally. "All right, it's gettin' along towards sundown, an' you just do that—get supper. An' listen, son—" He put one of his great hands on the boy's shoulder. "You want to stay bucked up, you know. This—these things can't be helped. You understand, Ted?"

The boy looked up at him soberly. "Yes, I understand," he said. "Maybe you'll—I forgot the horses pa took to town—"

"I'll get 'em in," said Buck quickly. "Don't worry about *any*thing."

Sneed followed Buck out as Ted went into the kitchen.

"Look here, Buck," he said gruffly, "I don't want that kid to know anything about me, understand? I'll tell him what I think he ought to know. You follow my lead." He swore softly, and motioned to Buck to go about his business.

While Buck was getting the horses and looking after them, and Ted Ryder was preparing supper in the lonely kitchen, Sneed walked about the meadow. The sun dropped behind the peaks and a rosy glow spread over the land, reflected from skies of gold and crimson. Ted called to them, and they went in to supper.

It was a quiet meal. Sneed did not wish to ask

the boy any more questions until after the burial. And he didn't know how he could comfort him. But he felt the boy should have some explanation as to themselves—he and Buck.

"I'm a stockman," he told Ted. "I'll be glad to help you any way I can. This is Buck, one of my hands."

The boy nodded with a faint smile.

"Haven't you got any relatives?" Sneed asked curiously.

"Nope." The boy said it quite as a matter of course.

Sneed remained silent. After supper he walked in the meadow while the twilight fell, and Buck insisted on helping the boy do the dishes. They went to bed early, Ted sleeping in his own bunk, Sneed taking the couch and Buck making a bed for himself on the floor.

In the morning Buck went to the mine for tools, and then dug a grave at the upper side of the meadow. Sneed himself took hammer and nails and saw, and fashioned a box from boards ripped from the tool-house floor. Thus they made a coffin and placed it with its burden in the grave.

Ted Ryder, dressed in his best, the bright morning sun shining like a benediction on his head, stood over the grave and read one of the Psalms of David, while Sneed and Buck stood uncovered opposite him. Then Buck put in the fresh-turned earth and Ted, holding the Bible in his hands, knelt down upon the grave. They saw his lips move, but heard no sound. Just as well they didn't, Sneed told himself. Afterward they went to the cabin.

"What are you goin' to do?" Sneed asked the boy.

"I hadn't thought," replied Ted, showing, for the first time, signs of worry.

"Have you got any money?"

The boy shook his head. "I can sell the mine," he said, brightening somewhat.

Sneed cleared his throat. He knew what selling a prospect amounted to. Well, the boy was up against it. Father dead, no one to go to of his own kin, alone and without money. Fine boy, too.

"Would you like to go to town?" he asked curiously.

The boy's eyes clouded. "I like the hills," he replied. "Pa always said God made the hills an' the Devil made the towns."

"Humph! Maybe he was right," said Sneed. "Well, you can't stay here all alone. An' it might be some time before you could sell the—the mine." He smiled wryly. "Ted, how would you like to live, an' maybe work a little, on a nice big ranch in the hills, where you could have horses to play with, an'—an' all the things boys want?"

The worry cleared from Ted's eyes instantly.

"That would be fine," he said with a smile that seemed to bring sunshine into the room.

Sneed rose. "All right," he said in the tone of a man who has made up his mind thoroughly. "You an' Buck get busy an' pack two of your horses with what you want to take along from here. We can lock the place up an' board the windows. You can ride your own horse—use your dad's saddle, if you ain't got one of your own. An' we'll get started. I'm goin' to take you to *my* place."

The bustle which followed caused the boy to forget his trouble, and Buck didn't give him a chance to mourn the departure from his home. Sneed boarded up the windows and saw that everything was put inside. He also locked the tool-house. Then they waited while the boy picked an armful of wild roses and placed them on the fresh mound in the meadow.

As the sun hung poised high in the zenith, Ted Ryder rode out of the little clearing behind Sneed, The Killer, with Buck whistling cheerfully in the rear.

Chapter IV

The Lesson

Ted Ryder's arrival at Sneed's ranch created a sensation in the rendezvous. The trio, having carefully avoided Morning Glory and the main road, reached the ranch after dark, having covered the long distance in good time. The bunk-house, where the men lived, was ablaze with light and resounded with laughter and shouts and snatches of song, showing that the members of the band were making carnival. They were observed by some men sitting before the bunk-house door as they rode past on their way to the ranch-house. Before they reached the house the noise behind had died away, and Sneed realised that their arrival was being discussed. His teeth clicked shut.

Buck took charge of the horses and started with them for the barn as Sneed led the boy inside. As they entered the big living-room a woman came in through another door. She nodded to Sneed and stared at the boy, who smiled wearily.

"This is Ted Ryder," said Sneed, giving her a warning look which she seemed to understand. "He's goin' to be with us for a spell. Ted, this is Miss Lucy. You must be nice to her an' do as she says."

Ted nodded up at him, and walking to Lucy Ware held out his slim, brown hand. "Howdy, Miss Lucy," he said.

Lucy took his hand and said something that was indistinct. Her surprise, however, showed plainly in her eyes, and when she looked at Sneed she did not have to put the questions which were on her tongue into so many words. But Sneed ignored her interrogating gaze.

"We're powerful hungry, Lucy," he said. "Suppose you scrape us up something while we're washing off the dust. Come on, son, an' we'll spoil some good clean water."

Later, while the boy was sitting in the living-room waiting for supper, Sneed had an opportunity to speak to Lucy privately. He told her briefly what had happened, but he made no attempt to explain the incentive which had prompted him to bring Ted Ryder to the ranch. He placed the boy in her care. "He seems to be a nice kid," he finished with a scowl.

Lucy Ware was no longer young, in the accepted meaning of the term, but she retained traces of a former beauty which had made her queen of the dance halls in the cow-towns. She had taken up with Sneed as her career—and it was no small thing, as such careers went—had dwindled. She was a capable housekeeper, and she had a good home on the ranch, with a coloured woman to help her with the work. She had a keen mind, was a great reader, and probably knew more about Killer Sneed than anyone else, although that wasn't saying much. But that was nevertheless enough to enable her to speak her mind, which she did when she thought the occasion required. She was a blonde, and somewhat pertly. And she possessed an invaluable gift—common sense. She spoke her mind this night quickly and sincerely.

"Sneed, have you brought that boy here to make another like yourself out of him?" she demanded, resting her hands on her hips and looking him straight in the eye.

"I brought him here because he didn't have no kin an' no place to go to," said Sneed, frowning heavily. "I'm goin' to take care of him for a while. An' I don't want you springing any smart jargon on him"—Lucy's eyebrows went up at this—"an' I don't want him mixing with the men, unless it's that young fellow, Buck. He's the best of the lot."

"If you're goin' to do the right thing by the boy you certain sure brought him to a fine place to do it," observed Lucy in fine scorn. "I suppose you think you can keep that bunch of cut-throats off him, do you? They'll ride him to death an' you, too, probably."

Sneed's face darkened in anger, but he was thinking, just the same. "You leave the cut-throats to me," he growled. "They won't bother him when *I* get through with them. An'—since when have they been ridin' *me?*"

"Oh, well," Lucy shrugged. "I suppose you know they thought they were goin' to have a week in town, anyway. Well, they're sure makin' up for it here. They must have stopped in town or sent somebody up there on the way back, for they brought home enough white mule to irrigate the Basin. Makes it nice for me, with you gone an' that Snark struttin' around like he owned the place. He's *one* man you want to keep away from that kid."

Sneed scowled deeply and went into the living-room. Ted looked up brightly; but Sneed saw that the boy had been thinking of his loss.

"You've got to make the best of it, son," the outlaw said. "Now this is your home. But there's one thing I don't want you to do. I don't want you to hang out much with my men, except maybe that fellow who was with us. An' if any of 'em says anything to you that you don't understand, I want you to come an' tell me—you understand?"

The boy nodded. "Yes," he answered. But he was puzzled.

"That's—er—because what you learn, I want you to learn from me," Sneed explained. "An' you'll find Miss Lucy a good sort. She'll look after you an' she's your friend. Now c'mon an' we'll eat."

Whatever else Ted's coming did, it furnished

Lucy Ware with a task she relished—although she might not have realised it. It was her opportunity—a woman's natural instinct—to look after somebody. She hovered about the table, seeing that the boy had plenty to eat, refilling his glass with milk, and brought him a large piece of wild strawberry shortcake with sugar and cream. And it was Lucy who arranged his room—a big, airy room in the front on the second floor—and who saw his clothes put away.

Sneed, rather bewildered by it all, went down and sat in the living-room. Lucy camc down finally with a queer look on her face. They stared at each other.

"He's goin' to bed," said Lucy in a loud whisper, "an' you know what he's doing? He's sayin' his prayers!"

Sneed fumbled for a match. "Well, why not?" he said brusquely.

Lucy nodded. "That's right," she said. "Why not?"

They were much alike, this pair, in some ways. Both had known only the wild life of a rough country in the making. And Sneed, strange to say, terrible man that he undoubtedly was, found his only comfort here on this ranch. So anxious was he to protect this sanctuary that he would not allow his men to go anywhere in the northern counties unless he accompanied them to make sure that they did nothing to jeopardise the pact he had made with the authorities. Of late he had been strangely inactive, and this had caused Lucy Ware to wonder to herself if he was growing tired of the game.

A burst of ribald song floated in through the open windows and Sneed got to his feet. “The celebration’s gettin’ hot,” was his comment as he took his hat and went out.

Yellow beams of light shone from the bunk-house door and windows. The wind stirred in the great cottonwoods and sighed in the lilac bushes. Overhead the stars hung in clusters and the moon rode the high arch of the night like a splash of silver. The shadows of the hills were softened, rounded, merging gently with the darker outlines of the mountains which rose to gleaming spires piercing the velvet sky.

Sneed walked across the yard to the bunk-house door and stepped within. The rays of the hanging lamps shone lurid through tobacco smoke which hung above the heads of the men in layers. On the table in the centre of the main room were several bottles and many glasses. The white liquor had been wantonly spilled and added its fumes to the odour of tobacco and the smell of lamp-wicks.

A shout went up as Sneed appeared. Most of the men were too far gone in their cups to recognize the dangerous look in their leader’s eyes. One, a large man with a wicked growth of beard, hailed him jocosely.

“Hey, chief, wha—what we doin’? Adopting the young ’un?”

Sneed stepped across to him. Then his mighty right arm straightened and his fist landed full on the man’s jaw with a crack that sounded like a muffled pistol shot. The man went backward and crumpled in a heap as silence fell over the room. The others stared and there were mutterings. Sneed paid no attention to them. Picking up a chair, he broke off its back and with the piece he swept the bottles and glasses to the floor, where they crashed.

Snark Levant had leaped to his feet, and suddenly Sneed turned on him. “Draw your gun!” he commanded harshly. “Do you hear me? *Draw it!*”

But Snark looked away and ignored the order.

Sneed laughed sneeringly. “All right,” he said shortly, his laugh dying as suddenly as it had burst upon their ears. “But any time you’re not satisfied you can get out or go for your gun—understand? You stay away from the house an’ away from that kid. I’m tellin’ *you.* Now you tell the *others.* Do you hear me? *Tell ’em!*”

“He says we’re to stay away from the kid,” said Snark loudly, his eyes glittering, snake-like.

The men had sobered and they avoided Sneed’s eyes as he looked about at them. The one who had been knocked down was sitting on the floor in a daze. Snark’s face was a picture of futile rage. Sneed regarded him narrowly. Snark Levant was valuable when there was work to be done. He could handle men, and the men were afraid of him. He was a gunfighter almost equal to Sneed himself! But in the planning of a raid in all its details, Levant was a failure. Sneed controlled him as much by his brains as he did by his strength of arm and gun. They were dependent one upon the other. And Sneed always gave his orders through his lieutenant.

"Tell them," he said slowly in a hard voice, "that the doings are over for to-night. Tell 'em to get in shape to-morrow, for we're goin' out on business." He saw Snark's eyes glisten with quick interest. "Tell 'em they can finish off somewhere in the south for a week or two when we've made our haul. An' tell 'em the kid is dynamite so far's they're concerned. If one of you bother him—" He picked up a piece of the ruined chair and broke it into bits with his hands. Tossing the remnants of wood on the table he went out, leaving them staring at what he had left.

Upstairs in the ranch-house Lucy Ware was listening, with her ear pressed against the door, to the regular breathing of the sleeping boy. She heard Sneed's step upon the porch and hurried back to her room.

Chapter V

Visitors

In the morning most of the men in the bunkhouse slept late, only Buck and the barnman being about when Sneed came out after breakfast. Sneed took advantage of the opportunity to take Buck aside for a little talk.

"I'm goin' to pay more attention to the ranch," he explained to the young fellow. "You're a cow-puncher an' I've got a bunch of cattle in here. I'm goin' to put you in charge of 'em an' you can let the kid, Ted, trail along with you. Teach him how to rope an' pick him out a good horse from my string in the south pasture. I've got a permit for five hundred head in the forest reserve, so you've got plenty of range. You're cow-boss."

Buck heard this news with visible pleasure.

"I guess the calves were all branded this spring but if you find any that're not wearin' my iron, put it on 'em." He looked at Buck closely. "I don't mean you're to go out of your way to brand strays off my range," he said pointedly. "Old man Burt will stay here at the barn an' that deaf hand, Smith, will be lookin' after the garden an' hay. You can use 'em if you need 'em. Be careful how you handle the kid."

Buck nodded to show that he understood his orders.

"I'm leavin' with the others to-night," Sneed went on. "You needn't worry about your share of any tricks we turn. I want you to keep an eye out here an' report to *me,* see? I'll be back in a week or ten days. The crowd is gettin' restless. If I shouldn't get back, Miss Lucy knows what to do. Did you hear Snark or any of the rest of 'em say if they'd stopped in town on the way back day before yesterday?"

"They sent a couple of men up to Morning Glory for some bottles," said Buck "They've been restless, like you say, I reckon. I don't think any of 'em meant to be fresh last night."

"That's right," said Sneed. "Stick up for your outfit, always. Well, it wouldn't pay any of 'em, or anybody else, to get fresh with me. Now you can take the kid down an' pick him out his horse. I suppose it's up to me to look after him considering what happened. Just remember that I'm a cattleman an' you're one of my hands. I wouldn't make any mistakes, if I was you."

It was a subtle threat to Buck to be careful to conceal Sneed's real business and the youth nodded wisely.

A short time after this Ted and Buck rode away towards the south pasture. The boy appeared thoughtful, as if he were just beginning to realise fully the loss of his father and the new life which had opened for him. He had evidently been sheltered and kept away from the rough element in those parts all his life. Lucy told Sneed that she had learned he had been born in the Snowy Mountains and that his father had crossed to these hills some years before, after the death of the boy's mother. His father had been fairly well educated and had taught the boy much.

"He asked your name," said Lucy when Sneed returned to the house after seeing the boy and Buck on their way.

"What'd you tell him?" Sneed growled.

"What *could* I tell him?" Lucy countered. "Wouldn't he hear me an' the men callin' you by your name? I told him the truth."

"Well, why not?" grumbled Sneed, although he was wondering at that very minute what the boy would think when he learned all about him, as he probably would, sooner or later. The thought put Sneed in a very bad humour and Lucy left him to himself.

When the men were stirring Sneed went out and ordered Snark Levant to be ready for the trail late that afternoon. Thus they were busy making their preparations the rest of the day. The cheerfulness these men exhibited would have done justice to a cattle outfit getting ready to go in to the fall rodeo in town. They were a hard-looking lot; and every man had proven himself fearless and toughened to hours in the saddle in all kinds of weather. Sneed would have no misfits in his band.

Each man put up a small pack of supplies and the cook served an early supper. Sneed bid the boy good-bye, telling him he was going out on range business with his crew, and rode away at the head of his men shortly before sundown. Lucy and Ted watched them go from the porch. It was at such times that Lucy's eyes clouded with worry; and it was only at such times, when the band was riding out on business, that Lucy showed visibly that she entertained a certain regard for Killer Sneed. She could never be sure when such an expedition set forth that Sneed would come back. And there was always the prospect of undesirable visitors at the ranch during his absence. Yet this time she felt somewhat reassured by the presence of Buck.

For more than a week Buck kept the boy busy. He picked him a fine black gelding from Sneed's string and Ted was elated with his splendid mount. The boy was a natural-born horseman, and he took as readily to the lariat. Buck was enthusiastic over his pupil, and found the ranch work and Ted's company more to his liking than the thrill of a raid. They rounded up the cattle, branded some late calves, cut out the beeves and herded them on forest range higher in the foothills. The next week they had less to do and Buck started breaking some horses. Here Ted showed his mettle by riding a bronco after the animal had thrown Buck. The boy changed rapidly in the unaccustomed companionship. He was already beginning to round out into a man, as Buck told Lucy.

"Listen, you," Lucy said, "don't be tryin' to push that lad too fast. He'll get old fast enough by himself. An' don't swear in front of him."

Buck raised his brows in surprise. "You figure he ought to sprout wings instead of spurs?" he asked.

"Don't talk to me like that," Lucy said sharply. "An' don't be askin' me questions."

Buck went away wondering just what the advent of Ted Ryder had done to Lucy Ware—and to Sneed, for that matter. Sneed was the last one he would have expected to take an orphan and try to bring him up right. Well, The Killer had some scheme in mind. Still, Buck didn't share Snark Levant's belief that Sneed had thrown the boy's father down the prospect shaft. And Lucy Ware would believe what Sneed told her. Even Levant was aware that Sneed didn't lie to his housekeeper. And Lucy Ware would have caught him at it if he had tried.

Toward the end of the second week Buck and Ted came riding in at sundown to find two horses standing with reins dangling in the yard. Buck's eyes hardened into an alert gaze and he swung in towards the barn as Burt and Smith, the only other hands at the ranch, save the cook, came out. They motioned to Buck and he leaned down to catch what Burt had to say.

"It's Sheriff Frost an' that smart aleck deputy from Mornin' Glory," he said in a tone that reached Buck's ears alone. "They're talkin' with Miss Lucy out in front."

Buck nodded and dismounted, the boy following his example. Buck told Ted to go into the kitchen and wait for him there. Then he hurried around to the front of the house where he found the two officers and Lucy Ware on the porch.

Sheriff Frost looked at him out of cold blue eyes and Buck caught a warning glance from Lucy. "This fellow was with them," the Morning Glory deputy said.

"What's up?" Buck asked, meeting the sheriff's gaze steadily. He had met Frost before. He knew nothing save a matter of grave importance would bring the sheriff to Sneed's place.

"My man here was up to the Ryder claim yesterday an' found the old man an' the boy gone," said Sheriff Frost. "There was a—, looked like a new grave in the clearing, didn't it?" He waited for his deputy's nod of affirmation. Then he again addressed Buck. "What do you know about it?" he demanded.

Buck sensed instantly that the deputy had thought much about Ryder's run-in with Snark Levant and Sneed and had gone to the old man's claim. Finding the man and boy missing and the cabin locked and boarded up, and seeing the mound in the meadow, he had gone to the county seat and reported the matter to his superior. Buck did not know just what explanation he should make. He wished Sneed were on hand to answer the questions. As it was, it was Lucy Ware who spoke first.

"I've told you what happened, sheriff," she said in an irritated voice. "If you want to know more than I do—if there's any more to know—you'll have to wait until Sneed gets back."

"Where *is* Sneed?" the sheriff asked her.

"I don't know," replied Lucy truthfully.

"Do *you* know?" Frost asked Buck sharply.

"No, I don't," Buck answered.

The sheriff frowned as if he realised himself that Sneed would not divulge any move of his in advance. "Where is the boy?" he asked next.

"Sheriff, you're not goin' to pester that boy with a lot of questions," said Lucy in a determined tone. "He's had trouble enough."

"I guess you're forgetting that as sheriff of this county I have to inquire into an affair such as this," said Frost soberly. "I shall have to ask the boy about it, especially as this man, who was with the party, don't seem to want to talk."

"Oh, he can talk," said Lucy with the trace of a sneer. "Tell him what he wants to know," she directed, nodding to Buck.

Buck wrinkled his brows, thinking hard and

fast. He only knew what Sneed had told them when they had ridden up to the mine dump after he had beckoned to them, and the explanation he had made to the boy. Which of these stories was he to tell? He decided to play safe.

"We were ridin' up that way—"

"Where were you headed for?" the sheriff interrupted.

"I don't know," said Buck with a scowl. "We were ridin' along behind Sneed, that's all. We—after a while when we were below this mine dump—we heard a cry an' went up there. Ryder had fell down the shaft—"

"How'd you know he had fallen down the shaft?" Frost broke in.

"Sneed heard something down there," said Buck angrily. "Then the boy came an' we—the boy an' me—went down the shaft. We found Ryder dead on the rocks down there. Sneed sent the others home an' we stayed there that night an' buried Ryder next day."

"Why didn't you send word about this to Morning Glory?" the sheriff demanded suspiciously.

"How do *I* know why we didn't do a lot of things!" exclaimed Buck. "*I* wasn't the boss. An' what good would that have done?"

The sheriff was interrupted by thundering hoofs before he had a chance to answer this or ask more questions. Sneed came galloping up to the house and brought his great horse to a rearing stop near the porch steps. He was alone. Buck sighed with relief at the timely arrival of his chief.

Sneed looked at the sheriff keenly, his eyes seeming to bore through the official. Frost appeared somewhat disconcerted. He cleared his throat but no words came readily and Sneed dismounted, motioning to Buck to take his horse to the barn.

"What's the trouble?" he demanded in a peculiar purring tone, glancing from one to the other of the trio. "Speak up, Frost! Why are you here?"

"I came to inquire about this Ryder business," said Frost. "I've heard two stories; now I'd like to hear yours." He did not appear to be afraid of Sneed; but he evinced considerable curiosity by looking at Sneed's dust-covered clothes and the tell-tale sweat-stains of a long ride.

"Fair enough," said Sneed, striding up the steps and across the porch. "Come in the house."

They followed him in and Lucy lighted the lamp against the falling dusk. Then she went out.

"What do you want to know about it?" Sneed asked sharply. "Want to know if I killed Ryder?" His gleaming eyes seemed to read the sheriff's mind. "Well, I didn't," he went on with a frown. "Ryder killed himself by fallin' into that shaft. I don't know what this young whippersnapper from Morning Glory thinks, but I reckon you know when I'm tellin' the truth. I don't have to lie!" A sneer came to Sneed's lips and stayed there while he surveyed the deputy coolly. "What do *you* think?" he asked harshly.

The deputy hesitated and then explained how he had discovered that something was wrong and that it was his duty to tell the sheriff about it. "An' I came down here because of the trouble you'd had in town," said the sheriff hurriedly, "an' because you rode out that way that morning."

"How'd you know I went out that way?" Sneed demanded crossly.

"Your men were seen going an' coming," said the sheriff quietly. "You don't think everybody in these hills but your crowd is blind, do you?" His voice took on a keen edge as he finished.

Sneed looked at him wrathfully. "An' just what do you make out of this business? Do you think I went up there an' killed Ryder so I could adopt his kid?"

"Is the boy here?" asked the sheriff coolly.

Sneed's eyes narrowed. He turned to the deputy. "Suppose you beat it to the bunk-house an' get your supper," he snapped out. "When the sheriff wants you, he'll call for you."

The deputy took a speedy departure at a nod from his superior.

Sneed closed the door and motioned the sheriff to a chair. "Looks like we've got to have another show-down," he grumbled, sitting down. "Ryder was a fool! Did you know that? Do you think a man would sink a shaft like that on a thin prospect if he'd had any sense? You been up to his place?"

"I was there last night an' at daybreak this morning," Frost replied. "I had that grave dug up, too. I know Ryder wasn't shot nor clubbed to death. He probably *did* go down the shaft. Sneed, I'm waiting for your story."

"An' here's where you get it," said Sneed grimly. He had no intention of permitting this affair to interfere with the carrying out of his pact with the north counties authorities. Therefore he told Sheriff Frost exactly what had happened on the day of Ryder's death, how it had happened and why it had happened. He omitted nothing, and even explained the trouble of the night before, of which, he felt certain, the sheriff had already had several accounts.

"And the boy?" said the sheriff when he had finished.

"He's here," said Sneed with a scowl. "He's got no folks, no place to go, no money. I brought him home with me."

"And do you think this is the place for him?" asked the official in a suggestive tone.

Sneed's eyes flamed. "Why not?" he flared. "The men ain't here, an', anyway, they've got their orders to lay off him. Miss Lucy can look after him an' he can learn from my cow-boss—that young Buck."

"No doubt," said the sheriff sarcastically. "And he can learn from you, too, Sneed. But the kind of education you'd give a boy wouldn't do him no good. You'll be fair enough to acknowledge that, I guess. The boy ought to be taken somewhere."

"Where would you take him?" Sneed asked.

"Oh—find him a home on some ranch," said the sheriff; "or in town. An' the State's got an institution—"

"Not by a—" Sneed swore. "None of that, Frost. I know what those places are. An' I know what he'd get on most of the ranches. He'd be better off here. As to teaching him, I'd teach him what he ought to know an' no more. I know what you mean by what he can learn from me. But you don't know what's in my mind, an' you never did. That kid would pine away in a town. What's more, I've sort of taken a liking to him. I may go in for cattle here on a big scale, later on. He'd have something ahead of him."

"I'd like to see the boy," said the sheriff, frowning.

Sneed rose and went to the dining-room door. "Lucy!" he called. "Where's Ted? Send him in here."

The boy came quick enough, looking at Sneed with a flush of pleasure at seeing him back. Lucy stared from the doorway.

"Son, this is the sheriff," said Sneed, speaking to the boy. "He's heard about your trouble an' he wants to take you away somewhere."

Ted's eyes clouded with instant concern as he looked at Frost. "Why—can't I stay here?" he said, looking up at the towering Sneed. "Where does he want to take me?" There was resentment in his voice.

"I don't know," said Sneed with an aimless gesture. "Don't you want to go?"

For a moment the boy hesitated while Frost looked at him in great intcrcst. "I want to find you a good home," said the sheriff.

"I've *got* a home!" Tcd blurted impulsively. "I can earn my grub, can't I?" He looked up at Sneed pleadingly. "I rode a horse that threw Buck yesterday," he said, more anxious than boasting. "An' I'm learnin' to rope."

"Not a bad thing to learn," said Sneed in a drawl, flashing a look at the sheriff. "Do you want to stay here, Ted?"

"Yes!" The answer came sharp and clear.

"Then run along an' get your supper," said Sneed with a signal to Lucy Ware.

When they were again alone, Sneed sat down and hitched his chair close in front of the sheriff. "Frost," he said, with a ring of deadly earnestness in his voice, "you an' I have got to understand each other. I reckon if there's goin' to be any one-sidedness to this thing, *you've* got to understand *me*. We've got a queer deal, you an' some others an' me. You keep on your side of the fence, an' keep your men along with you, an' I'll keep on mine. My word's good, Frost, an' you know it. I'm not goin' to answer any more questions nor spread this conversation out another minute. An' I'm goin' to tell you straight out an' for keeps—*the boy stays here!*"

Sheriff Frost got to his feet. "If you try to make an outlaw out of that boy, Sneed, it'll be the blackest and costliest thing you ever did," he said grimly. "An' I'll know it if you make one false move."

"Put your hat down," said Sneed dryly. "Soon's they're through in there, *we'll* have supper."

Chapter VI

Ted Learns

Sneed gave Sheriff Frost a room in the house that night, as the official did not wish to start on the long ride to the county seat at once. The Morning Glory deputy, however, after a short conversation with his superior on the porch, departed for the mining town where he was stationcd. His duty had been done and he was through. But during the night ride he mulled over thc cxtraordinary information he possessed. Sneed had taken the Ryder boy under his wing and the sheriff had permitted it! What a mouthful *that* would be for the camp gossips. And so it proved—with every last man believing that Sneed had killed the boy's father and intended to make a bad man out of the lad for revenge. But the mining populace was not too outspoken in its opinions. Sneed's name carried a power more significant than the law. None wanted to bring his wrath down on Morning Glory.

The sheriff left in the morning after he had seen Ted ride away with Buck to attend to range duties. He knew better than to ask Sneed where his men were, or where he had been on his long ride. In fact, Sheriff Frost was satisfied with the arrangement he had with the notorious outlaw, and, moreover, he was puzzled by a new quality which seemed to have permeated Sneed's being, even his speech. Could it be, he asked himself, that Sneed was becoming tired of the game? Might it not be possible that this clean, growing youngster would bring something into the outlaw's life which would cause him gradually to give up his nefarious expeditions? He did not know, of course, that Sneed, in a way, was bound by his men. It would not be so easy for the outlaw chief to step out of his role; and some of his men knew too much. Left to themselves, they might attempt something and fail—be captured and talk. There were counties far to southward that had posted rewards on Sneed's head; there were sheriffs in a bordering State that would give much to get him. Sneed's position was not an easy one, and his responsibilities were great.

But the sheriff could not resist one final word of warning at parting. "I'm looking for you to do the right thing by that boy, Sneed," he said soberly.

"Then don't do your lookin' at too short a distance," was Sneed's snarling comment as he waved the sheriff on his way angrily.

Sneed made a personal inspection of the south part of his big ranch that day, accompanied by Ted and Buck. The outlaw seemed to take a fresh interest in the great domain of his rendezvous.

"We need more cattle in here," he grunted. "I don't want any more to winter, but next spring I'm goin' to buy." That was all; but the remark interested Buck very much.

He repeated it to Lucy Ware that night when they sat alone in the living-room after Ted had gone to bed, happily tired.

"You sure you're goin' to *buy* 'em?" Lucy asked sceptically.

"That's what I said," replied Sneed with a deep scowl. "You're always on the off side, Lucy. It's been a long time since I stooped to rustlin'."

"There's no reason why you shouldn't go in for stock raisin' an' make good at it," soothed Lucy. "I reckon you've got the capital."

He looked at her suspiciously but her look was beguiling. "Yes, I've got it," he confessed. He leaned toward her and lowered his voice. "I took a bank this time—down in Wyoming. Sheep money!" He chuckled scornfully. "I left 'em half a dozen blind trails to follow an' told the boys to make their Fourth of July last a month. One more job this fall an' I'll turn 'em loose for the winter," he added thoughtfully.

Lucy Ware looked at him anxiously. "You're tacklin' bigger stuff all the time, it seems to me," she said in a half-worried tone. "You know there's such a thing as the game gettin' too big."

Sneed frowned impatiently. "The bigger the

stake, the easier it is to make terms," he said gruffly.

"I'm wonderin'," said Lucy slowly, "what's goin' to happen when you meet a man who won't make terms."

Sneed's teeth flashed in a sinister smile. "Do your wondering about the other fellow," he said. "He'll need sympathy, for he'll sure be lacking in brains. They don't call me Killer Sneed because they think it tickles my vanity, sister."

"Yes," said Lucy thoughtfully; "I know that."

It was two weeks after this that Buck had to shoot down a charging steer. The animal came for him as his horse stumbled and threw him. Buck undoubtedly saved his own life with his gun. It was good, quick shooting, too.

Ted Ryder came in with a very sober look in his eyes that evening. He was strangely quiet at supper and both Sneed and Lucy noted it. Moreover, they felt a certain concern. Sneed told himself angrily that he was a fool to worry about the kid, and that he must be getting childish or something. But something had happened and Sneed was curious. He elected, however, to let Ted broach the matter himself. He was conscious of a peculiar sensation of apprehension. Did Ted want to leave? Well, suppose he *did*. It would relieve him, Sneed, of any worry about him, wouldn't it? Probably best, too. And yet Sneed felt relieved when he learned the cause for the boy's thoughtful air.

"Something happened to-day, Uncle Jess," he said. He had taken to calling Sneed that—at Lucy's instigation, probably, for she was the only one who ever called Sneed by his first name. And Sneed, not knowing whether to be pleased or annoyed, had made no complaint.

"What happened?" Sneed demanded, his eyes narrowing. Had someone been talking to the boy—telling him things?

"Well, a steer—an' ugly devil an' a no-good long-horn—charged Buck when his horse stumbled an' threw him," Ted explained soberly. "Buck was afoot an' the steer coming at him like furies. I couldn't do anything for I was too far away. Buck had to shoot him. It was a close shave. I was wonderin' what would happen to me if *I* got in such a fix. Seems to me like I ought to have a gun."

Sneed stared open-mouthed at Lucy Ware; and Lucy stared back, a little frightened, it seemed. It might have been that both of them had expected this to come but had avoided the subject. Then Sneed scowled. Of course the boy had to have a gun! What man on that range *didn't* have one! Men had been known to save themselves from being dragged and kicked to death, with a foot caught in the stirrup, by shooting their own horse! Buck had found use for his weapon that day.

Moreover, a gun could be used in *self*-defence as well as in attack.

"Let me see that right hand of yours, son," said Sneed curiously, avoiding Lucy's eyes.

He took the hand Ted held out to him and his own eyes sparkled with admiration. It was a strong hand, a beautifully formed hand with strength where it was needed and firm, tapering fingers, and a good thumb. A perfect gun-hand!

"Grip my fingers as hard as you can, Ted," he ordered. "*Hard,* now."

His fingers were white with the contact when the smiling boy released them.

"I reckon you can handle a regular six-gun," said Sneed with a grunt. "Well, we'll see."

Sneed rode away next morning and didn't return that night. It wasn't until the evening of two days later that he came back. He had gone far—to a town that was safe—to make his purchases. And those purchases consisted of a gun-belt, holster, cartridges, and a perfectly-balanced forty-five that fitted Ted's hand as if made to order. And that night, when Ted stood before Sneed and Lucy, proudly wearing his new accoutrement, he suddenly seemed to have shaken off his boyishness. His flashing smile gave them a start. And Sneed stared again when Ted drew, not fast, to be sure, but in a free and easy manner, and tipped the blue barrel of the empty gun at his hip in a dead aim on the lamp.

"He's got it!" said Sneed in excitement as the youth went to put his newly-acquired property safely away in his room.

"Yes, he's got it!" Lucy snapped out. "Even *I* could see that. An' now all he needs is the polishing off you'll give him to make him a first-class gunman! I suppose that's what you want."

"If he's ever goin' to have any trouble," said Sneed with a gleam in his eye, "he might better know how to use that gun than not. It's more dangerous to be slow with a gun than fast, if you're goin' to pack one around."

Ted Ryder's lessons started bright and early next morning. First Sneed instructed him as to the care of his weapon. Then he made him practise holding it, spinning it, fondling it, playing with it—instinctively acquiring its "feel." This went on for two or three days before Ted ever shot the gun. From straight-arm shooting, Sneed gradually brought him down to the hip. Accuracy first! The draw came last.

And now Sneed entered into his work heart and soul. He spent hours with the youth and his very being glowed with satisfaction as he watched Ted's progress. Why, the youth was a natural-born expert! In a week he was drawing, aiming and firing almost with a single motion. Then Sneed filed the trigger-spring. Now the draw became a combined move of wrist, fingers and thumb, with the shot coming as soon as the gun was clear of its holster. By time the men had begun to drift back to the rendezvous in August, Ted was drawing and hitting targets with a speed denied to most men of the range. But he was still a novice compared with Sneed. And the older man began to teach him certain tricks. In fact, Sneed had determined to make this unsuspecting youth a veritable terror with his weapon, whether he was ever to have occasion to use his skill or not. But he also was careful to give meaty bits of advice.

"You're goin' to be fast, son," he told the boy. "But you want to remember that bein' fast is a danger to yourself. Never *start* things an' *never* touch your gun in a pinch *unless you're goin' to use it!* I just want to make you fast enough so you'll never have to draw *first,* understand?"

Ted understood. He got a great thrill out of these lessons and the hours upon hours of practice. And the day he beat Buck to it when they sprung a coyote in the hills and dropped the animal in its tracks with a shot from the saddle was—till then—the greatest day of his life.

Lucy watched and worried. If Ted had to be a gunman—because it was a protection, as Sneed insisted—he might as well be a good one. But suppose the boy's enthusiasm should carry him away and he should get beyond Sneed's control? Womanlike, she permitted her imagination to run riot. Then she began subtly to combat this enthusiasm by getting Ted to read in the evenings. She saw that he read the right books, too. And, as the days grew shorter and the evenings lengthened, he developed a passion for reading and for knowledge. Sneed would sit of an evening with an unlighted cigar in his mouth and watch Lucy Ware and Ted doing mathematical problems, or listening to Lucy explain the meaning of words that she, herself, had probably had to look up when she first encountered them—for lack of a teacher. Lucy sent an order to a mail order house, and in time several packages of books were received in Morning Glory and Buck was sent to get them with stern orders from Sneed to "keep his mouth shut!" With the arrival of a big dictionary, Ted relieved Lucy of the responsibility for unknown meanings of words and phrases.

By the first of September all the members of Sneed's band were back. A trip into the high mountains for big game was planned and encouraged by Sneed. Buck and Ted brought down the beef steers and the time approached to drive them to the shipping point in the north. Sneed, of course, would have to attend to the sale; but someone would have to go to Chicago with the cattle. He was wondering who to send with Buck when that individual broached the matter.

"Ted wants to go along," he said to Sneed. "I

can look after him, although he's pretty well able to look after himself. Anyway, I reckon it wouldn't hurt him any to see a little of the world."

Sneed and Lucy talked it over that night and decided to let Ted go. "A trip like that'll round him out a little," was the way Sneed put it. And Lucy agreed. But before they started with the beeves she had a serious talk with Buck and admonished him to keep Ted away from disrespectable places and not to drink. Sneed told him to use his brains or he'd "just naturally scatter 'em to the winds" when he came back.

They drove the cattle slowly, grazed them along, in fact, so that they wouldn't lose any weight. The steers were mostly three-year-old Herefords, with a smattering of four-year-old shorthorns, and some range stock. There were three hundred head exactly. The brand was a Lazy L with a bar through it. It was registered in Lucy Ware's name and, to all purposes, Lucy was the owner of the cattle and the ranch.

Now Sneed's name had carried far, but there was none he knew of who would recognise him at first sight in the town where they were to ship. He took the precaution, however, to camp just outside the town with his cattle, which was not at all unusual. He had written ahead to secure the cars.

He went into town and arranged the papers with the bank in Lucy's name, as he carried her power-of-attorney to sign her name and attend to all business matters. He used Buck's name, which, in full, was Fred Andrews, having warned him in advance that he so intended doing. This would also smooth matters for Buck at the eastern market.

He found that they were not the only outfit shipping that next day, for the S-S was also loading. This outfit came from the great ranch just below Sneed's place in the basin, owned by Nate Sinclair, a cattle baron of the old school, and one of the most important stockmen in the north range country. Sinclair knew Sneed by sight, but, so far as Sneed was able to judge, was friendly. They had never had trouble, for Sneed had never bothered stock or "worked" in the north counties. Sneed took care to ascertain if Sinclair was in town and learned he had gone back to his ranch, leaving his shipping in the hands of his foreman, Lute Balmer. If Balmer knew Sneed he made no sign.

The facilities were excellent and both outfits were loading next day when a Lazy L steer broke loose and dashed towards an S-S bunch of cattle with Ted Ryder in pursuit. The steer stopped short of the S-S bunch, and Ted, spurring his big black, dashed in and headed the animal about. But in doing so he disturbed the S-S cattle, set some of them on the run, and brought Balmer himself galloping to the scene.

"If you don't know how to work cattle get out of here!" the S-S foreman yelled in an enraged voice which carried to the chutes. He followed this with a string of oaths.

Sneed heard and sent his horse flying towards them.

"Dry up yore mouth!" came the boy's clear, ringing voice.

Balmer straightened in his saddle with the profanity dying on his lips. He was frozen with surprise. But Sneed had caught a note in Ted's voice which caused his heart to bound. The youth was a stranger to fear. Ted's face was white under its bronze and his eyes were flashing when Sneed arrived.

"Chase that steer back!" Sneed commanded sternly.

"Not till he takes back what he called me," Ted gritted through his teeth.

"Do as I say!" thundered Sneed.

The boy hesitated, then drove in his spurs and obeyed.

Lute Balmer was regarding Sneed steadily. But he said nothing. Nor did his face betray his thoughts. But Sneed was certain this man knew the brand on the steer; knew where they came from; knew *him.*

"I reckon you're willin' to let a kid learn," he

said coldly. "Learn the cow business, I mean, not language."

"He seems to be able to talk, *any*way," was Balmer's comment.

"But you see," purred Sneed, "*I'm* doin' the talkin' for the Lazy L, Balmer."

"That lets the kid out of it, I suppose," said Balmer wryly.

"Suppose is a triflin' word, Balmer," said Sneed in the same purring voice. "Don't suppose anything, Balmer—*know it!*"

"I'll take your word for it, then," said Balmer with a dark look. And he rode away forthwith.

Sneed took Ted to task when the cattle were loaded and the train was ready to start. "Throwin' it back at a man like that means gun-play," he finished, "an' you're not invitin' that—yet, anyway. Nor *any* time, if I have anything to say about it. I'm goin' to tell you for the first an' last time, while you're with me you'll do as I say. Keep remembering that. You'll obey Buck's orders on this trip."

He gave them a generous supply of money, allowing Buck a good surplus, and saw them off, Ted waving his hat from the rear of the caboose. He waved back and watched the train out of sight before he started on the long ride back to the ranch. He was thoughtful on that ride; for he knew what Ted didn't know—that the boy had made his first enemy.

Chapter VII

An Accident

Sneed forbore telling Lucy Ware of the incident in the shipping town as Lucy was already beginning to worry about the absent youth. Knowing, as she did, the many temptations which would beset an active young range rider like Buck, she feared that he might yield to them and show Ted a phase of life which might influence his future. But Sneed told her this was nonsense, for he had given Buck his orders and he had good reason to believe he would live up to them. Well, then, the train might be wrecked, according to Lucy, or Ted might get trampled in the pens in Chicago, or run over by a street car—he wasn't used to crowded streets, was he?

Sneed swore softly and looked at Lucy with new interest.

"I reckon that kid's sort of got us both milling," he said. "Well, I'm goin' to make a stockman out of him, an' if he can't get around without being hurt—" He paused, thinking of what had happened in town. Then he smiled queerly. "I've got a sneaking notion that Ted can take care of himself," he finished.

"You're always expectin' people to take care

of themselves, Jess Sneed," said Lucy. "Well, there's times when they can't. An' watch out that some time *you* don't get in that fix."

This amused Sneed at the time; but he had occasion to think of it afterward.

Ted and Buck would be away about twelve days or two weeks. He had given them permission to stay in Chicago a week, however, if they wished. One thing which had prompted him to permit Ted to go was that he would be away from the men. True, none of the band had tried to associate with him; they treated him decently enough. But Ted had evinced some curiosity as to them. Sneed had had to invent certain special duties they were supposed to have on another range in the south, and had told Ted that as his protégé—a word that had sent the youth to the dictionary for enlightenment—he lived in the house and was not supposed to be familiar with the men in the bunk-house. This was ridiculous and incongruous, but Ted didn't know differently. Yet Sneed found himself dissatisfied with having to lie to the boy. It was about this time that Sneed himself began to wonder if he could be changing in some ways.

It was the last week in September when Ted and Buck left with the cattle, and the first week in October the members of the band, led by Snark Levant, struck into the high mountains to hunt big game. Sneed told them to take a month of it and get in shape for an expedition which would mean a big "Christmas stake." The men grinned pleasantly at this, and Sneed realised more keenly than ever that it was the promise of profitable raids that held these outlaws loyal to him. Secretly, he held them in contempt; all save Snark Levant. His lieutenant was the possessor of a wicked cunning, a treacherous temper, and a certain amount of ambition. He was dangerous.

In about two weeks, perhaps a day or two over, Ted and Buck came back just before sundown. They brought an extra horse, which they had purchased at the shipping town, and the horse bore a heavy pack. Both Sneed and Lucy stood about, rather excited, while words streamed from Ted's lips as he and Buck took off the pack and opened it on the porch. Then Buck took the horses away, bestowing a significant wink on the thunderstruck leader of the outlaws, who didn't know whether to laugh or swear.

Ted had brought him a magnificent wallet! And on its side was a flamboyant S in gold!

For Lucy Ware there were lace collars, a string of large blue beads, a pair of ornate side-combs, a bracelet and—an ivory cigarette holder! This for Lucy, who rolled her own like a man! But she was immensely pleased and fluttered about in great excitement, while Sneed stood, holding his new wallet in his great hand, with a bewildered look on his face.

Further exploration of the pack brought to light a quantity of books, a collection of big, coloured silk handkerchiefs, a pair of expensive gauntlet gloves, some fine flannel shirts, clothing and haberdashery—all of the very best.

Ted stood up before them, his fine eyes sparkling. "How do you like the outfit?" he asked Sneed.

Sneed was looking him over from head to foot, and Ted was a sight pleasing to the eye. He wore a new pair of black, hand-made boots which he evidently had polished before riding in as they fairly glistened. He sported as sweet a pair of white angora chaps as Sneed had ever seen. His new, grey flannel shirt fairly sneered quality at the black sateen Sneed wore. On his head was a new, high-crowned, black, beaver Stetson that set his face off to its best advantage and shrieked "Fifty dollars!" to the high winds.

"How much for the boots?" Sneed inquired with a somewhat silly look.

"Twenty-five dollars," replied Ted with a proud glance down at his well-shod feet. "They'll last, too, for they've got the stuff in 'em."

"Humph!" grunted Sneed. "How much for the hat?"

"That stands us fifty," Ted answered cheerfully, spilling a little neat language he'd learned on the trip.

"Us? Who's *us?*" Sneed demanded. He was

making a swift calculation as to the probable amount spent.

"Why, Buck an' me," said the youth, surprised. "Buck said we could buy everything we wanted. He had plenty of money, besides what *I* had, an' he said there was lots more where *that* came from. We went to some shows an' put on the dog a little. Wasn't that all right?" Ted's eyes clouded for a moment.

"Of *course* it was all right!" exclaimed Lucy Ware. "You can have everything you want, Teddie boy. How'd you know I liked beads?"

"The girls was all wearin' 'em," said Ted with a shy grin.

"Well, I'll be—" Sneed sputtered. "How'd you get that other horse?" he asked curiously.

"Buck bought him," said Ted. "Only fifty dollars—but I reckon that was too much. We can use him, though. Buck says he'll be all right for a miscellaneous horse."

"I see," said Sneed, nodding his head. "So you've been to Chicago?" He looked at Lucy Ware who was smiling in a superior manner. "It's a dang good thing I instructed 'em to send the draft for the cattle to the bank," he declared, "or we'd never got a cent out of 'em. We'd have been paid in goods!" he finished with a snort.

"Jess!" said Lucy Ware severely. "You go get ready for supper!"

"Oh, I'll help the lad up with his purchases,"

said Sneed mildly. “I suppose you want to store all this in your room, eh, Ted?”

“Why—yes.” Ted looked at him soberly. “Did I do anything wrong, Uncle Jess?”

“Sufferin’ snakes, no!” Sneed boomed. Then, with something suspiciously like a twinkle in his eyes: “If you ever run short of cash change, son, don’t get what you need from Buck or any of the men. Just whisper to me or mention it to—to your Aunt Lucy.” He stamped inside with an armful of Ted’s belongings.

Later he listened with ill-concealed interest and amusement to Buck’s account of their trip. They had had no trouble with the cattle and they hadn’t seen Lute Balmer and his men in the market. Ted had been wildly excited and intensely interested in Chicago. No, they hadn’t gone in a saloon. Had Buck, himself, gone in any? Well, if he had, Ted hadn’t known anything about it. Ted went to bed early and slept soundly. Yes, he’d advanced him money; why not? He was dirty with money he couldn’t spend. Why, sure, he’d take it back. Thanks.

“They thought Ted was the son of some great stockman,” Buck finished with a grin. “An’ the kid didn’t tell ’em any different!”

Thus was young Ted Ryder’s position as a fixture in the peculiar household of Killer Sneed cemented.

Next morning there were warning signals

in the sky above the mountains where dark clouds scurried across the peaks and unfurled their grey streamers far to eastward. The sun climbed bravely into the thickening vapours and was drowned. Then a veil of misty white crept down out of the north and the land was soon mantled in snow. The wind caught the turning leaves of the cottonwoods and strewed them like golden spangles on the glistening robe of white. Dogwoods and wild cherries marched in ranks of crimson against the green of pines and firs. The fine flakes drove in on a blast with the coming of night and then for three days a mild blizzard, harbinger of harsher storms to come, held the hills and basin country in its chilling grasp.

The fourth day broke with the promise of that wonderful, mellow, colourful season of the semi-altitudes—Indian Summer. The snowy coverlet melted in the warm rays of a friendly sun. The landscape suddenly flamed as Nature lavished her golds and purples and crimsons on the trees and grasses, and spilled the contents of her paint-pots on the hills. A tang came into the air, crisp and cool at night, moderately warm by day. Grouse, gloriously plumed, whirred across the meadows, and great flocks of blackbirds swarmed and chattered of the coming pilgrimage to the south.

Such was the setting for Ted Ryder's sixteenth birthday.

He didn't tell them until the very morning of that important day. But Cloe, the coloured house cook, found time to make a great cake. Buck was invited to dinner in the house that day. Sneed, taken by surprise, announced that he would "stake" Ted to a few head of cattle for his own the next spring. Lucy Ware produced a gold ring of curious design—a serpent holding an emerald in its mouth—and told Ted if it fitted him, it would mean good luck to him as long as he wore it. It fitted the third finger of his left hand perfectly and the youth flung his arms about her and kissed her on the cheek.

Indian Summer lingered and the men remained in the hills until the second week in November. Then they came back under steel-grey skies, bringing venison and elk meat and many choice heads to adorn the bunk-house. They had stopped at Morning Glory and for three days following their return they celebrated moderately.

Sneed, beset with conflicting emotions and impulses, yielded finally to the lure of the danger-trail and gave Snark Levant the expected order. "We start to-morrow night," was all he said.

Once more Lucy Ware and Ted watched them ride away; and this time the woman was more agitated than before. She kept her arm on Ted's shoulder until they had passed from view.

"Where are they going?" Ted asked wonderingly.

"To—to close the lower ranch for the—the winter," Lucy said in a worried voice.

"When will they be back?" Ted persisted.

"I don't know," replied Lucy. "You might as well tell Buck to come in an' have supper with us." She wanted someone else to talk to Ted that night while she laboured with misgivings.

During the week that followed Lucy Ware could not shake off the vague premonition which obsessed her. She had been reared in an environment of superstition. She remembered the first time she had been given a piece of paper money after a song in a hurdy-gurdy where she was queen. She was afraid of the bank-note for she had been accustomed only to silver and gold. Sure enough, a man had been killed there that night. She thought of the cowpuncher who claimed to have been a sailor. He had said when they wanted wind at sea they cut a cross in the main-mast. So, since they needed rain, he proposed to cut a cross in the bar. It would work both ways, he had declared. Then he had cut the cross and rain had fallen in torrents within a day. She remembered many instances when her forebodings of disaster had proved well founded.

Late one afternoon a strong wind came into being as if at a signal. It marshalled the clouds in the north and hurled them before the sunset, bringing an early twilight. It rapidly grew colder; the wind strengthened and shook free the last of the sear, clinging leaves; night closed in, inky-black, and there were no stars. In another hour the snow was stinging the window-panes and the blast was howling in the naked branches.

Lucy Ware sat up late that night in the living-room and nursed her troubled thoughts. A keen, tingling sense that there was something wrong came over her. She felt that she would cry out in terror if she remained inactive. She rose and fell to pacing the room. The fire in the heating stove crackled. The house seemed to shake as the blizzard hurled its furies upon it. She dropped again into the chair and closed her eyes. She wondered afterwards if she had dozed and dreamed, or if it was a vision. She saw a short street with shadowy buildings on either side. Tall, gaunt trees reared against the star-filled sky. Then from one of the buildings came a burst of light and a thundering report. There were swift-moving shadows in the street now, spurts of flame and the sharp barking of guns. A huge man swerved in the saddle on a great, black horse, shouted hoarsely, slumped forward and dashed away followed by others. She could hear the hoof-beats—pound, pound, pound—dull, resounding echoes.

Suddenly she was sitting up, staring straight ahead. There it was—the pounding. Someone at the door! She ran to draw the bolt and open it. A great form lurched against her and into the room.

The lamp flamed and smoked in the draught and she closed the door with difficulty, shutting out the storm. Then she cried out.

Sneed, his face cruelly white under its tan and the thick stubble of beard, was leaning his left hand on the table. His right hung motionless, the fingers stained with the dark red of clotted blood. His eyes stared at her out of caverns.

"Get this coat off," he said thickly. "Bring water an' look after my right arm and hand. The *right,* do you hear?" His tone was terrible with futile rage. "They got me twice in the right."

He slumped into a chair and Lucy, with queer, unintelligible mouthings, cut the right sleeve and drew off his coat. She used the shears on his shirt and then, at sight of the wounds, she became suddenly calm. She brought water and iodine and clean bandages and set about her work while Sneed grumbled.

"My first night job since I don't know when," he muttered. "A bank. We cleaned it but they were out an' on us before we expected 'em. I was last to leave. They hit me where it'd do the most good. My right, Lucy, d'ye hear? *My right!*"

Lucy Ware heard. And she realised the significance of the wounds. For it was Killer Sneed's right arm and hand that held the power of his dreaded name.

"The men mustn't learn," he said in a hoarse

whisper. "An' there's one in particular who must be kept in the dark."

"I know," said Lucy with a nod. "Snark Levant."

"An' young Ted," he whispered. "We'll tell him it was an accident. The rest of the world can go to blazes. An' so help me, it's come! *I'm finished!* Lucy, get me some whisky."

In the barn, by the flickering yellow light of two lanterns, Buck and the wrangler worked over a horse that had been ridden nearly to the death to bring its master home through the storm.

Chapter VIII

The First Bluff

In the morning Sneed was tossing, a bit delirious, with a fever. His right arm was swollen and there was danger of blood poisoning; for he had ridden nearly a day, and more than half the night before, with little rest and but casual attention to his wounds.

Lucy Ware was greatly worried, and she realised that Sneed required the services of a doctor. But he was not in condition to ride to a town. The blizzard was raging with increased ferocity. Any thought of reaching the county seat or one of the larger towns in the basin was out of the question. One could not follow a given direction in the flat country in that blinding swirl of snow. But the trail to the Morning Glory road was blazed and the hills and trees afforded some shelter and, to a certain extent, broke the force of the blast. It might be possible for a man who knew the way to get to the mining camp where there was a doctor.

At breakfast Lucy explained that Sneed had been hurt; but she evaded Ted's anxious queries and intimated that he had been injured at the "southern place" attending to cattle or something she didn't know just how. Anyway, he was confined to his room and must not be disturbed. But Ted was to stay in and keep handy in event she should want him for anything.

She confided in Buck, however; told him what had happened and asked him if he felt he wanted to try to get to Morning Glory and bring back the doctor. Buck volunteered at once. He scoffed at the danger Lucy feared and said the only trouble might be in getting the doctor to return with him. "But I'll bring him," he added, with a significant nod. So Lucy saw him leave within half an hour.

The trip to Morning Glory wasn't easy; nor had Buck expected it to be. He battled with the storm across the open meadows, over the ridges, and found his only respites in the forest where the trail led through the dim aisles, somewhat protected from the merciless wind. His progress was necessarily slow. Night had fallen when he reached the road. Of course, the road was easy to follow, being bounded by timber and banks, and his horse was eager to reach the shelter of a barn and accordingly gave the best there was in him. Still, it was after nine o'clock when he rode into Morning Glory. As he left the barn he realised it was useless to attempt to go back that night. His horse was too far spent, for one thing; and the trail would be impossible to follow in the darkness with the snow stinging his eyes.

Now Buck was wise enough to know that it would not be showing sense to advertise his presence in town or let his mission become known. There were too many who would want to know how serious Sneed was hurt and how he had been injured. Let it be noised about that Sneed was down and out, and the rumour would spread on the wings of magic. None could predict what might happen. So Buck went to the hotel, took a few drinks quietly at the bar, and if any recognised him they said nothing, or assumed he was in for a few days "on his own." He took the precaution to seal the barman's lips with a yellow-back. He went to bed puzzling as to how he could handle the doctor.

Blizzards—and the worst of them, at that!—are often temperamental. Dawn came with skies of steel but with little wind and no snow falling. Buck sensed the redoubling of the fury of the storm in this lull, but he decided to take advantage of it. He had an early breakfast and made his way immediately to the doctor's cabin. The doctor had just made his fire and was starting breakfast. But he admitted Buck and asked his business, for he was not unaccustomed to calls at any hour of the day or night.

"Want to take a ride to-day, doc?" said Buck cheerfully. "Can't bring the—er—patient to town."

"Where is it?" the doctor demanded, motioning the young puncher into the kitchen, where he busied himself at the stove.

"South of here," said Buck. "Lazy L ranch, they call it."

The doctor shot a quick glance at him. "That's supposed to be *Sneed's* place, isn't it?" he asked shrewdly with a frown.

Buck saw that while the doctor apparently didn't know him, he knew of Sneed and the location of the ranch. The frown didn't promise well. There were many excuses the doctor could make to get out of taking the trip. He could plead patients in town—which, in itself, would be enough.

"What of it?" he asked. If it was going to be necessary to use stern measures Buck was prepared to attempt to compel the man to accompany him, even if he had to do so at the point of the gun.

"That's where the Ryder boy is, isn't it?" the doctor demanded with interest. "A shame!" he ejaculated at Buck's nod. "A bright boy living with a man like Killer Sneed. I treated that lad once—it wasn't anything much—but he was a bright one. What's the matter? Is the *boy* ill?"

Buck's method of procedure opened automatically as he saw the concern in the doctor's eyes.

"Yes," he said slowly. "I rode all night in the storm to get here, doc. It's more settled now an' I reckon you'd better go back with me. You'll be well paid, I can tell you that."

"I'm not thinking of the pay," said the doctor

in a grumbling tone as he put his breakfast on the table and started to eat. "What's the matter with him?"

Buck shrugged. "I don't know much about sickness," he said, "an' I don't live in the house. But I guess it's pretty bad for 'em to be sending up here for you."

The doctor complained and made more remarks about the inadvisability of keeping Ted on the ranch with Sneed. He was middle-aged, this doctor, and long in the hills. "I don't want to see his face while I'm there!" he cried belligerently, referring to Sneed. Then he made ready to go.

The lull in the storm lasted more than half the morning and they made good time. Shortly before noon the flakes began to scurry above the trees and then the wind came down and the world was a maelstrom of blinding white. Buck, in the lead, pushed on at the fastest pace possible. Acting on his advice, the doctor had not taken his regular horse but had accepted a mount chosen by the experienced barnman. They battled their way through most of the afternoon. It was biting cold and the blast seemed to pierce their heavy sheep-lined coats. The doctor was showing the effects of the ride and the exposure when they reached the ranch in the early dusk.

He shook the snow from his cap and coat, and pounded his hands to restore normal circulation, at the same time stamping his feet. Buck brought him a generous drink of whisky, which he took. Then Buck spoke.

"It's *Sneed* you've come to see, doc," he said, in a low, even voice. "Now don't explode or get rash with your talk. It won't do any good. I was afraid you'd back out if you knew it was Sneed an' then I'd have had to *make* you come. An' don't say anything to the boy."

"I won't treat that—that monster!" cried the enraged doctor.

"Oh, yes, you will," said Buck coolly. "You'll treat him the best you know how an' take your pay for it, an' keep your mouth shut! Now, just listen to me a minute. This blizzard is back on us with all it's got. It's good for three days straight at the least, an' you know it. If you fly off the handle I'll just naturally *turn you loose in it.* I reckon you can figure how long you'd last. You couldn't find your way back to Morning Glory, or back to the ranch, for that matter, within a mile of here. But that ain't it. If you get onery I'll turn you loose *in the basin!* You know what *that* means. An' when they find your bones in the spring, why—you got lost goin' back home, that's all. See how it is?"

The doctor understood. This was Sneed's work, of course. And Sneed never made any idle threats. It would be just like him to give the order to turn him loose in the blizzard. That would mean death! The doctor ground his teeth, but he had no alternative but to treat Sneed. He was madder than ever over the thought that Sneed had fooled him by using the boy.

"Let's go in," he snapped. "An' my price may be higher than you think!"

The doctor had made a decision. If it was a matter of life or death he would drive a hard bargain with Sneed. He would make him promise to give up the boy and to forsake his nefarious profession before beginning the fight to save his life. He knew men of Sneed's type were deadly fearful of a natural death. They preferred death with their boots on, when they couldn't see it coming, or have time to think about it.

But he received three shocks soon after entering the house. The first was the interior of the house itself. Instead of being the sort of place he had expected—untidy, with saddles and guns thrown about, empty bottles in corners, soiled, cheap lithographs on the walls, worn and dirty carpet on the floors—it was neat and clean and comfortable, well and tastefully furnished, with clean paper and good pictures on the walls, and thick rugs and excellent carpets.

His second shock came when Lucy Ware, a comely matron, came into the living-room followed by the tall, bronzed, broad-shouldered youth Ted, who he remembered as a much smaller boy with large, questioning eyes.

But he received the shock which nonplussed

and bewildered him when he followed Lucy Ware to Sneed's bedroom and saw the great form in the bed and looked into the eyes which men feared. The cruel, menacing glare he had expected, and which he was prepared to meet sternly, was not there. Instead, the light in Sneed's eyes was almost childishly wistful. And when he spoke it was in a tone of vibrant apprehension.

"It's my right arm, doc. Look at it. The *right* one, there." He looked down at the bandaged arm, and the doctor, being wise in the way of the hills and the range, understood.

He made a thorough examination. "Thank goodness, I brought some instruments," he muttered. His professional instincts were aroused to the exclusion of everything else. He leaned back finally and looked Sneed straight in the eyes. "May be gangrene there," he said slowly, "but I guess I can save your arm. It's pretty well smashed up. It'll never be the same, Sneed."

The big man turned away. Then a horrible curse came to his lips and he half rose in the bed. "I'm through!" he cried. "Do you hear that, doc? *I'm through!* Now I'll have the pack on me. The cowardly curs. I never was the first to draw in all my life, an' they call me The Killer!" His voice rose in shrill crescendo. *"They might better have shot me in the heart!"* He sank back exhausted.

Lucy Ware, hurrying down for warm water for

the doctor, saw Ted at the bottom of the stairs, looking up out of startled eyes.

"What did he mean by that shout?" asked the boy.

"He's out of his head," said Lucy in a shaking voice. "It's—the fever!"

For three days the blizzard raged with increasing fury while the doctor remained in the house and fought to save Sneed's arm and his life. Then, as the storm began to subside, the doctor saw he was winning. He stayed on another three days, and Sneed, sitting up in bed, pale and listless, heard him giving directions to Lucy Ware and announcing his intention to depart.

"What's the bill?" Sneed asked. "Make it plenty, doc; I suppose it's worth it." The doctor knew the man was thinking of his crippled arm as not being worth saving.

He had intended to ask certain things, but now he was in doubt. He had seen much while he had been there and had heard certain things from Lucy. He was surprised to learn that Ted knew nothing of Sneed's reputation and business. He was surprised that the boy had what seemed to be a good home. But not for one minute did he believe that Sneed was sickening of his profession. "Character once firmly established, can't be changed," he told himself, although he had the glimmer of a doubt. Perhaps Sneed, with his arm crippled, his lightning draw gone forever, *might* change. The thought that the boy's influence might have something to do with it never entered his head.

"I don't care so much about the bill, Sneed," said the doctor. "Us fellows don't work for money exactly, although we need some of it. But I should like to say that I hope this will be enough of a lesson for you to—well, to try and make amends for your past. As a gunman you're through, like you say. You'll find that out when your arm is out of the bandages. An' you're too old to teach your left hand what your right hand once knew. Maybe my telling you this will start you thinking."

Sneed wasn't looking at him. "Say, doc," he said, "would you mind promising me not to mention what's wrong with me aroun' town?"

"All right," said the doctor. "I promise. I suppose it would be like kicking a man when he's down."

"Lucy!" Sneed called. "Lucy! Oh, there you are. Pay the doc a thousand an' have Buck take him back to the Morning Glory road."

The doctor didn't offer to take Sneed's left hand, possibly because Sneed didn't extend it; and if he had looked back as he went out he would have seen the greenish, baleful glare in The Killer's eyes that he had expected to meet the day he had come.

The sun came out that noon and the weather

mended speedily. In a few days the snow was gone, save for in the ravines, under the thick timber and on the high peaks. It rolled on towards Christmas and Sneed went about with his arm in a sling. His mood now was terrible. His face was set in a perpetual frown. Only to Lucy and Ted was he civil. Then came the day when Snark Levant and several other members of the band rode in. They had waited for the snow to go off the trails so they wouldn't be leaving tell-tale tracks behind them. That day Sneed took his arm out of the sling.

There was a meeting in the bunk-house that night, with Sneed sitting at the head of the table, his arms resting on its top, his eyes roving over the men before him. Snark Levant sat at the foot, looking queerly at his chief. Sneed had no way of ascertaining if these men knew the truth, save through Buck, and none had hinted of any such knowledge to him. But Buck was no longer considered as being strictly on the "inside" by the others of the band, as he had not been along on the last two raids. Therefore, it was not likely he would be a target for confidences.

It was clear and cold, this night, and Lucy Ware, suspecting that it was to be an important conclave which might fly off at any tangent, had put on a fur coat and cap and slipped across the yard after Sneed. She stood now at a window where she was in the shadow of a tall fir, and where she could see Sneed's back and the faces of the men. It was Snark Levant whom she watched through the flimsy, cracked curtain.

There was some business talk in low voices and Sneed tossed a packet of bills to Levant with his left hand.

"Slip that around," she heard him say, "an' that squares us for the season."

Snark took the packet. "What're we goin' to do?" he asked with a scowl. "Lay aroun' all winter?"

"That's for you to figure out," Sneed replied crisply. "But there'll be no layin' around *here* all winter. I'd suggest that you bust up in small bunches an' hit for the towns across the range. We went pretty strong last two trips out, an' it's dangerous for us all to be hangin' out here. I'll keep Buck, an' the two old ones who've been here, to look after things. Probably I'll light out myself after a while."

Snark looked slowly about at the men. "Sounds like you was turnin' us out," he drawled with a mean inflection.

"You an' every man in the bunch has got a fat roll," said Sneed sternly. "I saw to that." His eyes narrowed and swept the crowd. "Anybody feel he's got any kick comin'?" Silence.

Lucy Ware felt a thrill. One hand came out of a sleeve of her coat and something flashed like silver in a ray of moonlight. Her breath came hard as she peered cautiously at the scene within.

"I was wonderin'," Snark began slowly, keeping his eyes on Sneed's, "if you takin' up that kid was goin' to change things for us."

There was a slight murmur from the men. Sneed tapped with the fingers of his right hand on the table.

"I reckon you've got a right to ask that," he said calmly, "an' you can make your own cake out of my answer. If you men can do better, or half as well, on your own hook, go to it."

"Meanin' you've gone soft on that brat an' want to get rid of us!" exclaimed Snark with a sneer.

In a breath Sneed had kicked back his chair, and was standing. His right arm was crooked so that his hand hovered, steady as steel, above the butt of his gun. Red fire flashed from his eyes—a flame from between the lids, which were narrowed to ribbons. His voice came hoarse with anger, yet fearfully strong with a clear-cut note of utter finality.

"I'm meanin' whatever you want to think!" he said. "You're not dealin' with a kid, Levant; you're dealin' with me—*Sneed.* If I'm turnin' you loose, to take the men an' do as you please, I'm doin' it because I don't think you'd ever have the nerve to double-cross me. If I thought *that,* I'd drop you in your tracks *now!*"

Snark Levant's face was working, the evil eyes were glittering; yet he seemed to be asking himself a question. None of them had seen Sneed after the bank robbery. They had gone in all directions, as was customary. Yet—what was there about Sneed which puzzled him? What was different; what was in the air, as it seemed? More than the boy. More than the hatred these two had for each other. What?

"You digested what I said?" asked Sneed sharply.

Snark's face cleared. "We'll be goin' in the morning," he said. "I'll take the bunch with *me*."

Sneed walked briskly to the door, his right hand remaining in its fixed position above his gun. He opened the door with his left. He knew what Levant meant. He was going to assume the leadership of the band. He paused for a final word.

"There's just one thing," he said in a voice that cut through the tense silence like a knife. *"Don't work in the north!"*

Outside he saw a dark form hurrying from the shadows toward the house. He overtook Lucy at the rear door. As she fumbled at the latch something fell from her grasp and lay glistening at Sneed's feet. He bent and picked it up with his left hand. He followed her in and held out his palm, with the small ivory-handled derringer in it, looking at her questioningly.

"I was at the window," she said breathlessly. "He'd never got you, Jess. I'd—have dropped him—for I had a bead on his heart. But I didn't know you could still draw."

A queer smile came to his lips. "I—I can't," he said, almost in a whisper. He looked down at his right hand above the gun. "It's stiff," he said. "I can't get it down lower without bending an' makin' a job of it. An' the *wrist* is stiff." He gazed quietly into her eyes. "It was my first bluff," he said calmly.

Chapter IX

The Blow Falls

Sneed had warned Buck and the two older men who were kept at the ranch not to say anything concerning the doctor's visit or to let an inkling of his injury escape from their lips. He trusted the tall, blond puncher Buck, and had ordered him to keep the other two under close surveillance to make sure his warning was heeded. In time, Snark Levant would know, quite likely: and Sneed realised that there would be no bluffing when that time came.

The men spent the next forenoon packing such belongings as they chose to take with them. To all appearances they were not loath to leave the ranch for a winter of carousal in the towns. Levant appeared cheerful enough, possibly because he had accepted Sneed's defi, and planned now to head the band. If he suspected any trick on Sneed's part, he gave no indication of it; if he knew the truth about Sneed's injury, he gave no indication of that either. He came to the house for a curt, businesslike good-bye after dinner.

An hour later the men rode away into the southwest hills with Snark Levant in the lead.

"It'll be time enough if they *never* come back," Sneed said to himself as he watched them out of sight from the porch.

During the week of fine weather which followed Sneed gave every evidence of a man distracted. He kept to himself, walking aimlessly about by day, sitting moodily by the stove in the living-room in the evenings. He thought many times about what Lucy Ware had told him concerning her vision or dream on the night he had arrived at the ranch. It was just about as it had happened, her description of what she had imagined. Queer business, that. Perhaps Sneed also was superstitious. These two were in many ways alike. He looked at her with respect of an evening when he recalled the pearl-handled derringer that would have made his bluff good the night he had challenged Snark Levant for the last time.

Four days before Christmas he announced that they would start the next morning for the shipping town north of the basin and there take train for Spokane to spend the holidays. Although surprised, Lucy Ware offered no objections. Once a year she went away from the ranch, but usually to one of the larger towns in the eastern prairie country. It broke the tedium, she told herself. Yet she was always glad to get back.

Buck drove them to the town in the spring wagon. Sneed told him to return for them in a month. They arrived in the city on the western side of the Divide the next evening, and Sneed told Ted and Lucy Ware to amuse themselves as they saw fit. He gave Ted a fine gold watch for Christmas; a set of expensive furs went to Lucy.

Ted explained to him that he thought something ought to be done about selling the mine so he would have some money of his own to spend and with which to repay certain favours. Sneed listened to this in approval and said he would advance him five hundred dollars on thc claim, but that it would be well to wait until the time was ripe before selling the property. The boy listened soberly, signed a paper which Sneed made out, took his money, and promptly bought Sneed a magnificent quirt and selected a bag for Lucy. Sneed tore up the paper Christmas Eve and sat in a stud poker game all night, emerging thirty-four hundred dollars to the good in time to wish them a merry Christmas in the morning.

Sneed now put in operation the plan he had in selecting the north-west city for the holiday. He visited specialist after specialist in the hope of having his arm mended. All to no avail. He left them for a week and went on to Seattle, where he called on more specialists with a like result. He tried Vancouver with no better success. He was permanently crippled. He returned to Spokane and gave himself up to an orgy of drinking and gambling till the time came to go home.

Buck met them at the shipping town and drove them home in a sleigh through a snowstorm. There was work for Buck and Ted after that. Baled hay had to be hauled from the basin for the stock and the stock had to be fed. The winter dragged on; days of blinding blizzard; periods of intense cold when the mercury dropped to thirty, forty, and even fifty below; weeks on end with the Chinook wind withholding the mercy of its warm breath. And during these months Ted Ryder became a strapping youth, merging into a man. Handsome, lithe, steel-muscled, with a natural grace of movement, he commanded admiration everywhere. Nor did he neglect his practice of gun-art. And Sneed redoubled his efforts to perfect the youth in the expert handling of his weapon.

None of the men returned that winter, nor was anything heard of the band. If Sneed, on his occasional trips to town for supplies, heard anything by means of that mysterious underground channel with which outlaws are acquainted, he said nothing. Secretly, Lucy Ware was glad. She knew better than to attempt to lecture Sneed; but she now and then hinted subtly that the country was getting too settled for men of his dubious profession. Sneed concealed his feelings behind a frown. But she sensed that he had little enthusiasm for the coming of spring; in a way, he seemed to have aged.

Spring came slowly, then suddenly. Rains drenched the hills and basin; the snow disappeared as if at the wave of a magician's wand; trees and shrubs budded, and soon the land was a flowing sea of green under a golden sun. May brought a riot of flaming blossoms.

Sneed shook off his lethargy, grumbled and swore under his breath, and then announced that if he was going to raise stock he was going to do it right. He ordered Buck and Ted to round up the cattle in the lower meadows, as the range between the house and the basin was called. He rode off to town to attend to some business.

Thus, on a fine morning, Ted Ryder found himself below the hills where the timber ended and the broad sloping plain flowed eastward like a carpet of brilliant green. He saw some cattle near some poplars along a little stream below him and rode down to inspect the brands. They bore the S-S iron, and he knew they belonged to the Sinclair herds. He was about to turn back when a horse came galloping around the trees, scattering the cattle, brought up close to him, and he found himself looking into a pair of large, violet eyes. He flushed and jerked off his hat.

"Oh! I didn't know there was a rider up here," said a surprised young voice. "Are you one of our men?" The eyes put the question in a deeper blue.

"What—whose men do you mean?" Ted stammered.

"Why, my father's!" The girl appeared more surprised. "Are you from the S Bar S?"

"Nope." The boy was recovering his composure. "I'm from the Lazy L up in the hills a piece."

"Oh!" She looked at him in approval. "I'm Dorothy Sinclair," she said gravely.

He nodded. "How do you do?" he said with a slight bow. "I suppose the S Bar S owner is yore father? I'm Ted Ryder an' I live up to my name." His teeth flashed in a smile.

She laughed. "You can't be more than a year or so older than me if you *are* so big," she said. "You've got a nice horse."

"That's nothing," he boasted, although he was visibly pleased. "We've got lots of 'em. I'll be helpin' to break more of 'em soon." He watched to see what effect this would have.

"Then you *must* be a rider," she said, with another nod of approval. "What—how do you come to be down here?"

"I was lookin' for strays," he answered, "an' saw some cattle in here. But they're yours."

"Of course," she said. "We're rounding up, too. I'm at the upper ranch with father, which is how I come to be this far up. I like to ride an' I like the hills."

"I love 'em," said Ted shortly. "I was born in 'em." A cloud passed quickly over his face as if at a memory. "I'm goin' to live in 'em all my life, I reckon."

"Oh." She looked very pretty as she said it, he thought. "Don't you ever go to the towns or cities?"

"I've been to towns," he answered, arching his brows. "An' I've been to cities. I've been to Chicago!"

Her eyes widened. "As far as that? It must be wonderful. I go to school in Wind Gap in the winter. I'll be through there next year an' maybe I'll go East to school then. Have you been to school? Of course you have."

"I read the books," he said in a superior tone. "Say, you know I think you're a right good-looker."

"Oh!" She tossed her head and a lock of golden hair shook loose from under her hat. "I suppose you learned how to talk like that in Chicago?"

He frowned at this and regarded her intently until she looked away. "My pa used to say it was always best to tell the truth," he said slowly.

"Well, Ted Ryder, you'll learn to lie to women before you're through," she said with a wisdom beyond her years.

Before Ted had time to reply to this amazing statement a third rider broke through the trees. The boy's face froze as he recognised Lute Balmer, foreman of the S-S. Buck had told him who this man was after the trouble in the shipping town the fall before.

"Dorothy," said Balmer sternly, with a hard look at Ted, "you go back to the house."

The girl's chin tilted and a flash came into her eyes. "You needn't be talking to me like that," she said. "You're not my boss."

"You do as I tell you," Balmer ordered angrily. "Your dad doesn't want you this far from the house. If I tell him he'll maybe send you back to the home ranch."

This had its effect, for Dorothy showed dismay as well as vexation. She turned to the boy. "Good-bye, Ted," she called with a smile. "Maybe I'll see you again."

"So long," he returned, and his gaze went back to Balmer as she rode away.

"What're you doin' here?" Balmer demanded, his eyes narrowing as he took in every detail of the boy's appearance, not overlooking the gun snug on his right side.

"Rounding up strays," replied Ted coolly. "Saw some cattle down here an' came down to look at the brands. They're S Bar S."

"Of course they're S Bar S, an' you keep well an' good away from 'em, d'ye hear," Balmer barked. "An' get off this range."

"I didn't see any *fence,*" said Ted pointedly, his face growing red with mortified anger.

"You didn't see—" Balmer broke off with a curse. "Are you goin' to slope back where you belong?" he shouted.

A sharp reply was hot on Ted's tongue, but he remembered Sneed's warning that day at the shipping point. "Throwing it back at a man like that means gun-play," Sneed had said. Ted bit his lip.

"Did you hear me?" roared the enraged Balmer.

For answer Ted whirled his horse and galloped up the long, easy slope. He did not look back. He said nothing about the incident at the house that evening. Sneed was not home; was not expected back from town before the next noon. Had he been there, the boy might have told him. But he had his doubts as to this when he thought of Dorothy Sinclair. It would seem as though—well, what would Sneed think of it? He remained thoughtful that evening, and the next morning he found an excuse to ride down to the rim of the basin again. He experienced a thrill as he saw the girl ride up along the trees after a time. He sent his mount down at tremendous speed and swept his hat low in approved cowboy style as he halted before her.

There was no bashful hesitancy about him this morning.

"Hallo, Dorothy," he greeted. "That's a mean foreman you folks have got!"

She looked at him soberly. "I was afraid I'd find you up here," she said gravely.

"Afraid you'd find me?" His tone betrayed surprise. "Why I came down *hoping* I'd find *you*."

“I said you’d learn to lie to women,” she said; “but you’ve already learned. I can’t ever see you again. Lute told me you—you’re bad.”

“What do you mean?” he asked, thunder-struck.

“You said you were on the Lazy L ranch,” she accused. “It isn’t so.”

“Who says it isn’t so?” he demanded hotly. “Did that Balmer tell you it wasn’t so?”

Dorothy nodded. “He said you’re on—on a man Sneed’s place,” she said.

“Well, what of it? That’s the Lazy L.”

Her eyes widened and he thought she looked horrified. “*That’s* the Lazy L,” he repeated. “It’s Sneed’s place. I know what’s the matter with Balmer. He had a run-in with me up in a town last fall an’ Uncle Jess took it up. He’s sore at him for that.”

“Is Sneed your uncle?” asked the girl, looking more horrified than ever.

“Well, not exactly,” the youth explained. “I call him that. He took me on when my pa fell down the shaft of our mine an’ got killed. He’s been good to me. He’s a better man than Balmer is.”

The girl shook her head. “He’s—he’s—” She hesitated, and the boy had to lean down to catch her whispered words. He heard, and his head came up with a jerk. It was his turn to stare.

“Balmer told you that?” he asked, dumb-founded. “Tell me again.”

She mumbled, and then in a stronger voice, with a toss of her head, she spoke clearly. “Yes, he told me that, an’ I don’t see why *he* should want to lie to me.”

“Well, it *is* a lie!” cried the boy. “An’ you tell him I said so an’ I’ll tell him it to his face!” Then, for the first time, Ted’s hand dropped instinctively to his gun.

Dorothy saw the flash of fire in his eyes and the swift swoop of his hand. She drew a quick breath, startled. Then she turned her horse and touched him with the spurs. Ted started after her but drew rein quickly. His jaw had clamped shut. It would only mean trouble for her to follow her. She must have slipped away against orders to see him. What did she think? What *could* she think? It was that mean, sneaking Balmer! Ted felt the hate swell within him as he dashed back up the slope.

It was noon when he rode up to the ranch-house and saw the barnman taking away Sneed’s horse. Sneed had just arrived. He came out on the porch as Ted dismounted and looked up at him, white-faced, his eyes hard.

“What’s the matter?” asked Sneed with concern.

“We’re goin’ to have to settle with that Balmer down at the S Bar S,” said Ted. “He lied about you.”

“Eh?” Sneed’s exclamation carried within the

house, and Lucy Ware stepped to where she could listen without being seen.

"I was down that way yesterday mornin' lookin' for strays," said Ted. "I saw a bunch of cattle an' went to take a look at the brands. They were S Bar S cattle, an' after I'd looked, a girl, Dorothy Sinclair, came ridin' along. We talked. Balmer showed up an' told her to go back to the house an' ordered me off that range."

"Yes?" Sneed was surprised and interested. "Maybe he thought you was goin' to run off with her," he said with a grin.

Ted shook his head impatiently. "I went down there again this mornin'," he continued, "an' she showed up. She said she couldn't see me again because I was bad. She thought I'd lied to her because I said I was from the Lazy L. Balmer told her I was from 'that Sneed place,' an' when I explained *your* place was the Lazy L she told me something Balmer said about you. He lied because he didn't want me mixin' with her, I reckon."

Sneed's crooked right arm was straining against his side. His face had hardened and the light in his eyes was like the glint of a naked knife.

"What'd he say about me?" he asked in a voice he strove to control.

"He told her you was an outlaw an' yore name was *Killer* Sneed!" said the boy bitterly. *"An' she believes it!"*

The silence seemed to grow and grow until it became an eternity. Then Sneed's breath whistled through his teeth.

"Go put up your horse," he ordered harshly.

Lucy Ware came out a few moments later to find him standing as though turned to stone, his burning eyes staring down at the blue mist of the basin, his gun clutched in the enfeebled fingers of that rigid right hand.

Chapter X

The First Draw

At dinner Sneed simulated a cheerful manner and contempt for the S-S foreman. He actually chuckled to himself to allay Ted's suspicions and soften his grave manner. Lucy took her cue from him and gradually the affair lost some of its importance so far as the boy was concerned.

"I reckon you rubbed Lute Balmer's fur the wrong way that day last fall," said Sneed with another chuckle. "An' maybe he thinks you're too rough company for Nate Sinclair's daughter. An' maybe he's jealous of me because I've got a place of my own—*our* own." He looked at Lucy. "An' maybe he's got it in for me because I horned in on the trouble last fall."

"He's a rotter!" exclaimed Ted unexpectedly. "If he says to me what he said to that girl, I'll just naturally bore him!"

Both Sneed and Lucy started at the venom in the boy's voice. Before Sneed could open his mouth to comment on this, Ted spoke again.

"I don't care so much for myself, or you," he said. "We can take care of ourselves. But that girl shouldn't be made to hear such things."

Sneed and Lucy looked at each other again.

There was a sparkle of appreciation in Sneed's eyes.

"That Dorothy," he said; "is she a good sort?"

"She's a nice kid," replied Ted, calling upon his Chicago vocabulary. "She's younger than me an' not so smart—or she'd known I wouldn't lie to her."

"Don't ever think you're smarter than women folks," was Sneed's growling comment. "You got lots to learn, Ted."

Sneed rode away after dinner. Hc struck straight down into the basin and spurred his horse at a ringing gallop for the S-S upper ranch-house. As he rode in he saw Nate Sinclair and the girl on the porch. Sinclair rose quickly and Dorothy looked at him curiously. He managed a smile which seemed natural enough.

"Hello, Sneed," the ranch owner greeted. "Get down an' have a chair on the porch."

The girl had risen hastily and now she disappeared in the house. Sneed's lips were pressed firmly together as he lowered himself from the saddle. "I've come over on business," he said to Sinclair. So far as he knew, Sinclair had nothing against him. He had never bothered S-S cattle or range, or had any trouble with any of Sinclair's men except for the brush with Balmer in town. He wondered if the foreman had told Sinclair about that.

Sinclair was himself a big man physically;

ruddy-faced, rough-voiced, a cattleman of the old school who understood men of Sneed's stamp and knew there were few of them. It was likely that through his political activities he knew of the pact Sneed had with the authorities of the north counties; knew, too, that it was being respected.

"I don't look very business-like this afternoon," he boomed. "Spring's got into my bones, I reckon. I've took to comin' in to dinner an' restin' afterwards. That's a sign of growing old, eh?"

"No sense in men like me an' you growin' old," said Sneed with a queer look as he took a chair. Then he came to the point. "I'm goin' in for cattle on a fairly big scale, Sinclair, an' I need some stock—young stock, an' breeded stock. I've got plenty of range up back of here in the hills, an' meadows for hay to feed winters. I'm in the market an' I thought you might have something to sell. This basin stuff is good stock."

Sinclair was looking at him intently. No doubt he was wondering at this change in the man. Was Sneed quitting his former game? He'd heard about the boy, too. Perhaps *that* was it. Well, Sneed had been square in the north; square enough to earn himself sanctuary and a certain guarded measure of protection. If he had decided to go straight—

"How many head you want?" he asked, pursing his lips.

"Two thousand to start," said Sneed. "White-faces. I'll be buyin' more here an' there later. Cash on delivery at the Lazy L."

A vague suspicion filtered through Sinclair's brain. But, nonsense! It was no trick. If Sneed wanted to rustle cattle he knew where he could do it; yes, and get away with it. Nothing was impossible for this dangerous man. Moreover, Sinclair believed what he had often heard—that Sneed's word was good.

"All right," he said in sudden decision. "I'll let you have 'em. An' I'll see you get good stuff. Fact is, I haven't got anything scrubby in my herds."

"Which is one reason why I come to you first," said Sneed. "Have your foreman, Nate Balmer, deliver 'em to me on the Lazy L. Send the bill of sale along. I want *him*"—his eyes glinted coldly—"to see that everything's regular."

Sinclair nodded. "That's agreeable," he said. "I'll send 'em along within the week."

Sneed rose. "I suppose you've heard about me takin' on that Ryder boy," he said. "His dad fell down his prospect shaft an' got killed. The young'n didn't have no place to go."

"Yes, I've heard," said Sinclair, showing keen interest.

Sneed looked at him hard. "He's a good kid," he said shortly, and started down the steps.

Within three days four men arrived at the Lazy L. "New hands," Sneed explained briefly.

"Takes punchers to run cattle." But Lucy thought she had seen one or two of these men before, and she knew Sneed would be very careful as to the men he hired. Then she had it. They were men who had at some time been on expeditions with him and proved safe. Even in a legitimate enterprise, Sneed was gathering men of his own kind about him. Two more arrived next day.

It was the sixth day after Sneed's visit to the Sinclair upper ranch that Ted rode up to the house and announced excitedly that a big herd of cattle was being driven up to their range. Sneed explained it was the herd he was buying. "You stick with me," he told the boy. Then he gave orders to the men as to the disposition of the herd when it reached the Lazy L range. He rode down with Ted and met Lute Balmer in the lower meadows.

"I'm delivering two thousand head," said Balmer, who had three men at his back. "I've got a bill of sale signed by the Old Man, a note, an' a receipt, an' I want twenty thousand cash"—there was a sneering hint of doubt that Sneed could produce this—"an' the note signed for the rest of it."

"Why not *all* cash?" Sneed snapped.

"I'm followin' out my orders," said Balmer with a scowl.

"Come along to the house," Sneed commanded. He called to Buck who had followed them. "Take charge of the herd," he instructed. "I'm accepting delivery on those cattle."

Sneed wondered about the note as he and Ted rode in advance of the three S-S men and their foreman on the way back to the house. Had Sinclair thought he didn't have the cash for the cattle? If so, it was rather white of the S-S owner, but Sneed smiled to himself. He had been a spender, but he also had been a good gambler; and he had won almost as much as he had spent. He had always taken a major share of his ill-gotten gains and he had saved much. He hadn't trusted banks much, either. He could put his hands on his fortune with little trouble. He was prepared at that very minute to pay cash for all the cattle. But if Sinclair wanted a note for the balance, he could have it—signed by Lucy Ware. He surmised that Sinclair did not want to have such a large amount of cash in his ranch safe.

They went into the living-room, Sneed, Balmer and the boy. Sneed looked at the bill of sale, noted the space for the buyer's name was left blank, nodded in approval. He took the note and left the room. Ted stood near the table looking hard at Balmer.

"You lied to that girl, Dorothy," he said suddenly in a low voice.

"What's *that?*" said Balmer with a dark look.

"You heard what I said," Ted replied. "Don't you take cover behind a girl."

Balmer glared at him in astonishment, but before he could frame a suitable reply Sneed came in briskly. He handed Balmer the note and put a packet of bills of large denomination on the table.

"Count that money an' hand over the receipt," he ordered.

"This ain't your signature," Balmer blurted.

"No?" Sneed's eyes narrowed. "You must have noticed that the bill of sale was made out in blank. The person whose name is signed there is buyin' the stock. She has an account in the bank at our shippin' town an' she owns this ranch. Now that you've found that out, count the money an' give me the receipt."

Balmer grumbled, but he counted the money. He looked at the receipt and scowled in perplexity as he saw the space for the name on that was left blank also. "I guess it's all right," he growled, handing the receipt to Sneed.

"I reckon it's a good thing somebody on the S Bar S has got some brains," said Sneed. "An' that somebody is Sinclair."

Balmer's face darkened and his eyes glared from Sneed to the boy. His gaze rested for a perceptible length of time on Sneed's right arm, crooked above his gun. Then he turned abruptly and stamped out the door. Sneed followed, with the boy behind him.

"Just a minute!" Sneed's words shivered keen-edged as Balmer was about to mount his horse. The S-S foreman whirled angrily. His three men were at the lower end of the yard, waiting. Ted stepped to Sneed's left. The boy sensed a current of feeling in the air that was almost electrical.

"You made a little mistake the other day," said Sneed in the purring voice which those who knew him best always recognised as a danger signal. "You told Sinclair's girl down there something that got to Ted, here, an' from him to me. Remarks like you made always travel to headquarters, Balmer."

Balmer remembered what Ted had said to him in the living-room; remembered, too, his meeting with Dorothy. So he had seen Dorothy again. And she had told him. His lips curled and the light in his eyes chilled. He had the power of the S-S behind him and Sinclair's influence was not to be denied. Also, he did not hold his own resources in light esteem. And there was something else! He suddenly laughed.

"I don't think I was mistaken," he said in a bragging tone.

"No?" The word came with a soft, hissing sound from Sneed's lips. He was watching Balmer narrowly, and he was stooping a bit. "It was a mistake to run off at the mouth like that, I mean, Balmer."

Ted held his breath as he, too, kept his gaze steadily on the foreman's snapping, black eyes.

"Meanin' you *think* so," said Balmer insolently.

"An' you ought to *know* so," said Sneed sternly. Then his voice fell again to sibilant accents. "People don't usually talk like you did so it'll get back to my ears, Balmer. I reckon you better tell the boy you was mistaken."

A jeering sneer twisted Balmer's lips. "You mean you're askin' me to apologise to that—"

"You understand me!" Sneed cut in hoarsely.

"Understand hell!" shouted Balmer. "You'd try to make me out a liar when *any*body'd know I told the truth? What's more, I'll tell more, I'll—"

But the demon in Sneed's heart had broken its bounds. Fire flamed from his eyes in maniacal rage. Everything was a blur but the derisive face of the man before him. He bent and the crooked right hand swung as if on a hinge. Balmer's lips crushed back white against his teeth and his right hand struck. Sneed caught a flash of a move at his left and then a gun roared in his ears.

Balmer staggered back two paces, half turning, his own gun exploding to send a harmless bullet over Sneed's head. He fell against his horse and the animal broke away to let him down heavily on the ground. Sneed looked with startled wonder at his own weapon in his rigid hand. He hadn't fired! That lightning move at his left! He turned to see Ted standing straight as a rocket, his face pale, his gun just slipping back into its holster from his fingers.

Sneed's left hand went up in a signal to the three S-S men at the lower end of the yard. They came at a gallop, punchers who had seen disputes on the range settled with guns before, and who were doubtless familiar with Sneed's reputation and therefore not altogether anxious to take up their foreman's quarrel.

"Look him over an' see where he's hit," Sneed commanded. "He—" He paused and looked hard at Ted. "He drew first an' *tried to beat me to it!*" he said in a voice that carried over the place.

Balmer was muttering as the men worked over him. "It's just below the collar-bone on the right," Sneed heard one of them say. He motioned to Ted to go in the house.

"Carry him over to the bunk-house," he told the men when the boy had gone. "I'll get some water an' bandages. I'll have the spring wagon hooked up to take him home. I guess the fool thought he could best me."

He hurried to the house and found Ted and Lucy Ware in the living-room. The boy's eyes met his squarely.

"Why'd you do it?" Sneed cried with blazing anger.

"You told me once that throwin' it back at a man like that meant gun-play," said the boy clearly. "I knew he was goin' for his gun, saw him start, an' I knew your arm wasn't right for such quick work. So—I beat him to it!"

Lucy drew in a long breath. “He’s got your trick,” she whispered. “I *saw* it. An’ your own trick saved your life.”

Sneed stared at Ted. It must be true. Now in the cold light of reason he realised that he couldn’t have drawn quick enough to have beaten Balmer. And Balmer’s strange bravado. Perhaps he knew! Another thought flashed through his brain. Was he doing right in trying to conceal his past from this boy? Would it not bring more trouble? He should *tell* him! He strove to speak, but the words would not come. He looked pleadingly at Lucy Ware—and she misunderstood. He braced himself and at last managed to speak.

“Ted, what—what would you think if I told you that what Balmer said was—true?”

“I wouldn’t believe it!” sang the boy, his eyes flashing. “What’ll they do with me, Uncle Jess?”

This brought Sneed to himself with a start. “Do? Do to—you?” he stammered. “Why, nothing.” He put his left hand on the boy’s shoulder, his gaze holding Ted’s fast. “Remember,” he said hoarsely, *“I shot Balmer!”*

Chapter XI

"Prove It to Me!"

Lute Balmer lapsed into unconsciousness while they were dressing his wound. Sneed was gruff and visibly worried and confessed to Lucy, who had insisted on taking charge, that it looked bad. He sent Ted for Buck, after cautioning him not to talk about the affair, and ordered the barnman to hook up a team to the spring wagon. Meanwhile one of the Sinclair men had started for the town nearest to the S-S main ranch in the basin to get a doctor. When Buck arrived, Sneed instructed him to drive with Balmer to the Sinclair ranch and bring the team back that night. He told the young puncher what had happened and gave him to understand that *he* had shot Balmer—in self-defence. As he was saying this, Sneed wondered for the hundredth time if Balmer knew who had shot him. The other S-S men had been too far away to see just what happened in those brief, hot moments. The money and signed note were in Balmer's pockets and Buck was charged with seeing that Sinclair got them. He also was given to understand what he should tell Nate Sinclair. So far, so good, thought Sneed as Buck drove away with the wounded man on a pile of blankets and quilts. One of the S-S men rode with Balmer in the wagon, his horse tied to the rear, and the other went on ahead to prepare for their arrival in the basin.

It seemed useless to Sneed to administer any severe lecture to Ted. After all, the boy *had* saved his life. Furthermore, Sneed felt that he was responsible. It had all come about through his desire to humble Balmer in the boy's presence; to convince Ted that Balmer had been lying, whereas the S-S foreman had told Dorothy a truth that Ted was certain to find out for himself sooner or later if Sneed did not tell him. It was more or less of an accident and pure luck that Ted hadn't learned the truth before this, Sneed realised. And now the outlaw took himself to task for his attitude and decided that Ted *must* be told. In a vague way he realised that he had wanted to make a good showing before the boy before Ted could learn the truth. Why? What was this youth to him? Aye—that was the point. That was what bothered this man of the lightning draw and the hot trail of the past. Did he owe this boy anything? He hadn't killed his father, as he knew Snark Levant and some of the other men who had been with him that fateful day believed. Yet, if he hadn't gone up there to teach Albert Ryder a lesson in his rage that day—

Sneed shrugged and growled and gave up the idea of telling Ted anything that night. He would watch his chance and at just the right time, when he was in just the humour and could explain to the best advantage, and when Ted was in the mood to receive such a confession—it would have to be a straight, man-to-man business—and circumstances were just right, he would tell Ted everything.

Meanwhile, he expected a visit from Nate Sinclair. The stockman would certainly come to ask the details. Sinclair was an old-timer. He would know that Sneed would not deliberatcly pick a quarrel with Balmer to try to kill him. Sneed felt sure on this point. In the end, Sneed brightened instead of becoming depressed under this trouble cloud. After all, the matching of wits, the stress of turmoil, and the thrill of danger were his very life's blood. But one thing he knew beyond the peradventure of a doubt: bend or swing or crouch as he might, he never could draw his gun again to enforce his wishes by covering a man, or to protect his life with that unerring aim and magical speed of which he had once been master. He must never forget himself again—*never!*

Buck came back at midnight. He had left Balmer at the upper ranch, where the S-S men had taken charge of him. He had not let him out of his sight until Sinclair had come in off the range and had taken the money and the note. Buck had explained, clearly and curtly, what had happened, as Sneed had told him. This was done away from the men. Sinclair had listened intently, quietly enough; but he had asked the same question several times and that question had been: "What was the trouble about?" On this point Buck had had no specific instructions and he had evaded it. He had told Sinclair that it all "happened in a minute" and that in the excitement he did not ask how it had started. But he pointed out that Sneed would hardly be deliberately picking a quarrel with Balmer to get him; that he had a reputation for never drawing *first;* that he didn't *have* to, because he was far faster with his six-gun than any man in that country. Sinclair had grunted and scowled and asked if Ted was there when the shooting took place.

"He asked that, did he?" Sneed broke in excitedly.

"Yes," Buck replied, "an' he gave me the idea, some way, that he thought Ted might have something to do with it." Buck laughed as he said this, but the merriment died cold on his lips when he caught Sneed's look.

"Turn in," said Sneed sharply. "In the mornin' take Ted out with you an' keep him away from the house all day. Move the cattle to the south range. I'm goin' to send the bunk-house cook over there with a wagon an' you men will stay with the herd. I want 'em branded with my iron first."

Sneed sent the cook with his outfit and the

bed wagon in the morning and then awaited the coming of Nate Sinclair. He felt so sure that Sinclair would come that he had framed every sentence he intended to speak. Noon came and the S-S owner had not arrived. Lucy Ware was strangely quiet at dinner, but Sneed took no notice of this, so busy was he with his own thoughts. After dinner he rode down to the meadows. He was rewarded in a short time by the sight of several horsemen riding up from the basin. Sinclair was coming, then, and bringing a guard!

Sneed rode back to the ranch and told the barnman to saddle a horse and be prepared to take a message to the men with the cattle if there should be any trouble. "Ride like the devil was after you if anything starts," was his parting order.

He told Lucy to stay out of sight as he did not want her involved in the affair in any way, and sat down in a chair on the porch. When the horsemen hove in sight at the lower end of the yard, Sneed's carefully prepared speech went on the winds and his left hand gripped the arm of his chair until the great, brown knuckles went white. Riding in the lead was not Nate Sinclair, as he had expected, but Sheriff Frost!

He got up and went down the steps, greeting Frost sourly as the official dismounted. There were four men with the sheriff, and these remained in their saddles.

"I sort of expected something like this would happen," was Frost's answer to Sneed's greeting. "But I don't know as I figured on it comin' so soon."

Sneed recognised the sheriff's manner, glared at the men with him, who were staring at him almost open-mouthed, and then motioned toward the bunk-house and started for it with Frost following him. He had decided quickly that whatever the nature of this conference, it was going to be carried on beyond the ears of others.

Inside the bunk-house Sneed stood on one side of the table while the sheriff took his place opposite him.

"Sinclair sent for you?" Sneed demanded, straight to the point.

"No," said Frost. "I was in town when one of his men rode in for a doctor an' he told me about it."

"I suppose he said I tried to murder Balmer," sneered Sneed.

"No. But I talked a little with Balmer this morning. He told me some things. I know what the trouble was about. Sneed, I'm not goin' back on my word to you, but I don't expect you to go back on your word to me. I expect you to play the game; but I've noticed a man of your stamp always runs true to the breed."

Sneed's face darkened at this. "You thinkin' I've double-crossed you?" he demanded.

"I'm goin' by what I've been told an' Balmer's flat on his back, punctured bad, for evidence," replied Frost, frowning.

"I suppose he just naturally said I popped him out of hand for nothin' at all," said Sneed with another sneer.

"No. And I wouldn't have believed him if he had." The sheriff raised his brows. "Where's that boy, Ted?" he asked.

"Ted?" Sneed was startled. "What's *he* got to do with it?"

"I want to talk to him," Frost answered sharply.

"Ted isn't here," said Sneed slowly, thinking hard. "What were you figurin' on doin' with me?"

"I haven't been thinking of that," said Frost curtly. "I want to talk to the boy."

"I told you he wasn't here!" Sneed thundered. "An' there's no use ringing him in on this. Your business is with *me,* an' you know good an' well that I never shot a man who didn't draw first."

The light in the sheriff's eyes sparkled a shade softer, but he shook his head. "No use, Sneed," he said in a tone of finality. "You didn't shoot Balmer. I got that straight from Balmer himself, an' I believe him."

Sneed's face had gone the colour of ashes. He wanted to ask Frost if Balmer had said Ted shot him, but he didn't dare put the question. He knew Balmer had told Frost the truth. But—

"How's Balmer goin' to prove I didn't shoot

him?" he asked. "He's flat on his back, as you say, an' I'm not denying I plugged him."

Again, Frost shook his head. "No use," he repeated. "Sneed, come square!" He rapped the table with the knuckles of his right hand. *"I want to ask that boy one question!"*

The sweat came out on Sneed's brow as he made his decision. "All right," he hissed through his teeth. "I'll send for him. Stick aroun' an' tell your posse"—this with a grim tightening of his lips—"to rest their horses."

Frost followed him out, saw him go to the barn and call out an order. In a few moments the barnman had galloped away. Sneed returned and asked Frost to go in the bunk-house and sit down. But Frost refused.

"If you've sent word to that boy to light out, Sneed," he said slowly, "I'll take it as breaking your—ah—agreement."

"I reckon you're a sheriff because you've got a naturally suspicious an' onery disposition," Sneed snapped out. "I sent for Ted to come here. I don't reckon you've heard any *more* bad reports, have you?" he finished with a curling lip.

"No. I thought the buying of those cattle was a good sign."

"I thought so too when I bought 'em," said Sneed. "But your sort won't let me believe in but one kind of signs. Maybe you'll notice this bunk-house hasn't been used much this winter.

There's only been two or three here. I hired some hands the other day to help work the cattle. But I can fill this bunk-house with men who aren't cowpunchers quicker'n you think!"

Frost's eyes narrowed slightly as he caught the significance of the threat. He looked away and his brow furrowed. Sneed was a natural-born leader; his power over men of an evil stamp was too well known. There was only one way to end such power. That way was to remove the man who possessed it. But Frost had given his word. Moreover, there were other authorities bound by the word that had been given Sneed in exchange for his own. After all, he had to be careful. Yet he was convinced that Sneed, in an indirect way, had betrayed him!

It was nearly an hour before Ted arrived at a thundering gallop. Sneed called him inside, where the boy stood looking wide-eyed and startled at them both.

"Ted, this is Sheriff Frost visitin' us again," said Sneed, holding the boy's eyes. "I've told him what happened here yesterday when—when Balmer was here. You remember?" There was just a slight emphasis on the last word, and Sneed's eyes bored into him. The boy nodded. "The sheriff wants to ask you a question," Sneed finished.

Frost was frowning during this speech, ready to interrupt if he thought Sneed was coaching the boy. Now his face cleared, and he gazed steadily at the youth.

"Who shot Balmer?" he asked, leaning forward suddenly.

The boy caught his breath, and at the same time he caught a piercing glance from Sneed. He remembered.

"Uncle Jess," he said in a gulping whisper.

Frost straightened. "You can go out," he said. His eyes met Sneed's gleam of triumph as the boy left.

"I didn't think you would do it," he said slowly.

"I *wouldn't* have done it if he hadn't gone for his gun first," Sneed declared.

"I don't mean anything like that," said the sheriff, shaking his head. "I mean I didn't think you would teach the boy to *lie* as well as make a gunman out of him."

Sneed glared. "You still figure—" He bit off his words and cursed.

"Balmer's men saw the boy an' you with him," said the sheriff. "You haven't denied the boy was there. You asked him if he remembered. He nodded. Balmer told me the *boy* shot him. I believe it. You threw the talk into Balmer, but you couldn't throw a gun with him yesterday, Sneed. You're not *able* to throw a gun. *I* know about your arm. You couldn't have *drawn* as fast as Balmer. But you've taught the boy. If you're still as fast as you once was, *prove it to me!*" The sheriff's voice rang in the room. "Prove it!" he repeated. "Prove it, an' I'll believe you. Sneed—*draw!*"

Sneed was shaking like a man afflicted with palsy. His eyes blazed with deadly longing. In the helpless realisation of the utter futility of his frenzied desire he was more terrible than ever he had been before a fearful retribution had struck the power from his arm. He wet his lips, but no word came.

"Never mind," said the sheriff, a bit unsteadily. "I have my proof. I'll have to take the boy—don't try to draw *now!*" Then after an interval: "He won't come off so bad, for I reckon Balmer's goin' to live."

"How—how'd you *know?*" Sneed asked hoarsely.

"The Morning Glory doctor told me when he was down in the county seat," Frost answered. "I was sort of glad to hear it. I told Sinclair one day. I reckon he thought you were goin' to go straight when he sold you the cattle an'—"

"You told Sinclair?" Sneed broke in. "Then Sinclair must have told Balmer. An' *that's* why Balmer was so brave!" His eyes again shone with triumph. "If Balmer knew my—my arm was bad, wasn't he figurin' on killin' me when he went for his gun? Didn't he *know* he had the best of it?"

"That'll have to be thrashed out," said the sheriff with a shrug.

"Would you blame Ted for tryin' to protect me?" Sneed persisted with an eagerness that was not inspired by any regard for his own safety.

"We'll go into that later," frowned the sheriff, starting for the door.

"Listen!" cried Sneed in a voice that brought Frost to a whirling stop. "If you take that boy, *I* go with him. An' if we go, you're callin' the turn!"

Frost scowled and hesitated. Then he went out the door.

"I reckon you'll have to go," he said shortly.

Sneed threw back his head. "All right, sheriff," he purred.

His call for Ted was not answered. He ordered his horse saddled and rode to the south range with the sheriff. Buck told them Ted hadn't returned there. They went back and began a search. In an hour they gave up. Sneed was as bewildered as Frost was suspicious.

Ted Ryder was gone.

Chapter XII

A Demonstration

Morning Glory woke to a day of strange rumours and queer events. Not since the new lead strikes had revived the mining camp and sent hopes skyward had there been such excitement. The sheriff of the county had arrived during the night. He had sent a posse into the hills at dawn in charge of his deputy there. He was organising another party of searchers. The word had gone out that young Ted Ryder was wanted!

Instantly all ears were alert. Gradually the rumours took form. There had been a shooting; maybe a killing. Lute Balmer, foreman of the great S-S, was the victim. He had been shot by young Ryder in a dispute over some cattle. Men who thought they were wise nodded to each other significantly. Rustling, more than likely. The whole town knew Killer Sneed had the same as adopted the Ryder boy. He had made a gunman out of him; now he was finishing him off as an outlaw. It was as they had expected. Weird tales circulated as to the marvellous skill of Ted Ryder. He had Sneed's trick of the draw; he was even faster! The sheriff was after the boy who was being protected by the famous Sneed gang. Sneed had taken him away from the sheriff at the point of his gun. Sneed was gathering his band for an attack on the town!

Then the most amazing report of all filtered through the camp and dazed its populace. Sneed's right arm had been injured. His uncanny command of his weapon was gone forever. Killer Sneed was through!

The complicated tangle of rumours gradually straightened into a new version. Sneed had lost control of the boy who had "gone wild." Sneed had quit his old game and gone in for stock-raising. Balmer had been shot when he had ordered Ted off the S-S range where the youth had gone to see Dorothy Sinclair. The S-S owner had offered a big reward for Ted's capture. Sneed had announced he was through with the boy. But it was feared it was all a trick of Sneed's.

So the rumours flew, bandied from mouth to mouth, embellished with flagrant details which did credit to the imaginations of those who repeated them. And more men went out into the hills. They went in parties as a protection against attack. The sheriff was powerless to allay the fears of certain mine officials and business men, and he could not quiet the rumours, even though he repeatedly stated that there was a question about the shooting, that he wanted the youth first to question him further, that Sneed was at his ranch. Morning Glory would not be cheated of its sensation. And then its nerves received another shock.

Killer Sneed rode into town at noon!

His bloodshot eyes—the result of a sleepless night of worry and watching—were mistaken for eyes blazing with rage; his ash-grey face was assumed to be pale with anger; the crooked right arm with the hand inside his coat meant that he held a gun in readiness. Men scurried out of his path. A stealthy whisper strengthened in a twinkling to a roaring rumour. Sneed had come to kill the sheriff!

But, strange to say, Sneed went directly to the doctor's cabin. This was almost more than Morning Glory could stand. Had Sneed been hurt again—in the same arm? Or—and more probable—he was *going to kill the doctor first!*

Such is the frenzy of primitive conjecture in the gulches in the high hills where law is often a myth, and justice is a home-made commodity.

Citizens thronged the street below the slope where was situated the doctor's cabin. The doctor was liked and respected, where Sneed was feared. But—was Sneed to be feared *now?* There were growls and a few Winchesters made their appearance. Yet the crowd was mainly quiet; for it was listening. It needed but the sound of a shot up there in the whitewashed log cabin to start the flame of riot where the sparks of unrest now flickered.

Inside the cabin, Sneed was standing before the doctor.

"So you had to tell, eh?" he snarled. "After givin' me that promise, you told."

"You asked me to promise that I wouldn't tell anyone in Morning Glory," said the doctor fearlessly. "I told no one here. I told the sheriff down in the county seat as I intended doing from the first. If you had asked me to promise not to do that, I would have refused."

"You tricked me!" Sneed accused vehemently. "I thought you meant you wouldn't tell *any*body. An' Frost told Sinclair, an' he told that fool Balmer, an' now it's got me an' the boy into trouble. That goes right back to you. An' I believe you made this arm stiff on purpose!" His hand came out from beneath his coat; and the hand held a gun.

"I didn't promise that I wouldn't tell *any*body," said the doctor stoutly. "And no power on earth could have prevented that arm with its torn muscles and ligaments from going stiff. Had I so wished—now *listen* to this—had I so wished, I could have let the blood-poisoning do its work and you would have died!"

Sneed stared at him darkly, yet showing that he realised what the doctor said was true.

The man of medicine saw this and he went on: "If I were you, Sneed, I'd give up the boy. I would—"

"You fool, I don't know where he is!" cried Sneed.

"No?" The doctor was puzzled. "Well, then, help find him. Frost doesn't want to jail him, although he'll have to if Balmer dies—so he told me. But you don't know the talk that's going around. They say you've made a gunman and an outlaw out of Ted. I don't know if that's true, and, in fact, I hardly believe it. I don't doubt but that you've skilled him in the use of his weapon; but I *do* doubt the other. A boy's viewpoint couldn't be changed so quickly. But it *will* be if you keep control over him. Now, hold on to yourself. Don't you see you can't trust yourself?"

The doctor's eyes now gleamed with earnestness and he leaned forward. "Put away your gun, Sneed, and listen to what I have to tell you," he said in deadly seriousness. "Every principle of psychology is against your complete reformation. A character such as yours, so firmly established, cannot be totally changed. The devil in you will crop out when you least expect it. In your heart of hearts you have *right this very instant* a wild yearning for the old life of outlawry—of swift death and rapine. How do you expect the boy to resist something which you cannot control yourself? Your peculiar regard for the boy is a false sentiment. I am speaking not as a friend, not as an enemy, but as a physician. I know that the heart of a killer cannot be cured!"

In the silence which followed the growling murmur of the crowd came up to them. Sneed's faculties, which had been concentrated on the doctor's speech, were diverted instantly. His eyes flamed and his lips curled as he turned to the door.

"What are you going to do?" asked the doctor anxiously.

"I'm goin' to give you a little demonstration of your—psychology, as you call it," said Sneed grimly. "That pack of wolves down there has heard about my arm. I saw it in their faces as I came into town. I'm goin' to slip my gun in its holster an' keep my right hand in plain sight! Then I'm goin' to ride through 'em, an' you watch 'em scatter."

As Sneed came down the short road from the slope, a towering figure on his great horse, every man in the muttering throng saw his gun and saw his arm crooked at his side; saw the rigid right hand. And every man swore afterwards that the narrowed, glinting eyes were looking straight at him. The muttering died. Sneed charged in among them, weaving his horse, and they scattered in all directions. He drove them up the street and down the street, into the spaces between buildings, into doorways. Then he pulled up his horse in the centre of the cleared space and, looking up at the doctor, who was standing in the doorway of his cabin, he waved an arm—his *left*.

From somewhere in the crowd which ringed the cleared space came a maniacal cry. It rose and wavered, eerie-like, and then was shattered by the sharp report of a rifle. Echoes climbed the crags and pinnacles and floated off the spires above the gulch.

Killer Sneed's arm dropped; he leaned forward and coughed. Crimson bubbled on his lips. Then he fell on his horse's neck, slipped and tumbled to the ground. He lay still, staring up at the high, blue bowl of sky, while a curl of dust unfurled and floated lazily above him, a golden veil in the rays of the sun.

The silence fell into the gulch, tempered only by the soft lament of hurrying winds in the marching stands of pine.

Then a shout went up, swelling into a cry long-drawn with wonder, consternation, horror. Men ran toward the motionless form in the dust of the street as Sneed's horse broke away. The sheriff came, hatless and profane, while a grizzled, wild-eyed assassinator dragged his Winchester by its hot barrel in a circle. He was led away by two who knew him.

The body was carried to the deputy's shack, where the sheriff was making his head-quarters. The doctor came down the slope on the run, his face a strange puzzle of conflicting emotions. He made a swift, almost needless, examination, and turned away from the lifeless form.

"In the heart," he said, blinking as though in a strong light.

The sheriff looked at the crowd in the doorway, outside the window, thronged in the street. "It's the way most of them go," he muttered, nodding wonderingly at the doctor.

Drama serves its ends through the medium of suspense, and achieves them with its culmination. Therefore, in the reaction from the sudden going of Killer Sneed, it could not be said that the appearance of Ted Ryder at this moment created any greater sensation.

The crowd broke away from the front of the shack with hardly a cry. It stared curiously, forgivingly, at the tall, handsome youth on the big, black horse, his eyes wide with suspicion, his manner wary. He had naturally hurried to where the crowd was on his arrival in town. A lonely night of mental torture in the one place where they hadn't looked for him—the cabin in the meadow by his mine—had sent him seeking the man who now stood in the doorway of the little shack, beckoning to him.

"Come in," said Sheriff Frost gently as he dismounted.

Ted went in and the crowd closed breathless behind him. He knew as soon as he stood in that little front room. Even in death the strong-willed spirit of Sneed made itself felt. The boy took off his hat, pressed his lips firmly together, looked straight in a disconcerting way at the sheriff.

"Who did it?" he asked in a voice which caused the doctor to look at him closely.

"I don't know—yet," said the sheriff. "It—really doesn't make much difference, Ted, my boy."

"Why not?" The words cracked like a whip-lash.

"Because—" The sheriff hesitated and frowned. "Ted," he said in a fatherly voice, "didn't you know the truth about Sneed? Didn't you know that what Balmer said was a fact?"

"No," said the boy firmly; "an' I don't know it now because you say so. It's a lie."

"Sneed was an outlaw, with a price on his head," said the sheriff earnestly. "That's why it doesn't make so much difference who held the rifle to-day."

"A rifle?" The boy's eyes widened. "Somebody shot him down unawares when his arm was crippled?" He seemed incredulous.

"It's the way most of them go," said the sheriff with a shrug.

"But it wasn't fair!" Ted's voice rang in the room and carried to the crowd outside. "He didn't have a chance!"

"There were men whom *he* didn't give a chance," said the sheriff grimly. "You don't want to get the wrong notion about this, son."

"I don't believe what you say about him," said

Ted defiantly. "I believe you're lyin' to cover up. I reckon you was afraid of him."

"You can ask the doctor," said the sheriff, showing a trace of irritation. "You can ask anybody here." He swept an arm toward the crowd.

Ted looked at the doctor and then his gaze roved over those in the crowd whom he could see. He read his answer in their eyes. He whirled on the sheriff.

"I want to tell *you* that *I* shot that man Balmer," he said in a loud voice. "I came here to tell you that. Uncle Jess—" He paused as a slight waver came into his voice. But the look he turned on Frost was that of a man come suddenly into his estate as such. "Uncle Jess wanted to take the blame. He was a *man,* an' not like this slinkin' coyote who murdered him, or like Balmer, who tried it. What do you want with me?"

"I'll want you later, I guess," said Frost, frowning. "This—changes things. I suppose you'll want to take Sneed home."

It was so arranged. Sheriff Frost did not attempt to question this youth who seemed suddenly to have aged beyond his years. Word was sent out to bring the posses back to town. The body of Sneed was placed in a spring wagon and two men were delegated to drive it home.

With the sunset fires flaming on the western peaks, Ted Ryder guided his horse along the silver ribbon of road toward the far-flung plain.

A purple twilight draped its mists above the basin as they swung about to climb the grassy slope. The stars broke forth in clusters and Ted looked up at them with a tightening in his throat. He was leading The Killer home.

Chapter XIII

Lucy Ware

It took all night and part of the next morning for the horses to pull the wagon bearing Sneed's body up the long slopes. Meanwhile, Ted's thoughts were divided between the desire to rush on ahead and prepare Lucy Ware for their coming, and the conviction that it was his place and duty to stick close to the remains of his dead friend. He started on several times, but always came back.

When they finally reached the ranch in the forenoon it was Lucy Ware who, by a cruel freak of chance, first saw them coming. She was in the yard before the house and her arms were filled with flowers. She just stood and looked, white-faced, as Ted rode up. After she had looked in his eyes, and before he could speak, she nodded.

"I know," she said in a strange, tired voice. "It had to come some time." She walked slowly towards the wagon and stood mute and awestruck while they carried Sneed's body into the house, deaf to Ted's fervid entreaties to go in and not feel too badly.

It was one of the men who had come from Morning Glory whom she asked for details. After they had started back she listened to Ted's passionate recital of his part in the affair, and what he thought, and what he intended to do.

"No," she said dully, "it wouldn't do to try to get his slayer. It had to come. But I thought it would be Snark Levant who would try it. No, Ted, you mustn't start this way. Jess was always this way; sort of—spectacular. They were all afraid of him and when they saw for sure that his arm was gone, one of them lost his head. Might be sorry now; can't tell."

"But what they said about him bein' a killer," the boy protested.

"All true," said Lucy. And then, with flashing eyes: "There wasn't one of them that would dare face him when his arm was right!"

Ted looked at the still form on the sofa in the cool, dim living-room, with the flowers heaped upon it; his eyes were wide and wondering, still expressing disbelief. But Lucy Ware would not lie.

"You'll have to help me," she said. "Go out in the kitchen and get some breakfast. Then ride down and get Buck before you take some sleep. Poor boy—you must need it."

Whatever her thoughts were as she sat those next few hours beside the couch no one could tell. Just once she gave way to tears. In her heart was a lurking dread; she feared the possible return of Snark Levant. She did not fear for herself so much as for the youth. Always she had been possessed of a feeling of security when Sneed was alive. Now, for the first time since those spectacular days of the wild cowtowns, this feeling deserted her.

They buried Sneed next day under the cottonwoods in the lower yard. Lucy Ware's face was white and drawn, but whatever emotion she experienced she concealed. That night she told Buck to return to his post in charge of the cattle; but she asked him certain questions about the men, and told him to be in readiness to return to the ranch-house on an instant's notice.

"I shall probably sell the place," she finished absently.

She pondered over this. Yes, she would have to sell the ranch. She didn't feel capable of managing it. It made her bitter whenever she thought of Sneed's intention to follow the cattle-raising business and give up his old life. And now, just when he had started he had been shot down. He had been killed, too, before he had had a chance to tell the boy everything. What cruel irony of fate!

"Jess was going to tell you with his own lips," she said to the tall youth that evening when they had lighted the lamp in the living-room, which seemed strangely deserted despite their presence. "Last night he was in terrible anxiety, Ted. We didn't know where you had gone and Jess just walked the floor all night. I could hear him muttering in his room. He missed you. He wasn't all bad, you know. He brought you here because he wanted to—well, to do something for you, I guess. We got to like to have you aroun'. It—it was sometimes lonesome here."

Ted nodded gravely. "I know he wasn't all bad," he said. "He treated me white. He even loaned me money on my mine!"

That remark brought the tears to Lucy Ware's eyes. "Oh, if you only knew, my boy, what we've been through. Why, it was really through *me* that he became an outlaw!"

They stared at each other in the shaded rays of the lamp.

"He shot a man who tried to take advantage of me!" Lucy cried fiercely. "Those were the days of the *real* cowtowns, Ted. An', oh, they were tough! The sights I've seen! You know I'm not young."

There seemed to be no answer to this outburst; and then Lucy Ware found the relief she needed in confiding in this youth, who listened wonderingly and intently.

"Listen, Ted, I've seen more than one man killed," she went on excitedly. "I've seen 'em killed in knife battles, in gunplays, with bottles. I've seen 'em fighting like tigers over nothing more than a stack of white chips, or a slip of the tongue, or a refusal to take a drink."

She paused, her breast heaving.

"Listen!" she leaned toward him confidentially. "They once called me the dance-hall queen. It isn't so long ago, either; an' this is a tough country yet. I was in a big place in—well, in a town where at that time there wasn't a soul in the graveyard that had died a natural death. We had a long bar, an' gambling tables, an' a dance floor in back. I had charge of the girls who were paid to dance with the men, an' I sang a few songs every night. It was a big glittering place an' when it was runnin' full blast it was a sight to see, an' something to listen to."

Her eyes sparkled with their old light of adventure as she drew back the veil of the past.

"After the round-up they'd come in. They'd come from *everywhere*—punchers, gamblers, prospectors, miners, hangers-on—oh, the whole crew. They'd drink, they'd gamble, they'd sing, they'd fight. An' the noise! Glasses clinking, spurs jingling, chips clicking, dice rattling, the man at the wheel calling the numbers; men laughing, shouting, swearing, singing; girls shrieking their orders as the men bought them their percentage drinks; the piano player doin' his worst; me givin' one of my songs—all under the hangin' lamps, with the smoke drifting in layers. Well, it was some exciting scene, take it from me. An' I thought that was the life—*then*."

The boy's eyes were gleaming as the word-picture unfolded before his eyes.

“It was Jess Sneed who took me out of all that, without knowing he was goin’ to do it,” she continued with a catch in her voice. “You see, Ted, I wasn’t a dance-hall girl, exactly; I was—well, maybe I was a little better. I wouldn’t let any man get fresh with me, an’ mostly they treated me right. But there was one who came along during a rodeo who stepped over the mark.

“This man was popular from the start. He had a good make-up, wore several big diamonds—which counted a lot in those days—and spent plenty, which counted more. He was good looking, had a way about him, an’ was a whirlwind of a gambler. I guess that was his trade, if you could call it a trade. Well, he tried to make up to me.”

Lucy Ware smiled wryly as she said this. After a spell she continued:

“One night he came out on the dance floor an’ when I’d finished a song he asked me to dance with him. I refused. Now, Jess Sneed was freighting down there then. He was a big man, an’ was known to be fast with his gun. He’d stopped a gang that had tried to hold him up once, an’ he wouldn’t stand for anyone tryin’ to kid him. An’ he kept pretty much to himself. I guess he had more personality than this stranger, but because he didn’t try to make a show of himself he wasn’t so popular.

“When I told this stranger I wouldn’t dance

with him, he tried to make me. When he took hold of me, Jess Sneed stepped on the floor an' called to him to let up. Well, this stranger was like a tiger in a split-second an' he swore at Jess. Jess handed it back to him an' he went for his gun. He might as well been picking flowers. Jess bored him for keeps before he could get his gun out of its holster. Then Jess vanished."

Lucy paused again, thinking, before she went on:

"It seems they liked this stranger better than Jess, an' the house was in an uproar in no time. They called him a killer an' went after him with posses. But they never got him. He stopped two of them an' they gave up. But he had the name Killer Sneed, an' it wasn't long before he was on the outlaw trail. Maybe it was in him, but I think he was driven to it.

"The affair had a bad effect on me. It—well, I just couldn't seem to sing after that. An' I lost my nerve. I quit. I didn't do any too well from then on, an' I was in a little town in the south, working in a hotel—mind you!—when Jess rode in with his band to take the bank. He saw me an'—well, he asked me how I came to be there an' I told him. He told me about this ranch he'd just got hold of an' how he needed somebody to take care of the house, an' asked me if I wanted to come. Me, *I* wanted a home. So I came. I've had a good home, an' he always treated me right in his way. But the thing most people—nobody, I guess—knew was a thing we had to keep secret, because it was the best policy."

She looked above the youth's head as if seeing afar; and there was a mist in her eyes.

"You see," she said softly. "I was Killer Sneed's wife. An'—an' now—I'm his *widow*."

With this she leaned upon the table and her shoulders shook with sobs.

Ted, his eyes wide with wonder and pity, rose quickly and put his strong arms about her, trying, awkwardly, to soothe her. When she looked up he kissed one of her wet cheeks.

"Never mind, Aunt Lucy, we'll make out," he said earnestly.

"I don't know what'll become of you when I sell the ranch," she said, after a time.

"Sell!" His voice rang. "We—you won't sell, Aunt Lucy. Buck's teaching me the business an' we'll make a go of it. Don't you see? This is *your home.* Where you goin' if you leave here? An' it's my home too. We'll just stick to it. Won't you stick, Aunt Lucy?"

She was staring at his sparkling eyes, at the height and strength of him; and his enthusiasm fairly filled the room.

"All right," she decided; "I'll keep the ranch."

Chapter XIV

An Unscheduled Visit

The discovery of Sneed's real business, and Lucy Ware's remarkable story, made a great impression on Ted Ryder. Truth was, that he felt the loss of Sneed more keenly than he had felt the loss of his father. Perhaps this was because his father had been a hard, silent man, and their life in the little meadow above the mine had been more or less monotonous; whereas there had been more excitement at the ranch, and Sneed, in his way, had been kind. He had been sympathetic, too. However, Ted gave up all thought of trying to avenge his death. He felt a keen sympathy for Lucy Ware, after her extraordinary disclosure. Then, too, Ted had had no mother for years, and a woman who looked after him, as Lucy did, was bound to have influence over him. Now that she was left alone, he wanted to do all he could for her.

But another thing bothered Ted. After all, Balmer *had* told Dorothy Sinclair the truth about Sneed. Certainly her father had confirmed it, too. And then, with the shooting of Balmer, what did she think of him—of Ted? She would naturally assume he had lied; that he had shot Balmer purposely. He worried about this that night of Lucy Ware's confession, and next day. And then he decided upon a bold move. He would see Dorothy and tell her the truth!

It was with this end in view that he rode away from the ranch, down to the lower meadows, and to the timber screen of the river down there late in the afternoon of the next day. He kept well within the shelter of the trees as he made his way eastward. He passed the upper ranch, which now was practically deserted, and continued on to the main buildings of the S-S. These were situated in the bottoms with the bench sheltering them on the north. He followed along the river and reached them just at dusk.

It seems that a mysterious element of luck naturally attaches itself to the activities of youth. Ted rode along the shadow of the trees and had hardly secured his first view of the house when he caught a tell-tale flash of white in the yard. As if some latent instinct told him that this signified the presence of Dorothy Sinclair, he rode into a little clump of poplars, left his horse with reins dangling and scurried about the shrubs until he stood, hat in hand, before the astonished girl.

Dorothy was too surprised to speak.

"I came to tell you," Ted said, "that what Balmer said about Uncle Jess was true. An' he was killed in Morning Glory three days ago. I didn't know about him when you told me that, an' I didn't want you to think I'd lie to you. That's all, I guess—except that he wasn't as bad as some of them thought, an' he was always good to me."

She looked at him gravely and tossed her head. "You shot Lute Balmer," she accused. "An' some time you'll be hung because that bad man's made you a gunman."

"That's what they're tellin' you, I suppose," he said scornfully. "Well, you tell 'em I said I'd take care of myself. If I hadn't stopped it, Balmer would have murdered Uncle Jess. Tell 'em I said that, too!"

"Who'd believe you?" she scoffed.

He thought this over. "Listen, Dorothy," he said finally; "just because Jess Sneed took me in when my father got killed they're against me. Now Jess Sneed is gone. Do you reckon they'll still keep after me?"

"Father says you'll have to go away," said Dorothy. "He says you're dangerous. Don't you think you'd better go away?"

Ted shook his head. "Nope. I reckon I'll stick. Anyway, I couldn't go while Balmer—how *is* Balmer?"

"He's going to get well," Dorothy replied. "But father says you'll have to go. He heard about that man getting killed."

"So he'd drive *me* out!" Ted cried indignantly. "Why, I couldn't go if I wanted to. Don't you see that would be running away?"

He looked very big in the failing twilight, and his voice and eyes impressed her.

"I'll be going away next year myself," she said vaguely.

"I reckon that'll be too bad," decided Ted promptly.

"Oh, you couldn't ever see *me* again, anyway," she informed him. "Father says I can't have anything to do with you because you're—well, you're bad!"

Ted laughed, forgot himself and slammed on his hat. "What yore dad don't know would fill a lot of books!" he jeered. "How'd I come to see you to-night?"

"If they knew you were here they'd chase you away—maybe they'd shoot you," she said earnestly.

"I'd take my chances!"

She shrank back as his hand dropped swiftly to his gun. There it was! The gesture of a gunfighter! Dorothy knew; she had been born and reared in that very country; she had listened to men talk—and she was smart. But she felt a certain exhilaration in her young heart. Ted, standing there above her, unafraid, was not unlike a young knight—a knight of the open country.

"You—must be careful," she murmured.

"Listen, Dorothy, don't you let them kid you along none," he said in a tone of confidence. "An'—" He stepped toward her and grasped her hand impulsively. "Don't you let 'em tell you I'm bad!" A quick pressure of his strong fingers and he started away.

As he hurried toward the trees where he had left his horse, a shout came from behind the house. He broke into a run. A man came down the yard.

"Hold on there!" came the sharp command.

Ted didn't recognise the voice, but he realised its import. They had been seen, or *he* had been seen, by some member of the S-S outfit who knew him by sight. He increased his pace. As he reached the trees a shot rang out and a bullet clipped the leaves above his head. Dorothy's scream came to him then. It gave him something of a thrill. She feared for his safety! He laughed boyishly as he gathered his reins and threw himself into his saddle.

There were no more shots, for he was under cover now. He raced for the river. Darkness had closed in; but as he looked back at the house, he could see the yard fairly well in the starlight and could not distinguish the form of any moving thing. Nor could he descry the tell-tale splash of white which would have indicated Dorothy's presence. He leaped to the conclusion that she had called off his pursuer.

He cantered easily along the trees and walked his horse up the long slope to the bench. This delay brought trouble. As he reached the top of the bench three riders came pounding up the road from the barn. He heard their horses, then their yells, and knew they were after him. He straightened out on the open plain and the race westward began.

In selecting a horse for Ted, Buck Andrews had chosen one of the best animals in Sneed's string—and Sneed had been noted for the speed and endurance of his mounts. His business had required the best horseflesh obtainable. Thus the horse that Ted rode this night was far superior to the ordinary range stock. But Sinclair, old-timer and lover of horses as he was, also had some splendid stock; and he liked to see his men well mounted. Therefore, Ted soon found that he wasn't going to have any easy time of it.

He thrilled from head to foot with his first chase. What they wanted him for, he didn't know, didn't care. They were not shooting at him, anyway. Wanted to capture him and take him back to Sinclair probably. Then Sinclair would have an excuse to make more trouble for him. Might even hint that he was on his range bothering his cattle! Well, they wouldn't get him.

As Ted let his horse out to its swiftest pace, tail and mane flying, the wind rushing past, the vast expanse of plain alive with dancing shadows, he felt a wild exultation. He looked back. They were coming on, a racing trio who figured on getting him before he could get back to the ranch. It was possible they would have a chance when they reached the long slopes leading upward to the lower meadows of the Lazy L. What would Sneed do in such a case? Ted pondered this and realised that Sneed's raids must have put him in a similar predicament time after time. But they'd never caught him! Why? Because Sneed had used his brains, of course.

And now Ted gave evidence of possessing that instinct which often comes natural to those born in a wild, free country—the same instinct which had been Sneed's, although he didn't know it. He wouldn't wait until they reached the slopes; he would trick them!

He was some distance out on the plain from the river; but now he turned suddenly and headed for the dark band of trees along the stream. The shouts came again, and, as he neared his objective, shots broke on the wind. Ted laughed and drove in his spurs for a furious spurt. They were not going to shoot him down or they would have tried it the first glimpse they'd had of him. They were trying to frighten him? Perhaps not; but it made little difference. He gained the shelter of the trees without hearing the whine of a single bullet.

He swung west just within the deep shadow cast by the timber and sped along until he spied an opening. Here he rode in on a trail which he believed would lead to a ford. This proved to be the case and he crossed the stream. As soon as he emerged from the trees on the opposite bank he turned *down* the stream. He was soon around a bend where he would be out of sight of his pursuers when they crossed after him. They could assume either that he had gone up-stream—as would seem natural—or had hidden in the timber. But at the first likely-looking opening in the trees he crossed back to the other bank.

He rode out cautiously, but could see nothing of his pursuers. Here Ted exhibited a degree of cunning beyond his sixteen years. He told himself that the S-S riders would figure that he had crossed the river in desperation and was riding up toward the west, or that he was hiding in the timber. They would not give him credit of being capable of a bold ruse. It would be most natural for them to decide he was hiding; for Ted had thought of doing that very thing, at first.

He rode slowly up-stream until he was nearly at the spot where he had entered the timber. There he listened, and finally the sound of voices came to him dimly from the other side of the ford. He rode on past the opening and then spurred his horse at break-neck pace. Any delay was to his advantage.

He kept close to the trees until another bend favoured him and then he spurted. He called on his horse for everything there was in him, rode like the wind, and at last gained the first slope. As he climbed he continued to look back and finally he saw them coming, one on each side of the stream; the third man missing. They had doubtless left their companion at the ford to keep watch there. But the delay, while they were in conference and deciding what to do, had won success for the ruse. They could not catch him now. He doubted if they could even see him as he kept putting clumps of aspen and bushes between him and the land below. It would do them no good to come to the ranch. They would have sense enough for that.

He reached the first stand of bull pine and reined in his horse. Far below, two shadows moved uncertainly about the stream. Then one of the shadows disappeared and soon came out on the side where the other shadow was. The shadows ceased to move. Shortly afterward they separated and soon there was again the shadow of a rider on each side of the stream. *But now they were going back!*

Ted laughed joyously. "They'll have to wait till daylight to make sure they haven't got me trapped," he sang aloud.

Then he continued on up toward the Lazy L meadows over the first ridge, chuckling happily.

But his merriment might not have been so keen if he had known what the outcome of this enterprise was to be.

Chapter XV

The Demand

While Ted Ryder was eluding the men sent to capture him a strange scene was being enacted at the Sinclair ranch-house. Nate Sinclair had been in his little office when he heard Balmer, who was in bed in a downstairs room, propped up so he could look out the window, call out. He ran in to see what was the matter and Balmer told him excitedly that Ted was in the yard. He had spied him leaving, had caught a flash of Dorothy. Then Sinclair had rushed out and it was he who had chased the youth and fired a shot in an effort to halt him. He had thrown Dorothy off as she ran to him and clung to his arm; had ordered out the horsemen to get Ted and bring him back. Then he confronted his pale, trembling daughter in the living-room.

"What was he doing here?" he demanded furiously.

"He came to see me," Dorothy replied coolly.

"And you didn't call *me!* Why didn't you *call* me?"

Dorothy flushed slightly. "He didn't ask to—to see *you,* daddy. He—had something to tell me."

"And you listened to him!" raged her father.

"After what I told you about him and about that outlaw up there; after I told you never to speak to him again? After he tried to kill my foreman?"

"I don't believe that," said Dorothy slowly. "He came to tell me he—he didn't know about that bad man up there when I told him what Balmer said. He didn't want me to think he'd lied to me. He said Balmer would have murdered that man and that he—did what he did—well."

"Stop!" her father interrupted. She was almost frightened at the sight of his darkened face and flashing eyes.

"Do you, my own daughter, mean to stand there and contradict me?" he said sternly. "Don't you suppose *I* know what that bandit of a Sneed's been up to? Good thing he was killed. I know the breed. I tolerated his being up there because I almost *had* to. But I won't tolerate this young ruffian who's following in his footsteps coming here, or *even looking* at you. You've never disobeyed me before. I—I can't understand it." His look changed from one of anger to pained perplexity.

"Well, daddy," said Dorothy in a low, earnest voice. "I don't believe Ted is a ruffian and what you say. It wasn't his fault he lived on that ranch with that bad man when he didn't know anything about him."

Sinclair was aghast. "You're sticking up for him?" he said incredulously. "Of course he knew it. He couldn't *help* but know it, with Sneed's gang coming in and out. Why, Dot, child, that boy's another killer!"

Dorothy shook her head, although she paled as she remembered how Ted's hand had dropped to his gun when she'd hinted they might try to shoot him if they knew he was there. Then she started and looked at her father with wide eyes.

"You shot at him," she accused.

Sinclair's brows knitted. "I shot over his head, thinking that would stop him," he said gruffly. "I had no intention of hitting him."

"But he wouldn't know that, would he?" the girl asked. Then with a little thrill in her voice: "He didn't stop. He said he could take care of himself." There was a note of triumph in her tone which Nate Sinclair did not miss.

"Oh, he did, did he?" said her father, his frown deepening. "Well, we'll see about *that.* Go to your room."

Dorothy turned away, but at the bottom of the stairs she hesitated. "I don't think it's right, daddy, to make trouble for him now that that bad man Sneed is gone."

"Go to your room!" her father thundered.

Upstairs at her window, Dorothy sat looking out at the branches of the cottonwoods weaving against the stars. "Don't let 'em tell you I'm bad!" His words echoed and re-echoed in her ears. She remembered the look in his eyes. She was old enough to know when a man's eyes were right. She had heard her father's shouted orders to the horsemen. "They won't catch him," she murmured, resting her chin in her hands upon the windowsill. "An'—I don't believe he's bad." Then tears obscured the weaving branches and the stars.

Nate Sinclair paced the living-room, an unlighted cigar clenched tightly in his teeth. He chewed it savagely by spells. How long would it take his men to catch the young rogue? He didn't know exactly what he'd do and say when they brought him back. Well, the kid had nerve—and courage. Coming right to the house to see Dorothy! Ignoring the shot! And Dorothy sticking up for him. Sinclair became extremely thoughtful—more thoughtful than he had been for years. The principal thought which was in his mind—that this youth might defy him and try to see Dorothy again—perhaps often—was intolerable. He was dangerous, this young fellow. He was too good-looking, for one thing; he was well set-up, a good rider; he had a dashing way about him; and girls—especially *young* girls—attached a false glamour to men who were supposed to be a little irregular in lawful conduct. Sinclair frowned heavily and clasped and unclasped his hands behind his back nervously. Why didn't they return with him? Would he trick them? Did he have a better horse? Sinclair swore and dropped into a big arm-chair.

He woke suddenly. Daylight was streaming into the room. He rubbed his eyes, hardly believing that he had slept. Then there were footfalls on the porch and a sharp rap at the door. He opened it hurriedly and looked eagerly at the rider who touched the brim of his hat.

"We didn't get him," the rider said shortly. "He tricked us in the timber along the river. Three of us couldn't watch *every*thing in the dark."

Sinclair stared. "Couldn't watch *every*thing?" he roared. "Couldn't watch *any*thing, you mean. I should have gone myself," he added with an oath.

"He had a good hoss," said the rider stoutly. "And he's no fool. We could have brought him back dead, if we'd had orders."

"Get out of here!" shouted Sinclair, and slammed the door in his face.

Sinclair ordered the housekeeper to prepare his breakfast immediately. Then he went into his office and took some papers from his desk. He looked them over and muttered to himself: "I reckon there's another way. Still, Sneed offered to pay cash for the cattle." He sat thinking steadily until the housekeeper told him his breakfast was ready.

While eating he instructed her to put him up a substantial lunch. After the meal he took the packet of food and went out. He ordered a man to get his best horse from the pasture and shortly afterward he rode away up the road to the bench, where he turned westward and went on at a steady lope.

Lucy Ware heard a vigorous rapping at the front door about midforenoon. She paused with misgiving before she answered. Always, these days, she was fearful of visitors; for there was one whom she expected to come and whose coming she viewed with alarm—Snark Levant. But when she saw the huge bulk of Nate Sinclair on the porch she breathed a sigh of relief. After all, perhaps she had no reason to be so beset with this abiding fear. She welcomed the rancher and invited him in.

"I've come on a matter of business," said Sinclair grimly, taking the chair she offered him. "I believe your name is Lucy Ware?"

"Ah—yes," Lucy replied.

Sinclair reached into a pocket and withdrew a slip of paper. "This," he said, waving it before him, "is a note signed by you for the balance due on the two thousand head of cattle which you, or Sneed, purchased from me recently. It is payable on demand."

Lucy's face went a shade grey. "Yes," she said. "I signed it; I own this place. What about it?"

"I shall have to have this money at once," Sinclair announced.

Lucy started, and then her eyes flashed angrily.

"So *that's* it. Now that Jess is dead you're scared about your money. Well, you have plenty of security so you needn't worry. You can find out for yourself up at the shipping point. If Jess were here he'd probably pay you on the spot. He—" She ceased speaking abruptly as an alarming thought struck her.

"No doubt," said Sinclair. "But since he isn't here, I reckon you're prepared to do the same."

Lucy Ware stared at him. "Of course I'm not prepared to do any such thing," she said indignantly.

Something suspiciously like a gleam of triumph came into Sinclair's eyes. "Sneed offered to do it," he said with a shrug. "I've got to have this money, Miss Ware."

"Maybe you're afraid for the cattle," she said scornfully. "Well, I have a good foreman an' some good men, Sinclair. We can run this ranch. I don't see why you should demand this money so soon after the sale."

Sinclair raised his brows. "I have my reasons," he said shortly. "But I'm willing to be reasonable. I'll give you forty-eight hours in which to pay."

"Forty-eight hours!" Lucy exclaimed. "Aren't you the Santa Claus. You don't need this money, Sinclair. You're doing this for some reason that has nothing to do with money. What is it?"

Sinclair compressed his lips. It was very probable that Lucy Ware knew nothing of Ted's visit to the S-S the night before. If he was to issue an ultimatum to the effect that the youth was not to go upon his range it would probably do little good. He wanted them out of there entirely.

"I have another proposition to make, Miss Ware," he said slowly. "I don't suppose you figure on keeping on here. You can go somewhere and be—well, be rich. If you say the word, I'll buy you out."

Lucy's eyes widened and then grew thoughtful. Sell the ranch? And where would she go? She liked the hills. As Ted had said, she *had* no place to go. And Ted wanted to stay. He was enthusiastic about learning the stock business. Why, she could leave him the place some day. And here she had a home. Moreover, there was a touch of sentiment about Lucy Ware. Sneed had brought her there after he had married her.

"No," she said firmly. "I won't sell the place, an' you can't *make* me sell it!"

"Very well," said Sinclair stiffly, rising from his chair and taking up his hat. "In that case I want this money within forty-eight hours, or I'll take back the cattle under the terms of sale."

"That would be robbery!" cried Lucy indignantly.

Sinclair smiled. "It seems to me," he said mildly, "that that is a—ah—peculiar word for *you* to use."

Lucy's face went white and she clenched her

palms. "I know what you mean," she said fiercely. "You're taking a dig at Jess. You wouldn't dare open your mouth if *he* was here. Now that he's gone, you'd take advantage of *me.* You're no better than he was, if you're as good!"

"Don't talk to me like that," said Sinclair, his face darkening with rage. "Remember who you are and who *I* am. This is business."

"Of course I remember who *we* are," said Lucy smoothly. "We're stock-raisers. Don't think for a minute, you double-crosser, that you're any better than *I* am. Now you leave my house!"

Sinclair fumed with hot words on his tongue. But as he opened his mouth to speak, Lucy's hand came out from under her apron. The ray of sunlight which filtered through a window sparkled and gleamed on the little ivory-handled gun.

"You going?" she asked quietly.

Sinclair stamped out with an oath.

When he had ridden away, Lucy dropped weakly into a chair. She was unaware of Sinclair's real reason for making his demand and thought he merely wished to acquire the ranch as an addition to his own big property. But where was she to get a matter of fifty thousand dollars? Sneed had been prepared to pay cash. She had no doubt of that. But where was the cash? In the bank? She decided not. Sneed was none too sure of banks; perhaps because he knew how easily they could be looted in the isolated towns. He was a hand to hide money. And now her brow clouded with grave concern. It was the first time she had had to think about such matters since Sneed's death.

And she didn't know where Sneed's money was hidden!

Chapter XVI

The Search

Within the hour, Lucy Ware, grimly determined not only to keep the ranch, but to disconcert Sinclair by paying him his money, began a thorough search of the house. She went through the few papers he had left without finding a clue as to the whereabouts of the hidden treasure. She sent for Buck and Ted and put them to work helping her.

"Have you *any* idea where he would hide this money?" she asked Buck.

Buck thought and thought, and shook his head. "He wouldn't hide it in the bunk-house where the men hung out, that's a cinch," he pointed out. "Fact is, I don't believe he'd hide it in *any* building because there's a chance of fire. I'd say it's buried. But we could dig up the whole ranch an' maybe not find it. It's probably somewhere in the hills. But that's like trying to rope a needle. I don't know what, Miss Lucy."

And that evening after an all-day's search to no avail, Lucy was ready to give up. But the money to pay Sinclair had to be found somewhere.

"I don't know what to do," she told Buck, who had been fully acquainted with the situation.

"An', you know, since this came up, I've been thinking that when Snark Levant hears that Jess is gone he'll come back here thinking to get some of this money. Night an' day it worries me—this thought that Snark will come back."

"You needn't be scared of him if young Ted is aroun'," said Buck with a grin. "Ted would fix him."

"Why, Buck," said Lucy, "Snark was almost as fast as Jess with his gun!"

"I know," said Buck, with a nod. "But I've seen Ted practising. He was natural-born to it, I'll say. I'd bet my hoss an' saddle against a cancelled postage stamp that he's as fast as Sneed was right now."

Ted came into the room at this juncture and no more was said on the subject. Lucy looked at him curiously. Why, this sixteen-year-old boy was a man! So she told him about Sinclair's demand.

"I reckon it's all my fault, Aunt Lucy," said Ted contritely.

Then he told them of his visit to the Sinclair ranch the night before, his purpose in going, and the result. Of course, he knew nothing of the meeting of Sinclair and his daughter.

"I guess it's because he wants to drive *me* out of here," he concluded. "He told Dorothy I'd have to go."

"That settles it!" Lucy exclaimed. "We stay

till the cows come home with roses around their necks!"

"I've been thinkin', Miss Lucy," said Buck, "an' maybe for once I've got a ripe idea. You know when we shipped last fall Sneed took me over to the bank where I got some papers to use in Chicago. Maybe he's got money in that bank. Maybe there's more there than you think, Miss Lucy. An,' anyway, why wouldn't the bank lend enough money to pay up on the cattle? They're good for it. Of course, we haven't got much to ship this year, maybe nothing. The chief bought young stuff to build up a herd. But just the same, I've got a hunch that banker up there would do something. He's an old-timer an' he acted plumb courteous."

Lucy Ware's eyes lighted. "Why didn't I think of that before?" she said wonderingly. "Why, of course. At a time like this the place to go is to a bank. What're the banks for? That's a good idea, Buck. We'll learn this game yet. You order the buckboard an' Ted an' I'll go up to town in the morning."

That night in her room Lucy Ware lay sleepless. Was she making a mistake? There was no doubt but that Nate Sinclair wanted them to get out. By staying she would make an enemy of him; very likely she had already done that. She had been infuriated when she had drawn the small gun she always carried. And her reason for carrying it caused her more worry. It was fear of the return of Snark Levant that prompted her to keep the weapon always at her hand. Still, in drawing against Sinclair she had made a mistake. On the other hand, did the rancher have the right to come into her house and insult her? Was it to be his privilege to drive her from her home? She knew why he wanted Ted away, of course. It was because of Dorothy. Well, Dorothy could do much worse than get Ted someday. And Sinclair's assertions that Ted was bad, that Sneed had made a man of his own stamp out of him, caused Lucy to sit up in bed and look out of the window with a hardened gaze. No—she wouldn't go. Nor would Ted go. Why, Ted was all she had left. The old spirit of adventure, of self-protection, of fighting for her rights flamed within her. After all she had gone through was she not entitled in the autumn of her life to have someone to love, to look after, and, in time, to look after her? Tears—too often strangers—came into her eyes.

She rose, slipped on a dressing gown, stole quietly to the door of Ted's room. She opened it softly. The soft moonlight filled the room, disclosing the features of the sleeping boy, and the tumbled mop of chestnut hair, dark against the white pillows. A sob swelled in Lucy's throat. She had come to look upon him almost as her own boy. Here he was home. What would become of him if he went out into the world?

She closed the door and went out upon the little balcony over the porch. She looked eastward. The basin was a dark, hazy blue, an island adrift in the light of the hanging moon and stars. The dark shadows of the hills loomed on either side. A breeze whispered secrets of the universe in the ruffled foliage of the trees. A night owl voiced its plaintive cry and from afar came the staccato barking of a coyote. The air was sweetly scented.

Lucy Ware drew a deep breath and still looking out towards the far-flung domain of the S-S she spoke softly, tremulously.

"I've a card up my sleeve, Sinclair, that you haven't thought of; and if you drive me too far—I'll play it!"

Then she went back to her room and sleep came to her.

Right after breakfast, Lucy and Ted started for the shipping town in the buckboard behind two splendid greys. Ted had learned to drive since he had been on the ranch, and he promised Lucy they would be in town before the afternoon was well spent. Lucy got a great deal of pleasure out of Ted's enthusiasm on this drive. They'd fool Sinclair. They'd have one of the best ranches in the foothill country. There would be plenty of hay for the winter. They were moving the stock on forest range where the feed was splendid. That would save the lower range for the winter, too. Next year they would put in more oats.

"And what do you think of this Dorothy Sinclair?" Lucy ventured to ask.

"Nice kid," he replied promptly, with a flourish of the whip.

Lucy Ware smiled to herself. She would be more interested in a romance than in all the cattle, hay, oats and ranches in the world.

Ted kept his word and by three o'clock they were in town. He put the team in the livery barn, and, after Lucy had freshened up her appearance in the hotel, they went to the bank. There she ascertained that she had a balance of fifteen thousand dollars. There was no account in Sneed's name.

Lucy considered for a few moments. Sneed had had five thousand dollars in his money-belt when he died. There was fifteen thousand more in the bank. That was twenty thousand at her disposal. She made an immediate decision.

"I want to see the president," she told the cashier.

"He's in the back room, ma'am," said the cashier. "I'll tell him."

He walked to a door behind the cage, opened it and went in. A few moments and he came out, motioning Lucy around the cage. Ted followed her into the little private office of the banker. He rose from behind his desk as they entered. He was a formidable-looking personage; a stocky man of bulk, with a large head, aggressive chin, thick moustache above firm lips, and bushy, black eyebrows which lent a fierce aspect to his features. But the eyes were a kindly hazel.

"You're the president?" Lucy said nervously.

"I'm Armstrong, and I own this bank," he said in tones which precluded any doubt as to the truth of his statement. "Sit down, Miss Ware. Who's this young man?"

"This is Ted Ryder," said Lucy, feeling more at ease. "He lives at my place."

"Likely looking lad," said Armstrong. "Well, Miss Ware, what is it?" He sat down in his swivel chair, filling it completely, and leaned his elbows on the desk.

"I—I want to borrow some money," said Lucy.

"Ha! You know, Miss Ware, I guessed that very thing. About the only people who come in here who don't want to borrow money are those who want their notes renewed, or extended. Sometimes I do it, an' sometimes I don't." His eyes twinkled under those terrible brows, reassuring Lucy. "How much do you want?"

Lucy began to explain, and as the banker showed more and more interest, she began to add details, even to the point of confessing that she believed she had made an enemy of the powerful Nate Sinclair.

"Humph!" the banker ejaculated. "Sinclair hasn't got his rope on *me.* Now let's see, Miss Ware. You need fifty thousand. I think he hooked

Sneed on those cattle, at that. You've got five thousand cash an' fifteen thousand on deposit, which is twenty thousand, an' a ranch. You ought to have at least five thousand on deposit for running expenses. So we'll say you've got fifteen thousand. That leaves you needing thirty-five thousand."

He paused, frowned, and did some figuring on a pad on his desk.

"You've got two thousand head of thoroughbred cattle an' some hundreds odd of scrubs. Well, I'll lend money on thoroughbreds any day. There ain't enough of 'em in the country yet. You won't have to mortgage your ranch, Miss Ware. You want around seventeen-fifty a head on your good stock. Now, you'll have to look after these cattle mighty careful, Miss Ware. Thirty-five thousand." He looked from one to the other of them, pursing his lips.

"I'll let you have it," he said suddenly.

Lucy gasped and Ted slammed his hat on his knee enthusiastically. Armstrong looked at him with a scowl. "Don't be too gay, young fellow," he admonished. "Borrowing money is a serious business. Always think three times before you borrow. An' if everybody did that, I don't know how I'd make any money," he added humorously. "But it's right good advice, just the same."

He opened a drawer and took out a pad of notes. With pen and ink he filled out a blank. He also made out a cheque and a deposit slip. Then he looked up at Lucy.

"Now, Miss Ware, there are four things you must do. You must sign this note, you must sign this cheque for fifteen thousand, you must turn in your five thousand for deposit, an' you must consult me in any emergency concerning the cattle. Do you understand?"

Lucy nodded. "Yes, I understand," she said soberly.

"All right," said the banker cheerfully; "now move your chair up an' get busy with this pen. About the only enjoyment I get out of life is watching folks sign on the dotted line!"

When Lucy had signed the note and cheque, and turned in the five thousand, Armstrong made out a cheque for fifty thousand dollars in her favour. He blotted it carefully and handed it to her.

"See that Sinclair endorses that note as paid, Miss Ware," he instructed.

"I—I believe he expects cash," said Lucy, taking the slip of paper.

"Tell him to present the cheque!" snapped Armstrong, rising.

As they reached the street, Lucy and Ted looked at each other. Lucy was dazed at the ease and rapidity with which the transaction had been completed. Ted was jubilant.

"Aunt Lucy," he said joyously. "We've pulled

out all Sinclair's tail-feathers with one jerk!"

They stayed at the hotel that night, and in the morning Ted had the buckboard and team ready at sun-up.

"Drive down the south-east road," said Lucy as they started.

Ted had to ask a direction and as they turned into the road he looked slyly at Lucy.

"Where we goin', Aunt Lucy?" he asked softly.

"Straight to the Sinclair ranch," was the answer.

"Come on, *ponies!*" sang Ted, shaking out the lines.

Chapter XVII

The Arrival

Southward the sweeping billows of green rolled on and on, with the wind ruffling the grasses until the flowing plain took on the rhythm of a following sea. Here and there, glowing like topaz or rubies, the yellow and red flowers of the prairie cactus sprinkled the plain with splashes of colour. In the west the mountains marched, trailing their purple robes, holding their silver crowns aloft in the great, blue arch of sky. Golden sunshine bathed this world of beauty, brought out the colours sharply, widened the horizon until the sense of distance was lost and the plain seemed limitless. A single butte stood off in the east, pale blue and pink, like a prairie bulwark. The air was warm, delicious, sweet with the scent of spring.

Lucy Ware was happy. The enthusiasm, the bubbling vitality of the youth beside her, served to ameliorate her sense of loss and loneliness. A new life opened to her. She drank in the beauty of the land—the only land she had ever known. Leave it? Her eyes sparkled. Why, she had had a part in the making of it! Drive her out? Her head went up instinctively and she smiled at Ted, who threw an arm about her shoulders and gave her a bearish hug.

Although it was a long drive to the Sinclair ranch, the distance was not as great as to the Lazy L in the south-west hills. Moreover, there was a good road, and the horses made excellent time. Therefore, they were on the bench above the S-S ranch buildings by noon, and, as they drove down the winding road, they saw Nate Sinclair come out on the porch of the ranch-house, shading his eyes against the sun with his hand, looking up at them.

"I'll go in," Lucy told Ted. "You wait with the team."

Sinclair came down the porch steps as Ted brought the team to a halt with a flourish in the courtyard. He scowled darkly as he looked at the youth, who returned his stare coldly, and nodded to Lucy Ware without attempting to help her down.

"I've come to see you," Lucy announced, "on business."

Sinclair appeared nonplussed, and Ted smiled serenely. This was one time when the rancher couldn't order him from his domain.

"You can water an' feed your team in the barn," said Sinclair gruffly. He could not overlook common ranch courtesy. "You'll find a man out there to show you around."

"Thanks," Ted returned dryly. "I'm carryin' some feed an' I reckon we'll be stopping at the river springs west of here to eat."

Sinclair swung on his heel. “We’ll go inside, Miss Ware. I suppose you come about the money owing on the cattle.”

“I’ve come to pay it,” said Lucy, following him up the porch steps. She was unable to keep a note of triumph out of her voice and it caused Sinclair to bite his lip.

As they went in, a golden-haired, blue-eyed slip of a girl came around the corner of the house, stopped short, and heard a strong young voice greeting her.

“Hello, Dorothy. Here I am again. I reckon I won’t get chased this time.”

“I knew they wouldn’t catch you.” There was a sparkle of welcome in her eyes. “Who—what—”

“Aunt Lucy’s with me an’ we’re payin’ for our cattle,” said Ted proudly. “I guess yore dad thought we couldn’t do it. Listen, girlie, we’re goin’ to have *some* ranch.”

“Oh, I’m glad,” said Dorothy, who couldn’t resist the impulse to clap her hands. “I hope you show daddy you’re not bad, because I told him you wasn’t.”

“You did?” His eyes widened. “Good for you! You just stick along an’ we’ll show him something.”

Thus, unconsciously, did Ted link the girl with his interests. Perhaps she realised this; but, if she did, she didn’t resent it.

“Can’t you come up some time an’ see us,”

he urged. "You must have a good horse an' you could make it between breakfast an' supper. Aunt Lucy's real folks, an' if I'm not there, she'll get me in to the house quick."

"I'd get killed," breathed Dorothy, with a flush.

A stamp of boots in the hall and Sinclair's huge form was framed in the doorway. "Dorothy!" he roared. "Come in here at once. Do you hear me? *Come in!*"

Dorothy went meekly, while Ted began to whistle a range lullaby. If Sinclair's glare of rage could have killed, Ted would have been struck dead in the seat of the buckboard.

"Go to your room!" the rancher thundered, as Dorothy passed him.

Lucy, standing just within the door of Sinclair's office, caught sight of the girl and smiled. Dorothy smiled back on her way to the stairs.

"Look here, Miss Ware," said Sinclair angrily as he entered the office, "I can't have that young—that—" He paused, fuming.

"Yes?" said Lucy sweetly.

"Sit down," he said harshly. When she was seated he took the chair by his roll-top desk and looked at her darkly.

"What I want to say is that I can't have that fellow speaking to my daughter," he said evenly. "She is not only the heir of the S Bar S, she is—she has been brought up different. She doesn't know about such things as you an' Sneed—er—

well, I won't have that scamp talking to her."

"Why don't you tell him so," was Lucy's comment.

Sinclair sputtered and bit off the oath that came to his lips.

"I guess you're forgetting that I came here on business," said Lucy coldly.

"Well, have you got the money?" he snapped.

Lucy opened her purse and brought out the cheque, which she had already endorsed. "Here's your cheque," she said, again unable to restrain her exultation.

"Cheque!" exclaimed Sinclair. "I didn't say anything about a cheque. I asked for the cash. Where is the cash?"

"Present the cheque!" said Lucy haughtily.

"I don't *have* to take a cheque," he announced. "I was at the county seat yesterday an' saw my lawyer. I can demand cash. How do *I* know you're cheque is good, anyway?"

"Oh, if it wasn't you could still take the cattle," said Lucy dryly. "Look at the signature on that cheque, Sinclair. I've endorsed it to you." She handed him the paper, and as he looked at it, his face grew darker.

"Armstrong, eh?" he muttered. "Well, there's a way to get to him, too."

"Look here, Sinclair," said Lucy in a strange, stern voice. "Do you aim to keep on making trouble for me?"

"Business is business," he growled. "Sneed said cash. I want cash—an' your time's up."

Lucy's laugh rang in the little room, singularly free from mirth. "You're going to take the cheque, Sinclair," she said in a low, earnest voice, leaning toward him, "an' you're going to get that note out an' cancel it. But that isn't the point. Are you going to lay off of me an' that boy? I know what you want to do; you want to drive us out. Well, you can't do it. Get that straight, Sinclair. *You can't do it!* We're up there to stay. Now get that note out an' cancel it."

"What makes you think I'm trying to drive you out?" he demanded.

Lucy Ware's eyes flashed. "Why, you fool, don't you think I know what's stinging you? Do you think I'm simple?" She laughed scornfully. "What do you think I learned in the days when this country was a-fire?—a-fire, do you hear? I learned about men. I had mostly to do with men an' most of 'em braver men than you! I can read you like a book—*like a book,* do you hear? Now listen, Nate Sinclair, if you want hell on this range you can have it. I can give it to you. I have the means. *Do you want it?*"

"What can you do?" he sneered, although his face paled.

"Do?" Lucy's voice rang with menace. "Do? Nate Sinclair, you cancel that note, as you'd have to do anyway, an' you let me an' the boy alone; if you don't—if you don't—" She paused, her lips drawing into a fine white line.

"Yes?" he said hoarsely.

"I'll send for Jess Sneed's band!" she cried shrilly.

Sinclair sat gripping the arms of his chair, his features working, his eyes narrowed and blazing with wrath. No word came from between his clenched teeth.

"Jess Sneed is dead," Lucy went on softly; "but his spirit lives in the wild hearts of the men who followed him. I know those men, Sinclair. They'll follow me if I but say the word. I've but to snap my fingers an' the north counties pact is broken!"

Sinclair snatched open a drawer of his desk and took out a slip of paper which Lucy recognised. He wrote rapidly across the face of the note and handed it to her.

"You're still The Queen, eh?" he said grimly.

Lucy didn't answer. She put the cancelled note in her purse and, without looking at him, went out of the office and the house. Ted looked with wonder at her white face and jumped out to help her into the buckboard.

"What's the matter, Aunt Lucy, did he—"

"Drive out of here," Lucy ordered in a strained voice. "I want to get home."

They rested at the river springs where Ted unhooked the horses, watered and fed them and tied them in the shade of the trees. Then he and Lucy ate the cold food they had brought with them. They talked; but Lucy did not tell Ted of the threat she had used against the powerful rancher. Indeed, now that it was over, there was doubt in her mind as to whether she could carry out such a threat, even if she so wished. But she believed it would protect them. And yet—why did they now need protection? Sinclair and his lawyer in the county seat! The cattle were paid for; the ranch was clear of debt. Her smile returned as they resumed their journey.

It was late that night when they reached the ranch and Lucy went straight to bed, after a warm supper which the coloured housekeeper had kept against their return. She was tired, but satisfied.

But peace was not yet to come to the Lazy L.

At four o'clock the next afternoon, Sheriff Frost rode up to the ranch accompanied by two deputies. He dismounted and met Lucy on the porch. He greeted her gravely.

"I've got to take the boy down to town," he announced.

Lucy stared, white-faced. She had, for the time being, forgotten the shooting of Balmer. Then she brightened.

"Frost," she said slowly. "You can't touch Ted. I saw that whole business from just inside the door here. I saw Balmer go for his gun first when he *knew* Jess was crippled. He might have shot the two of them, if it hadn't been for Ted."

The sheriff's eyes roved about uneasily. He didn't like this business. There was the matter of the rewards connected with Sneed's death. There was a big probability that the thing would be negotiated so that he would profit by that unexpected happening. Like many sheriffs, he was not altogether above taking blood money.

"I can't help it," he said. "Sinclair made the complaint, day before yesterday. There's a warrant and an indictment coming up. But the boy won't be there long. He'll probably be back to-morrow. I'm pretty sure that county attorney will send him back on his own an' likely the whole thing will be quashed. But I've got to take him down to-night."

"So *that's* why Sinclair went to the county seat," Lucy said, as if to herself. "All right, Frost, I'll go along. *I'll* get him out if I have to put up all my cattle an' the ranch for bail!"

"No need to come, Miss Ware," said the sheriff. "We're riding fast. If he shouldn't be back by to-morrow, why—*then* you can drive down."

At this moment there came a pound of hoofs and Ted came galloping in from the range. His gaze darted from one to the other of them, and to the two waiting deputies. Then he understood.

"You wantin' me, sheriff?" he called cheerfully.

"I reckon I'll have to take you in," said Frost wryly. "But I don't think it'll be for long. You'll be back soon."

"When we startin'?" Ted asked.

"Soon's you're ready," replied Frost.

"That'll be in about a quarter of an hour," said Ted as he started for the barn.

"Honestly, Miss Ware," the sheriff began, "I—"

"Stop!" cried Lucy in a fury. "You're nothing but Nate Sinclair's tool. Don't you know, you fool, that he doesn't care a rap about Balmer's being shot. It's that girl of his—Dorothy. She's sweet enough an' all that; it isn't any of *her* fault. But Ted's seen her an' talked to her a time or two, an' he's furious. He thinks Jess wanted to make a bad man out of Ted an' that's a lie, Frost, an' you know it! Sinclair offered to buy my ranch. He was sore to-day when I paid off the note for the cattle we bought from him. He wants to drive us out of here an' he can't! Listen, Frost, if Sinclair wants trouble on this range, he'll *get* it. An' sooner or later I want to know who *you're* siding with!"

She left him and hurried inside to get some things together for Ted, who was arranging for a fresh horse. He came in to find her almost in tears. He put his arms about her.

"It'll be all right, Aunt Lucy," he said, "we might as well get it over with now as later."

She kissed him before he left, and she stood on

the porch and watched them ride away—watched until all she could see was a thin spiral of dust which the sun touched with gold. She went into the living-room and sat in a chair, rocking ceaselessly; but no tears came to her eyes. Lucy Ware had long since learned to bear her sorrows in silent, undemonstrative suffering.

She ate little supper; and again she sat, rocking and thinking, while the twilight gathered and the night wind stirred in the trees.

In time she made up her mind. In the morning she would send for Buck Andrews who was with the cattle. She would have him drive her down to the county seat. She would see the county attorney and place every resource at her command at the disposal of the court to secure Ted's release. And once again she felt a poignant pain in her heart because Jess Sneed was gone.

The dusk deepened into night and the stars broke through the purple canopy of the sky. The coloured woman came in and lighted the lamp. She had hardly gone out of the room when a rolling sound as of thunder came to Lucy's ear. She started and sat erect. The thunder sharpened into the staccato of flying hoofs on the road. Lucy gripped her chair, but she did not rise. She did not seem to have the strength to do so. Then horsemen were swarming in the yard. Lucy heard hoarse commands voiced. The stamp of boots and jingle of spurs came from the porch steps.

Then a slight figure in the doorway and a pair of eyes that held her gaze as a shudder swept over her.

Snark Levant had arrived!

Chapter XVIII

The Break

Levant closed the door softly and came in. He stood for some moments looking at Lucy Ware, who, although she had dreaded his advent, now was cool and collected at his coming. He took off his hat and put it on the table; then he dropped into a chair and looked at her steadily.

"Hallo, Lucy," he said.

She did not answer—merely looked at him curiously. Not once did her thoughts revert to the gun she possessed. Now that he was there, it seemed quite natural. She relaxed.

"Don't want to be sociable, eh?" he commented. "Well, we ought to be for old times' sake."

"What did you come here for?" Lucy asked.

"I heard about the way Sneed went," said Levant. "It was a dirty trick—them takin' him off that way. Same time, he sort of did us dirt—us men, I mean—after we'd stuck to him so many years. He kicked us out, you might say. It was that kid, I guess. Sort of felt sorry for him after him killin' his dad, an' wanted to—change."

"Jess didn't kill Ryder," said Lucy. "He told me about it. Jess didn't tell me such an awful lot, but what he *did* tell me was always the truth."

Levant shrugged and compressed his lips. “Well, we won’t argue that,” he said. “I didn’t come here to argue about that, anyway. You know, Lucy, we was with Sneed in all his deals. Us fellows took just as many chances as *he* did. We stuck by him too. Now he’s gone. We ain’t lightin’ any Christmas trees for joy, but we’ve got a notion or two. Sneed left a lot of money, Lucy. We helped him make it—or *get* it. We feel we should get in on the divvy, now that he’s gone. We’re entitled to it. You’ve got to split with us, Lucy; for we took risks where you sat snug at home.”

Lucy Ware leaned forward in her chair with interest. “You mean,” she said slowly, “that you expect me to give you money?”

Snark Levant’s eyes hardened. “There’s no use beatin’ aroun’ the bush, Lucy,” he said meanly, “we know Sneed left a big cache of cash, an’ we’re entitled to at least half of it. We’re keepin’ true to Sneed’s agreement to lay off the north counties, but we need cash. It’s up to you to split with us. You’ll have plenty left. An’ we won’t bother you nor work the north counties.”

“That’s a threat!” cried Lucy angrily—and suddenly she laughed shrilly, while Levant stared darkly. “Why, listen,” she said, controlling her mirth, “do you know what I was about to say? I was going to say that if *you* knew where Jess

Sneed could have hidden his money, I'd give you half!"

Levant half rose from his chair, his eyes flashing evilly. "Don't try any tricks with me, Lucy," he said hoarsely. "I'm not as big a fool as you think. We're entitled to half that money, an' you *know* it! We helped to get it. You've got to give it to us!"

It was then that Lucy Ware remembered. Her right hand came out like a flash and the yellow glow of the lamp gleamed on the little gun.

"Don't get up!" she commanded. "An' don't make any queer motions, Snark Levant! I've gone through a lot—about as much as I *can* go through, I guess—an' I'm getting so I don't care much about *any*thing, except this kid, as you call him. I was afraid you'd come—afraid for *his* sake—but now that you're here, I seem easier. You can't threaten me, Levant, an' if you try to do me dirt—*I'll shoot you in your tracks!*"

The gun was steady in her hand. Levant stared at it as if fascinated. Then he looked into her eyes, and the dark look on his face faded until it was replaced by a yellowish pallor. He wet his lips.

"Well, anyway, Lucy," he said in a milder tone, "there's no use in us quarrelling. You know I can't stop the boys thinking an' they—well, they—"

"They want half what Jess left behind," Lucy

interjected scornfully. "An' you think because I'm a woman, you can come here an' bulldoze me out of it. If I had a million dollars, Levant, you couldn't bully me out of a penny. But—" She paused and lowered the gun. She recalled what she had told Nate Sinclair.

"Suppose," she said softly, "I had wanted some help from the men who had worked with Jess an' had sent word. Would I have got it?"

"In a minute!" exclaimed Levant, his eyes glistening; his thoughts still on the money he knew Sneed had left somewhere.

"Well, Levant," said Lucy in a tired voice, "I'll tell you square I don't know where Jess left his cache—an' I could have used some of it. Yes, I could have used a lot of it." The gun dropped into her lap.

Levant scowled suspiciously. It was preposterous that Sneed should not have provided for such a contingency as would arise in event of his death. Of course, Lucy Ware knew where the money was; she probably had it. She was saving it for the boy, Ted, likely. Yet he realised that threats would avail him nothing. Moreover, he saw there was something on Lucy's mind besides Sneed's death and the money.

"Where's the kid?" he asked curiously.

"Ted?" Lucy's laugh was an uncanny thing to hear. "He's in jail, I reckon," she said dully, as though to herself. "Frost took him away this afternoon. He shot Sinclair's foreman, Balmer, when Balmer tried to kill Jess. I don't know—now, after it's all over—but that it might have been just as well if Balmer had done the job."

Levant's eyes had widened in astonishment. "So they grabbed him?" he said wonderingly. "Balmer an' Sneed had a run-in an' the kid stepped into the play? What—well, I'll be—" He stopped short and a light of cunning came into his eyes.

"Frost came up here an' took him to jail?" he asked softly.

Lucy nodded. "You see I've no bed of roses, Levant; an' that's one reason why I'm not scared of you or your gang. You can't bring me more trouble than I've got. An' you can't do any good for yourself here. *Get that!* You might just as well push on. If you don't believe me, *I'll show you!*"

She hurled the wicked little gun across the room.

Levant leaned back in his chair, his cruel, little eyes gleaming. Ted Ryder in jail! If he should take him out, he would *then* be able to threaten Lucy Ware! He could hold the boy as hostage; or he could menace her with the threat that he could persuade Ted to join the band. His eyes glistened. It was a way to make her give him half the money Sneed had left and which he firmly believed was in her possession.

"Well, I guess you've got your share of trouble,

old girl," he said in a smooth voice which he meant to be comforting. "Maybe I made a mistake. I know Sneed was a secretive cuss. What do you want me to do?"

"Clear out," said Lucy Ware wearily.

Levant rose. "Remember what you said about—well, you might need us sometime?" he said craftily. "If you do, just send the word. I reckon you could manage to get a message to us, for you're no fool."

He went to the door and let himself out softly, while Lucy continued to stare vacantly at the farther wall of the room. She heard the stir of the horsemen as they left and breathed a short sigh of relief, although she knew in her heart that Snark Levant would return again. But *next* time, she would kill him!

In the hills above the Lazy L the band, with Snark Levant, came upon the reserve horses they had cached there. Always there were fresh horses near, now that Levant was the leader. He lacked the intrepidity that had been Sneed's prominent characteristic; but he possessed a greater sense of caution. The men changed horses and then rode swiftly eastward.

It was the hour before dawn. The moon had gone down and the stars had dimmed in lustre. Lamy, the county seat, was a dark blot upon the surface of the plain with no light showing, save for a pale yellow glow in a front window of the county jail.

Within that jail—an old wooden frame building, improvised for its present purpose—Ted Ryder lay upon a bench in one of the two cells. He had blankets under and over him; for he had been well treated by the sheriff and county attorney, who felt none too comfortable over the situation. But Sinclair was a power; jobs were jobs; and votes were votes. It has ever been so.

From each end of the short main street a number of horsemen rode silently into town, the hoof-beats of their mounts muffled by the deep dust. Some remained at each end of the street; others stationed themselves at intervals. Three went on to the jail and dismounted. One remained outside, holding an extra horse which was saddled and bridled.

In the little front office a deputy, serving as jailer, dozed in an arm-chair. The two men who entered the office fell upon him, tipping him over in his chair to the floor; one holding his arms, while the other swiftly gagged him with a bandana handkerchief before he, in his dazed condition, could cry out. Then they bound him hand and foot, and one of them took his keys.

The two men went through the door into the space where were the two cells. A dim light was burning and they looked into these cells. One of the men swiftly turned a key in the lock of one of the cells, entered and shook Ted Ryder rudely by the shoulders. The boy awoke with a start, sat up, and heard a hissing voice in his ear.

"Keep quiet! Get up an' come along out of here."

Then Ted recognised the thin features, glittering black eyes and voice of Snark Levant. He shrunk back against the wall.

"I'm not goin' with you!" he declared in a vibrant voice.

Instantly Levant slapped a hand hard against the lips of the youth. "Listen!" he hissed. "I've been sent to get you out quick! It's Lucy Ware. *She* sent me. She's in trouble! You've got to come!"

Ted's eyes glowed with suspicion and Levant removed his hand from the boy's lips. "Don't you believe me?" he said hoarsely, playing his trump card. "Then *stay!* I've done my part."

He turned to leave, confident of what would follow. Nor did his cunning betray him. Ted threw off the blanket and leaped from the bunk. He hurriedly donned his coat and hat and followed them out of the cell, out of the building. As they mounted the men at one end of the street came riding toward them. They turned up the other end of the street to join the others. From somewhere came a hoarse shout. Then the barking of a six-shooter. Men were in the street. Guns roared and they dashed out of town in a cloud of dust with blazing weapons winking red fireflies of death in the first grey light of dawn.

Chapter XIX

A Ruse Fails

Ted rode with Snark Levant on his left and another of the band on his right. The others closed in behind, returning the fire of the men of the town who had been roused by one or two citizens who were early abroad. But the town was soon left behind and the cavalcade raced across the open plain, undismayed by signs of swift pursuit. It would take some little time to organise a posse.

Ted found himself splendidly mounted. Sneed had been noted for the excellence of his horses, and the band had inherited a string of fine mounts. As they literally flew along the grassy reaches, with the rosy dawn behind them, the foothills seemed to march toward them out of the mists.

Worried as he was, Ted could not throw off the feeling of suspicion which took possession of him. The mention of Lucy Ware's name, the hint of trouble, had sent him bounding from his cell. But now, in the chill of early morning, his thoughts freshened. What trouble could Lucy Ware be in? And would she send Levant to get him out of jail? It seemed preposterous. It was not logical. His suspicions grew until, within the next hour, he became convinced that he had been tricked, betrayed.

They continued to race toward the mountains, but *not* in the direction of the Lazy L. They were riding north-west, whereas the Lazy L was in the south-west. Indeed, they headed almost on a dead line for the Ryder mining claim north of Morning Glory. As they approached the foothills, with the sun mounting in the eastern sky, Ted saw that Levant had no intention of turning to the south, in which direction the Lazy L now lay. To assume that he proposed to circle through the hills was ridiculous; for the road to Morning Glory would have to be passed and the chances of being observed, and tracked, were ten to one. Also, if Lucy Ware was in trouble and had sent for Ted, would it not naturally follow that Levant would make a spurt for the ranch?

Ted upbraided himself mentally for his folly. He tried to catch Levant's eye, but the outlaw looked steadily ahead. The others were riding more or less about them now, and Ted was hemmed in. He realised he was a prisoner—the victim of a ruse. What did Levant want with him? His hand dropped against his empty holster and his jaw clicked shut. He was unarmed. His weapon had been taken from him at the jail, naturally. And there was another thought which bothered him. More than likely Levant had been recognised in the county seat. It would be known that he had rescued Ted from jail at the point of the gun. Ted would most certainly be linked with Levant and the old band. The boy ground his teeth. It was unfair. It was heaping more trouble, not of his own making, upon him. Then, too, it would mean more trouble for Lucy Ware. And there was Nate Sinclair ready to add his word against him and say: "I told you so!"

They entered the foothills at a point about a mile north of the Ryder claim. Here the order of riding changed. Levant moved in ahead with a man behind him. This man continually peered back over his shoulder at Ted, who had fallen next in line. The others brought up the rear. The cavalcade was in single file, following a narrow trail that wound about the hills, mounting steadily into the higher mountains. All thought of Levant taking him to the ranch now was abandoned by Ted. He was beset by an overpowering curiosity as to what Levant wanted with him; what he intended to do with him. It was something important, he knew; or Levant would not have taken the trouble and risk to take him out of jail.

They climbed steadily and Ted, who knew something of the lower hills in the vicinity, surmised that they were making for Smoky Lake pass, a deep gash in the high, rock-bound ridge below the Great Divide. They stopped when the sun was hanging directly overhead, watered their horses in a little stream, loosened the saddle-cinches, and permitted the animals to graze on the luscious grass while two of the men made coffee and others got food from their slicker packs. Ted approached Levant.

"Where are we going?" he asked mildly.

"You'll find out soon enough," said Levant cheerfully. "Don't worry. Just take things easy. We're safe enough."

"I'm not worrying about our being safe enough," Ted retorted, "an' I know you lied about Aunt Lucy sending for me. But I'm wondering what you want with me, Levant."

"Oh, you'll find that out soon enough, too," said the outlaw with a slight frown. "But I'll tell you *one* thing, kid, an' that's that I don't want you slingin' any questions at me now. An' I don't want you talkin' in front of the men. What we've got to say, we'll say when we're alone. Savvy?"

He strode away and Ted realised it would be useless to attempt to learn anything until Levant was ready to talk.

After they had eaten and taken a short rest they resumed the trail. They were in the big pines now, and the basin was a sea of blue haze far below when they occasionally glimpsed it from the top of a ridge. Ted was paying strict attention to the trail. No detail of the winding path was lost to him; he noted landmarks as they proceeded and he noticed, especially, that the trail had, at times, been well-travelled. Plainly they were going to one of the mountain rendezvous for which Sneed had so often found use.

The afternoon wore on and, with the passing of every minute, almost, they gained altitude. Higher and higher they climbed; through narrow aisles of forest, over rock-ribbed ridges, through gravel-strewn ravines, across treacherous patches of shale—upward toward that wicked gash in the great Smoky Lake ridge.

The sun slipped down the western sky, gathering momentum as it neared the pearly peaks, and then it dropped behind the mountains, splashing the high skies with crimson, flooding the valleys and washing the ridges with waves of colour until the horses seemed to wade knee-deep in a sea of purple gold. They came abruptly upon the pass, a narrow defile through the crest of the great ridge. As they passed through and came out upon the down-trail on the western side, they saw Smoky Lake beneath them, the filmy haze from which it took its name hanging over it like a veil. Down the steep trail they rode; but instead of entering the valley proper, they turned off to the left up a narrow ravine and came into a broad meadow, rimmed with rock walls, creased by a small stream, sprinkled with alders and clumps of fir, and studded at its upper end with a number of small log cabins. This, as Ted suspected at once, proved to be the rendezvous.

They rode up the stream to the cabins and dismounted. The upper end of the meadow was fenced off and there were a number of large posts grouped about outside the cabins with pegs, upon which the saddles and bridles were hung. The horses were turned loose and the gate in the fence closed.

Snark Levant beckoned to Ted to follow him. He led the youth to a cabin and threw open the door, motioning to him to enter. When Ted was inside, the door closed after him, and he heard a bolt shot into place. He looked first at the window through which the fading light of the sunset filtered, and was not surprised to see that it was barred on the outside. This, then, was his prison.

He looked swiftly about the interior of the cabin. There was a bunk with a quilt and some blankets, an oilcloth-covered table on which was a lamp with a smoked chimney; in a corner was a high bench with a pail of water on it, a wash-basin, some soap, and a soiled towel hanging on the wall above it; there was a fire-place at the side of the room opposite the bunk, and three rough stools. On the walls were a number of old calendars and some pictures clipped from magazines. There was a piece of frazzled rope under the bunk. The beams which supported the dirt roof were sagging. Evidently, years gone, it had been the abode of a prospector. There was no glass in the window, and Ted tested the bars, only to find them rigidly secure.

The boy put his hat on the table and sat upon the straw tick of the bunk. So far, he was none the worse off than if he had been in the cell in the jail at the county seat. But he found it hard to think. He was relieved in that he knew Lucy Ware was not in trouble. Whatever had caused Levant to take him from jail it certainly had nothing, so far as he could see, to do with the Lazy L. Nor did Ted believe that Levant had any personal spite to vent upon him. With the dogged nonchalance of youth he gave up trying to solve the riddle and lay back upon the bunk, content to rest until Levant should see fit to visit him and explain the purposes he had at hand.

He had had little sleep the night before, and the day's ride had fatigued him; he dropped off to sleep. He was awakened by being rudely shaken, and sat up, rubbing his eyes. The lamp was burning on the table and beside it were a number of dishes. The odour of food was in the air. The window was dark, for night had fallen. He looked quickly at the man beside the bunk, expecting to see Levant. In this he was disappointed. The bearded ruffian who looked at him out of small, beady eyes was merely a member of the band. This man pointed to the table.

"There's your supper," he growled. "Hop to it while it's hot."

He stamped across the board floor to the door, gave Ted another look, went out, closing the door and shooting the bolt.

Ted got up and drew a stool to the table. He was hungry. His eyes lighted as he saw the fried grouse, potatoes, biscuits, stewed apricots, and the steaming can of coffee. There was salt and sugar, and a small can of condensed milk. He fell to eagerly. Whatever Snark Levant had in mind, he apparently had no intention of starving him.

He hadn't long to wait after he had finished his meal when he heard steps outside and then the bolt was drawn and the door opened. The man who had brought his supper came in and gathered up the dishes. As he went out, another entered and closed the door after him. It was Snark Levant.

The outlaw looked at Ted quizzically, drew up a stool and seated himself across the table from the youth. He continued to flash glances at him as he drew tobacco and papers from a pocket and leisurely built a cigarette. He snapped a match into flame with a thumbnail and lighted his smoke. He inhaled deeply and smiled wryly.

"I reckon this is better than jail, eh?" he said amiably.

"As near as I can make out, I'm still in jail," replied Ted, with a glance at the barred window.

Levant chuckled meanly. "You don't need to hang out in here if you're ready to show some sense," he said. "I suppose you know what you're up against."

"No, I don't," said Ted. "I don't know what you want with me or what you intend to do with me. An' I'm curious."

Levant waved his cigarette in a gesture of irritation. "I'm not meanin' anything about you being here," he said. "It's down below where you're up against it."

He leaned an elbow on the table and gazed at the youth keenly. "Don't you know that they're out to get you?" he said with a frown, holding the boy's eyes. "They had you in jail, didn't they? Well, listen, kid, they were fixed to railroad you along to the big house, that's what. Sinclair wants your hide, an' he can get it—if you let him. He holds that fool sheriff in the hollow of his hand. He wants to put you away where you'll be out of the picture. Then he'll make things hot for Lucy Ware an' in time he'll drive her out an' get the ranch. He'll fix the evidence, an' anyway Balmer's got a perfectly good hole in him for a clincher. The jury would know Sneed took you up an' made a gunfighter out of you—"

"That's a lie!" Ted exclaimed.

"Oh, is it?" Levant could not repress a sneer. "You mean to tell me you can't sling a gun?"

"I can handle a gun some, yes," Ted confessed. "But that doesn't mean that Uncle Jess intended for me to be a gunfighter like you say."

"How you goin' to prove it?" Levant snapped out. "Think you can make that cattle crowd believe you? Sinclair would pack the jury with his crowd. You wouldn't have a chance. I hear everything that goes on aroun' here. You shot Balmer all right. An' you made some talk in Morning Glory the day Sneed got his. Everything's against you. I'm tellin' you that you wouldn't have a chance. Do you want to go to prison?"

He eyed the boy closely and saw his gaze shade to worry.

"That's where you're headed for," he continued. "That's why I got you out. I did it partly because you're an able lad an' partly because I believe Sneed would want me to look after you if he could say so. There's just one thing for you to do."

His small, cruel eyes glowed with evil cunning. Ted looked at him questioningly.

"You've got to keep out of reach for a while, quite some time, I'd say," Levant said in a low, impressive voice. "You might as well trail along with us. I'm giving you a chance I wouldn't offer to anybody else I can think of right this minute. But you've got some stuff in you, an', as I say, I feel I owe it to Sneed. You'd have an easy enough time of it with us; all the money you wanted to spend; a chance to play the towns up the line, an' a chance to see Lucy down at the ranch once in a while with us to protect you. I reckon Sneed would have taken you into the outfit, if he'd lived."

Ted stared at him, startled. So *that* was it. Levant wanted him to join the band. Why? He didn't for a minute believe that the outlaw was making any such proposal because of any sense of loyalty to Sneed's memory. In what way did Levant want to use him? Instantly he discounted the outlaw's statements about Sinclair wanting to send him to prison. He suspected that Sinclair's move in having him taken to jail was an effort to frighten him. In any event he did not propose to join the band.

Levant continued to look at him, and if Ted could have read the man's mind he would have had more cause for worry. For Levant had good and sufficient reason for trying to link him with the band. It was Lucy Ware against whom his scheme was directed. With Ted as a member of the band, he could go to her and offer to persuade the youth to return to her if she would give him half of the fortune which Sneed had left. He was convinced in his own mind that Lucy Ware had the money or knew where it was. And if Ted refused to join them, he could hold him a prisoner and refuse to give him up unless Lucy came to terms. He smiled evilly as he thought of the alternative. The game was in his hands. Even if Ted gave in and joined, he would be closely watched and would still virtually remain a prisoner. And after he, Levant, had obtained the money, Ted and the others would find themselves without a leader; for half of Sneed's ill-gotten fortune would be enough to keep Levant very comfortably in some far-away place for the rest of his life.

"Well, what have you got to say?" Levant demanded harshly, rousing himself.

"Nothing," replied the youth shortly.

"So?" Levant's eyes flashed fire. "Well, listen to me, kid," he said in a hissing voice; "I've put the proposition to you straight. I won't make it again. You can take it, or leave it, an' I'll give you till day after to-morrow to make up your mind. I'm figurin' you'll show some sense; because if you *don't,* I can promise you *one* thing—you'll never see the Lazy L again!"

He rose and kicked back the stool, glaring at the boy who gazed at him calmly. "When you're ready to send word to Lucy that you've joined up with us, we'll be ready to protect you, an' her, too. But don't think I'm goin' to all this trouble on your account for nothing. I'm tryin' to do you a good turn, an'—" He paused and his eyes narrowed. Then he laughed brutally. "I snatched you out of jail an' you rode away with us. That makes you one of us so far as that outfit down in the basin is concerned, an' gives Sinclair the last bit of evidence he needs. I reckon you've got sense enough to see that."

He moved to the door and with another laugh went out.

Ted sat staring at the door, the rattle of the bolt throbbing in his ears. His face had paled. It was Levant's parting shot that had told. For it was true. He *had* ridden away with the band after he had allowed them to take him out of jail. That would be hard to explain. It gave Sinclair a formidable weapon if the rancher really wanted to do him harm.

He got up from the stool and paced the cabin. But the more he thought, the more hopeless his situation appeared. If he could only talk it over with Lucy Ware. He stopped by the table and his eyes roved aimlessly, finally coming to rest upon a thick beam above the door. He stared at this timber, unseeing at first, and gradually becoming aware of the fact that one end of it had almost rotted away. It diverted his thoughts, this beam which had given way to time. He looked curiously at the other end under the sagging roof. Some time it would fall, this heavy timber. And if anyone happened to be going in or out of the door at the time—His eyes lighted and he sat down on the bunk. He continued to stare at the timber and at the door. After a time he removed his coat and boots, blew out the light in the lamp, and curled up in the blankets. He had a plan.

The golden dawn was streaming in through the cabin window when he awoke. He rose at once and after a short session with the soap and water he looked out of the window. There were no other cabins to be seen, as the habitations of the outlaws were all above in a semicircle. He saw horses, however, grazing on the rich grass between the cabin and the rock wall which hemmed in the meadow.

Soon he heard footfalls without, the bolt was shot back and the door flung open wide. The man with his breakfast on a large board slab made sure he was on the farther side of the table, then he brought in the food and placed it on the table. He went out without speaking.

Ted ate heartily and waited by the window until the man had removed the dishes. Then he set to work. Bit by bit during that morning, and in the afternoon after dinner, he worked with the huge beam over the doorway, standing on a stool, ready to get down and over to the window or the bunk on an instant's notice. He loosened the beam until it barely hung in place. Meanwhile he had concealed the frazzled rope in his bunk lest it should be seen on the floor where it had lain and be taken away.

Levant did not visit him this day and Ted wisely surmised that the outlaw leader thought that by staying away he would cause him more worry and perhaps thus force him to agree to join the band. Ted also thought that it was because of his skill with his gun that Levant wanted him with the band. And the youth was not so troubled this day. He believed that if he returned to Lamy and told the sheriff everything he would get a square deal. And he had bethought himself of a man whom he believed would be his friend in the emergency—Armstrong, the banker at the shipping point. But first of all, he wanted to talk with Lucy Ware.

Sunset came and flooded the cup in the mountain wherein lay the meadow with a rosy light which faded rapidly, owing to the high surrounding walls. Ted affixed one end of the rope to the end of the beam, which was literally hanging by a hair. The rope just reached down across the end of the cabin to the bunk. He sat upon the bunk with the rope lying at his feet and waited.

The twilight deepened speedily in the rock-walled meadow. It was almost dark in there when there was still light on the ridges. He did not light the lamp. There was just a faint glow in the window when he heard the tell-tale footfalls outside. His heart leaped. He leaned down and grasped the rope as the bolt was drawn and the door swung open.

"Eh! Where are you?" growled a voice.

Ted simulated an audible yawn. "Here—here," he said. "That supper?"

The man grunted and stepped inside just as Ted jerked the rope with all his might. There was a rasp of wood against wood, a shower of earth from the roof, and the beam plunged down. It struck the outlaw on the shoulders behind and he was knocked forward on his face, the dishes containing Ted's supper crashing on the floor.

Instantly Ted was upon him, his strong hands about the man's throat. But there was no need for rough tactics, for the man was knocked senseless. His legs were pinned to the floor under the beam. In a thrice Ted had the rope tied about the outlaw's wrists behind his back. He gagged him with his own bandana handkerchief. Then he took the man's gun, slipped it into his holster, and rapidly extracted the cartridges from his captive's gun-belt, thrusting them into his own coat pockets.

He stole out of the cabin, closing and bolting the door. It was now dark, and though light streamed from the windows of the other cabins among the trees along the stream, he saw no one about. He slipped to a post where a saddle and bridle hung. He swung the saddle over his shoulder, took bridle and saddle-blanket and hurried to the rear of the cabin where he had been confined. Here he dropped the saddle, took the rope from it, and soon he was leading in a horse from the west side of the meadow there.

His heart pounded and he shook with excitement as he quickly bridled and saddled the horse. He mounted and rode slowly down the meadow in the shelter of the trees. When he reached the narrow entrance to the rendezvous, he heard a shout and a dark form loomed ahead of him. He drove in his spurs and his horse lunged ahead. There was a spurt of flame almost in his face and a gun roared in his ears. His own weapon leaped into his hand. He fired over his shoulder and the dark form melted into the shadows. His horse galloped madly, its shod hoofs ringing against the rock floor of the defile. And then he was out on the trail and turning up towards the star-filled gash in the ridge which marked Smoky Lake pass.

Chapter XX

At the Ranch

There was no false conception of security in Ted Ryder's mind as he rode up the steep trail. His youthful features had hardened; his lips were pressed firmly together; his eyes were alert and gleaming. He knew pursuit was as certain as the coming of another day. Snark Levant was not one to be thus circumvented in his evil designs. The man at the entrance to the rendezvous had been a look-out, of course. The shots would rouse the camp. Someone would ride down to ascertain what was wrong and find the guard, wounded or dead. They would rush to the cabin where Ted had been held prisoner and would find him gone. Then they would take to their horses and start after him. At that very moment the outlaws might be running for their mounts. So the youth pushed on, grimly determined to reach the Lazy L in good season ahead of the band. He did not for an instant doubt but that Levant would head for the ranch if he didn't overtake his quarry.

As Ted reached Smoky Lake pass and cantered through the gash in the rock-ribbed spine of the ridge, a new moon edged up out of the dim eastern horizon like a silver disc, its cold, clear light shining along the trail that led down through the stands of pine and fir and cedar. His horse took the down-trail willingly, eagerly, knowingly. Although he did not know it, Ted had taken one of the best horses in the outlaws' string; an animal which ordinarily was ridden by Levant's right-hand man. He soon found that the horse knew the trail. It was a splendid bay, full of spirit, fast and sure-footed. And Ted made time, galloping across such open spaces as he encountered, trotting through the forest aisles, mounting the ridges at a fast pace; he had reason to thank his stars for the training in horsemanship which he had received on the Lazy L range.

There were no sounds of pursuit. He realised that the timber growth would muffle such sounds; but he was also convinced that none of the outlaws could make better time than he was making. And he had got a fair start. He was going down much faster, of course, than he had come up two days before. He recognised various landmarks which had impressed him on the way to the pass, but he really had no need of these, for the trail was easy to follow and the rising moon favoured him with its silvery light, aided by the clusters of stars that hung in the night sky.

He extracted the empty shell from his gun and inserted a fresh cartridge. Now and then he flung a look over his shoulder. His alertness and tension never slackened for so much as a moment. It was a different Ted Ryder who rode this night. Gone was the youth with the winning smile and the sparkling eyes. Instead, here was a *man,* full-grown and mature in the hour of emergency and danger. He was ready to shoot at the first warning. And, if it came to a matter of guns, he did not intend to waste bullets.

It was barely midnight when Ted came out upon the trail in the foothills which led southward toward the mining claim his father had left him, and the Morning Glory road. Here he was on familiar ground. He spurred his horse and dashed along the trail to the meadow where was the cabin where he and his father had lived. He did not stop, but raced across the meadow into the trail leading down from the mine. Then he pushed his mount to the utmost of its powers on the firm trail until he had crossed the Morning Glory road and hit the trail which led to the ranch. He did not spare his horse. He expected the animal to be spent by time he reached the Lazy L, but there it would be well cared for and he could get a fresh mount for the ride to the county seat. Ted did not doubt but that Lucy Ware would advise him to go to Lamy and make a clean breast of the affair. Surely he owed no allegiance to Killer Sneed's former band. Sneed was dead and the men had gone off with Levant. Lucy Ware herself would have nothing to do with them.

He made fast time on this trail, taking advantage of every opportunity that presented itself to call for all the speed his mount could muster. He blessed his luck that he had chanced to pick such a horse. But, then, the bay had certainly been wildly ridden before. Not once since his escape from the rendezvous had he heard or seen anything to indicate that pursuit was near. When he crossed the last ridge and came upon the straight trail to the ranch he used his spurs and streaked for home. The first grey glimmer of the dawn began to dispel the mists over the basin. Gradually the rim of the eastern horizon flushed; the sky blossomed like a rose, first pink, then flaming crimson. The sun rose out of a sea of colour, showering the plains with gold. And then Ted broke through the last clump of trees, checked his horse and cantered to the barn of the Lazy L.

The barnman was already about, and Ted, dismounting swiftly, ordered his spent mount blanketed and stalled, and asked that a fresh horse be brought in from the pasture as quickly as possible and saddled against his departure.

The barnman, who had listened to him round-eyed, took up the reins of the horse Ted had ridden and found his tongue.

"There's two men here," he said with some excitement. "They're in the bunk-house. They've been here since day before yesterday. I don't know much about it, but I guess they're some of Frost's outfit from the county seat, an' I think they're sort of expecting you."

Ted's thoughts raced. It seemed logical that the sheriff would send men to the ranch to watch in event he should return. They were probably deputies. Frost himself was likely leading a posse north towards the Canadian line, or in the hills. Ted frowned. He had no wish to go back with any deputies. He wanted to go in to Lamy alone to give himself up. It would create more of an impression in his favour.

"Listen," he said; "get the horse an' saddle it out beyond the house an' I'll leave from there. I don't want to see this pair."

The barnman nodded knowingly and led the spent horse into the barn. Ted stole to the rear door of the ranch-house and let himself in. The coloured cook was already up, and he sent her to call Lucy Ware and to warn her she must hurry. As the cook went up the stairs he set about getting some cold meat and bread to appease his hunger.

The coloured woman was back shortly with the information that Lucy Ware would be down at once. Ted gulped his food and entered the living-room as Lucy Ware, in slippers and dressing-gown, came down the stairs. She gave a little cry and hurried towards him. He put his arms about her shoulders as she stifled a sob.

"Listen, Aunt Lucy," he said quickly, "we have to hurry. I'm goin' back to Lamy. You heard what happened?"

"Yes. There are two men here looking for you. Oh, Ted, why—why—"

"Listen!" he interrupted. "I want to tell you as quick as I can." He stepped back and in short, crisp sentences he explained what had happened, while her face paled and her look hardened.

"Levant lied," she said when he had finished. "He was here. He wanted money. He went as suddenly as he came. I didn't know what he intended doing. I didn't send him. Yes, you'd better go back. There are lawyers in this country that Sinclair hasn't got tied up, an' I reckon I can still raise money. I'll be down there to-day, Ted, boy—don't worry."

"Get Buck," said Ted, "an' have him drive you like fury up to see that banker, Armstrong. He'll know what to do. I reckon—I wouldn't be surprised if Levant came along this way lookin' for me. He's got some kind of a scheme. But he won't dare touch you. The man at the barn's gettin' me a fresh horse. I'll be starting. It's *you* that mustn't worry. An' the only thing that worries me—" He paused and a steel-blue light shot from his eyes. "Aunt Lucy," he said slowly, "I'm afraid I'm goin' to have to *kill* Snark Levant!"

Lucy Ware, startled at his tone and look, groped for words and failed to find them.

"I'm off," Ted announced, and, kissing her hurriedly, he ran for the kitchen and went out the back door.

But Ted was too late. He had been right in assuming that Levant would take to the trail in pursuit at once. This was just what the outlaw had done. And he had pushed his mount as hard as Ted had pushed his. So fast had been the pace that only five of the band had been able to keep up. The others had been compelled to follow some distance behind. And the interval while Ted had given his instructions to the barnman, and had remained in the house, comparatively short as it was, had given Levant time to close the gap between them. As he stepped out into the courtyard at the rear of the house, Ted heard the thunder of flying hoofs, and then the riders burst through the trees with a chorus of yells.

They swept towards the youth, their guns swinging. But they held their fire. Evidently Levant was bent on a capture. Ted hesitated for the barest of a brief space. He half turned back towards the door. But out of the corner of his eye he saw the barnman with a horse in the trees behind the house. He started to run in that direction and instantly the first shot broke upon the morning air. A bullet whistled past him.

Ted's teeth came together with a click and his gun seemed to jump from its holster of its own accord. Then it spoke sharply, and one of the outlaws went tumbling out of the saddle. Ted darted around the corner of the house, paused and shot again. A horse leaped high in the air and came down on its knees, flinging its rider over its head. The rider lay motionless on the ground, while the other four outlaws swung into the courtyard, putting the house between them and Ted.

The youth ran along the length of the house to its front and started to climb up on the porch. As he did so, Snark Levant came racing around the other side. Ted's gun barked again, and Levant's hat was torn from his head by the impact of a bullet. His horse reared to the tight rein and Ted dashed around the end of the porch, seeking another shot. For a short space Levant had to give his attention to his mount, but as Ted reached the porch steps, his gun flaming, he whirled his horse. Ted caught sight of the blazing eyes and the distorted features of the outlaw. Before he could shoot, Levant's right hand came up like the snap of a whiplash and his gun roared. Ted shot wild and fell upon the steps, his gun dropping dully on the wood.

From the direction of the bunk-house came the staccato of more pistol shots. Wild yells broke above the barking of the guns. The front door of the house opened and Lucy Ware, white-faced, came out on the porch with a rifle. The butt came up against her shoulder and the big gun roared as

Levant, with a final look at the motionless form of Ted, drove in his spurs and dashed for the road leading down into the trees. Lucy worked the lever of the rifle with a sob. She had missed. Again the Winchester roared its message, but the hot lead failed to find its mark, and Levant, riding like mad, disappeared down the road.

Lucy flung the gun down and ran to the end of the porch. The guns were barking again and two riders dashed past, making for the road after Levant. The two men who had been in the bunk-house were out, one of them shooting after the fleeing pair, the other leading a man—the man who had been hurled from his horse when Ted's bullet had done for the animal—across the courtyard. Two of the outlaws lay still on the ground of the yard and their horses stood off at a distance with reins dangling.

"Ted! Where's Ted?" Lucy Ware called shrilly.

She ran to go down the steps and stopped with a weird little cry, a clutching feeling in her throat. Ted lay sprawled on the two lower steps. Lucy went down, mumbling, whimpering inarticulately. She grasped Ted by the shoulders and turned him over, his body slipping from the steps to the ground. On the first step was a little pool of red.

Lucy sank upon her knees, calling hysterically for help, as one of the deputies came running to her aid.

Chapter XXI

The Rim of the Shadow

The two deputies carried Ted Ryder to his room, where they undressed him and got him into bed. Lucy Ware came with warm water and bandages. After a time the flow of blood from the ugly wound in the youth's left side was staunched, and Lucy bandaged him as best she could. One of the deputies took the horse which the barnman had saddled for Ted and went to get Buck Andrews from the range at Lucy's request. When he returned with Buck the two deputies, realising the futility of pursuing Snark Levant, started for Lamy with the outlaw who had been captured. They were under instructions to send the doctor from the county seat at once. Meanwhile, Lucy dispatched Buck to get the doctor at Morning Glory. Buck took the fastest horse on the ranch and set out at a furious pace.

Again Lucy Ware stole silently about the house and sat at the bedside of one she held dear. She bore up with fortitude, dry-eyed; denied the relief of tears by her curious, patient nature. Hers had been a lonely life, even when Sneed was living. Now if Ted was to go—Hopeless, forlorn misery swam in her eyes. Once she left the bedside and went to the window, wringing her hands. Then her hand went gently back to Ted's hot brow as if she would smooth away the injury.

All morning Ted remained unconscious while Lucy watched over him and the messengers raced their horses for the prairie men of medicine. Then, shortly after noon, the boy opened his eyes and his lips framed the request for water. Lucy gave it to him and he lapsed into coma. The afternoon wore on with Ted recovering consciousness at intervals for a very short time. Once he whispered to Lucy:

"I'd have—got him—if—his horse hadn't—kicked up—a ruckus."

And Lucy smoothed his hair and kissed the bronzed cheek. No one could know how much she regretted her poor aim when she had thrown the heavy rifle to her shoulder and turned it on Levant. If Levant should ever come to the Lazy L again—A tigerish gleam came into Lucy Ware's eyes. She would shoot from ambush, or she would shoot on sight; but she, herself, would kill Levant before Ted could do so—if Ted got well.

Sunset came and lighted its crimson fires on the peaks. Gradually they burned away and the skies cloaked themselves in gold. The tones softened to rose and amethyst, and the twilight rode in on the gentle, evening breeze. Lucy Ware maintained her vigil as the shades deepened, and then, as night descended with its beacon of stars, she heard horses in the courtyard and hurried downstairs.

The doctor from Morning Glory came up the porch steps as she opened the door. He pushed past her with a gruff greeting as the coloured housekeeper came in with a lighted lamp.

"Where is he?" the doctor demanded of Lucy.

"I'll show you," said Lucy, taking the lamp and leading the way upstairs.

The doctor made an examination, frowning all the time. "Too bad," he muttered. "But I expected it. Well, he's a strong specimen. He may make it. He's built like a Greek god. That man of yours was saying you'd sent for Butler, too." He looked askance at Lucy.

"I sent for the doctor at Lamy," said Lucy. "I wanted to be sure of getting one or the other of you as soon as possible."

"That's Butler," growled the physician. "I'm glad you sent for him. I'll wait till he gets here before starting after the bullet the boy's got in him. Two heads are better than one in a case like this." He took Ted's pulse.

"You're not looking any too pert yourself," he said, bending his professional gaze on Lucy. "I'll give you something."

But Lucy shook her head. "It isn't medicine I'm needing, doctor. I'm wanting to know if you think Ted will pull out of it."

The doctor shrugged. "He's hit hard in a bad place," he told her. "Hang it! why do they allow these cut-throats to roam aroun' this country? I'm for calling out every man that can tote a gun an' hanging Levant an' his crowd without a trial." He glowered at the lamp on the table. "Butler ought to be here by midnight," he ruminated. Then, pocketing his watch, "The best thing we can do right now is get something to eat."

Although the doctor ate heartily of the supper the coloured woman served, Lucy could eat nothing. The doctor insisted that she drink a cup of strong, black coffee before she returned to the sick-room. "We'll need you as nurse," he said. "By the way, do you know my name?"

Lucy shook her head.

"My name's Craven," he announced. "You know—I liked that boy. Now drink your coffee and then you can go back up there."

After supper Doctor Craven attended Ted until finally, just before midnight, the Lamy doctor arrived behind a pair of spent and sweating horses. The Morning Glory physician met him in the living-room and after he had taken a cup of coffee they went upstairs. Lucy Ware was excluded from the consultation and at its conclusion the physicians procured several more lamps to furnish more light, and other things which they needed, and proceeded to extract the bullet from Ted's side, thoroughly cleansing the wound and bandaging it properly.

This done, the fight to save the youth's life began in earnest. His temperature had risen steadily and now he was in the throes of wild delirium. The doctors took turn about at the bedside during the early hours of the morning and in the forenoon. Lucy Ware was ordered to lie down for a few hours to conserve her strength. Buck Andrews was sent post-haste to the county seat to obtain certain medicinal supplies from the drug store there. He cut through the S-S both going and returning, and it was on the way back that he encountered Dorothy Sinclair.

Dorothy didn't know him, but she knew he was not of the S-S outfit and she had sufficient suspicion to stop him. As Buck had heard certain things, and knew of the trouble with Nate Sinclair and the reason for it, he told her grimly in a few words what had happened. Then he galloped on his way, leaving her sitting her horse with blanched cheeks and troubled eyes.

That afternoon Sheriff Frost arrived at the ranch with the county attorney and Nate Sinclair. The rancher's eyes glowed sceptically as he entered the Lazy L living-room with the officials.

Lucy Ware greeted them in a listless voice, but Doctor Craven, who came hurrying down the stairs, was indignant.

"This is no time to be coming here, Frost," he

said with heat; "you ought to know that. We have a fight on our hands here that is more important than any business *you've* got."

Frost held up a hand. "Easy, doctor," he said in a mild voice, "we don't want to bother you. But if Miss Ware doesn't mind, we'd like to ask her just a few questions that are in the interest of the community at large."

"If you want to do something for the community at large, you'll get this Levant and his gang and hang 'em to the nearest cottonwoods," the doctor snorted.

"You're forgetting that two men were killed here yesterday and young Ryder shot, I reckon," said Frost sternly. "I have to investigate. I've been trying to get Levant's gang and have two posses out now. I can't let you interfere with my duties."

"And I'll not let you interfere with mine," the doctor retorted hotly. "I'll give you ten minutes with Miss Ware, if she wants to talk to you. Don't forget that *I* have a few prerogatives as a physician." He turned and went up the stairs, looking significantly at his watch.

Frost introduced the county attorney and asked Lucy to tell them what had happened.

With her tired eyes on the carpet Lucy slowly recounted what Ted had told her about the jail break, his escape from the rendezvous in the mountains—the location of which she could not give them—and his arrival at the ranch. She described what had happened afterward.

Sinclair moved in his chair. "I believe when you were down at my place you threatened to send for this Levant," he remarked dryly.

Lucy looked up quickly. Then the fire flashed in her eyes. She rose, trembling with anger. "You bring your dirty grudge up here at a time like this!" she cried. "Listen you—you beast! If I ever threatened you, the threat stands! I have men on this ranch an' I can get more. I ordered you out of my house once, an' I'm ordering you out again, for ever! If you ever come on my range again, I'll put the Indian sign on you for keeps an' they can *bury you with it!*"

The sheriff had stepped quickly beside her and put a hand on her arm, flashing a warning look at Sinclair. "Don't get excited, Miss Ware," he soothed. "You better go, Sinclair. I guess we've heard all we need to know, Miss Ware." He turned to the county attorney. "What do you think?"

For answer the attorney drew some papers from an inside pocket of his coat and tore them lengthwise and then across. "I refuse to indict the boy," he said, "for *any*thing. Miss Ware, there is no longer any charge against him."

Sinclair rose smartly to his feet and went out. Whether or not he believed Ted was seriously wounded none could tell. He did not wait for the others but galloped down the road.

Lucy Ware dropped back into her chair, murmuring her thanks.

"I reckon that's all, Miss Ware," said the sheriff in a friendly tone. "We had to know what happened, and we hope the boy comes out of it all right. We've got one prisoner and if we can make him talk we'll make things hot for Levant yet, although I wouldn't be surprised if he was near enough to the Canadian line to throw his rope over it right now."

Lucy Ware made no sign that she had heard. The two officials went out the door. She heard them ride away. She rested her head upon her left hand. Her breast heaved and her lips trembled. Then suddenly came a flood of tears.

Doctor Craven came down the stairs, saw and went out upon the porch where he swore deeply and fervently. Yet his cursing lacked the irreverence of profanity.

The Lamy doctor remained that night also, but in the morning he left for the county seat where he had patients whom he could not neglect for a longer period. Doctor Craven, however, stayed at the ranch. Buck Andrews was sent on another errand to Morning Glory to leave word with the deputy there that in event of a serious accident or illness word was to be conveyed to the doctor at the Lazy L. Craven had no cases requiring his immediate attention.

He remained almost constantly at Ted's bedside. The boy was running a fever of a hundred and four, and was raving with delirium, tossing about, rarely still or silent. But toward morning of the next day he became more quiet and his temperature dropped slightly. This the doctor accepted as a good sign and sighed with relief. He lay down upon the couch in the room for a few hours of rest. By noon of this day, Ted was sleeping and the doctor hinted that the first crisis had been passed. Then Lucy Ware went to her room and did something she hadn't done since the death of Sneed. She knelt and prayed.

In the afternoon she went out to cut some flowers to take to the sick-room against the time when Ted should open his eyes with his mind cleared. She looked up quickly from a rose bush as the sound of hoofbeats came to her ears. Her eyes widened with surprise as a girl came riding up the road, turned into the yard and reined in her mount near her. It was Dorothy Sinclair.

The girl spoke first. "Are you Aunt Lucy?" she asked in a sweet, young voice.

Lucy Ware started. So Ted had been telling the girl about her. "Yes," she replied, "I am." She noted the trim figure of the girl, the golden wisps of hair that peeped from under her hat, the clear skin of her cheeks in which fragile roses bloomed, the soft eyes with the frank look of youth.

"How—how is Ted?" asked Dorothy.

"We hope he is better," Lucy answered. "He's been out of his head, but he's sleeping now."

A glimmer of gladness shone in the soft eyes. "That's good," said the girl. "I—I just had to come up and ask."

"Do you like Ted?" asked Lucy.

"Yes—I do," Dorothy replied with a defiant toss of her head. "And I don't believe a word of what they say about him." She nodded soberly.

Lucy smiled for the first time in days and stepped nearer to Dorothy's horse.

"Ted's a good boy," she said with a wistful look. "You can believe me, Dorothy. You see, I know quite a bit about men and I know a real man in the making when I see him and have a chance to study him day by day. Ted's pure gold and he can be trusted. These people who—who say things about him which are not true, maybe have reasons of their own for trying to harm him. He hasn't had a square deal, and he's worth the peck and parcel of them that's against him."

"I guess—I don't think daddy understands him," said the girl hesitatingly, and waited breathlessly for Lucy's answer.

But Lucy had no intention of saying anything to Dorothy against her father. She was too sensible for that. "Your father will come to like him in time, I hope. We should all be good neighbours here where there are so few of us." She smiled again.

Dorothy's eyes lighted and she held out a hand impulsively. Lucy took it and pressed it, a warm feeling about her heart.

"I hope he gets well soon," said the girl. "And when he's better I'm coming up to see him. Can I?"

"Why, of course you can, girlie," said Lucy. "And it would do Ted more good than any medicine he could take."

Dorothy smiled in appreciation. "I have to go now," she said with just a trace of trouble in her eyes. "I can't stay long because I started late. Good-bye—Aunt Lucy."

Lucy Ware stood looking after her as she rode away; watched until she was out of sight down the road. Then she turned again to her flowers. But Dorothy's visit had taken much of the bitterness out of her heart. The tired look in her eyes disappeared. A new, fresh interest seemed suddenly to have come into her life.

"Bless the child," she murmured, looking vacantly over the sweeping sward of green. "I wonder—I wonder if it'll be her who'll bring Nate Sinclair to his senses." Her troubles waned with the memory of the warm pressure of Dorothy's hand.

Meanwhile Dorothy had passed the lower meadows and was riding down the long gentle slope. When she reached the creek she crossed, and it was then that she saw her father galloping towards her. He drew rein when he met her. His face was dark with anger.

"I saw you riding away," he said harshly. "Where have you been?"

"I often ride up here towards the hills, daddy," the girl replied.

This retort added flame to the fire of the rancher's wrath. "I've told you to stay away from the west range," he said sternly. "To-morrow you start for your teacher's place down in Big Bend, an' you'll stay there the rest of the summer."

Dorothy's head went up. "No, daddy," she said soberly, "I won't. I love you and I've always obeyed you; but I won't go." Her words came with a spirit that was not to be denied. "I won't go, do you hear me? The S Bar S is my home and you can't send me away from it. If you do, I'll come back first chance I get, if I have to steal a horse!"

They rode furiously back to the ranch-house in silence; and Dorothy didn't go.

Chapter XXII

The Remedy

Ted awoke that night with the light of reason in his eyes. His temperature had gone down five and a half degrees; his respiration was twenty-four. He had passed the great crisis, and now Doctor Craven's chief concern was to keep the wound in the boy's side drained and properly dressed to guard against gangrene. With victory in sight, the doctor, after his kind, was very severe. He would not permit Ted to talk, and his rules were strict. Ted went back to sleep, and in the morning Doctor Craven left for Morning Glory, stating he would return next day.

Then followed the period of early convalescence, with the doctor making regular visits to dress his wound. Ted had lost weight, naturally, and some of the bronze on his hands and face had faded. But he soon was taking nourishment, and gradually his appetite assumed proportions which caused the coloured cook and housekeeper to wear the broadest smile she had displayed in years.

"Just you stop fussin' aroun' this yere kitchen, honey bird," she told Lucy Ware. "Ah knows what that boy wants. He wants good su'stantial victuals, that boy does. An' Ah knows how to cook 'em, Ah does. You just keep out of the way an' don't bother me, an' I'll put that boy back on his hoss as big an' strong as the day he went to bed!"

So Lucy laughed and did not again try to assist in the culinary department.

Summer had come and Buck had driven the cattle to forest reserve range. A deputy came from the county seat, bringing Ted's horse, saddle, bridle and his gun. Nothing had been heard of Snark Levant and his band after the flight from the Lazy L. It was assumed that he had circled around, had met the others of his crew and had made off over the range or up into Canada. It was Sheriff Frost's opinion that he would never again be seen in that locality. The man who had been taken prisoner could not, or would not, give any information. He proved, however, that he had joined the band but a month before his capture. This was doubtless why Levant made no effort to aid him. He received a six months' jail sentence and appeared content to serve it out. The horse which Ted had ridden from Smoky Lake pass, and the saddle, were never claimed, of course. There was peace on the north range.

These were happy days for Lucy Ware. She looked years younger, though her grey hairs had multiplied while Ted lay on the rim of the black shadow. She went about the house singing. Every little thing she could do for Ted gave her a pang of joy. She mothered him and fluttered about watching over him. She kept his room gay with the most beautiful blooms in the flower garden. And Ted read, and slept, and ate, and grew strong, and permitted his imagination to run riot regarding the wonderful ranch they were to have, and the money they were to make, and the trip they would sometime take—maybe clear to New York!—while Lucy sat with her needlework in her lap and listened in sheer delight.

Came the day when Ted first left his bed and sat in a chair by one of the windows. His eyes glowed with a fierce light of joy as he looked out over a land flooded with warm, summer sunshine. The grass about the front of the house was being watered and was a brilliant green; the rose bushes were splashed with white and pink and crimson blossoms; the tall, graceful cottonwoods murmured in the breeze, their leaves shivering; a blue veil of haze drifted over the basin, pierced here and there by the broad summits of pink buttes; a single string of fleecy, white clouds drifted in the sky like billowing sails of vagrant ships.

The boy drank in the beauty of landscape and sky with an eagerness that filled Lucy Ware's cup of happiness to overflowing. She hovered over him, adjusting the pillow at his back with little pats, tucking the robe in about him, employing those hundred and one little devices by which a woman can make a man comfortable.

Suddenly Ted sat up straight in his chair, looking down the road. Then he turned and exclaimed excitedly: "Go downstairs right away, Aunt Lucy. Somebody's coming."

When Lucy Ware had hurried down to the porch she saw Dorothy Sinclair dismounting near the steps.

"Hallo, Aunt Lucy," Dorothy greeted. "Can Ted see any visitors yet?"

"He's sitting up," said Lucy, going down the steps, her face beaming. "He saw you coming from the window and sent me scooting down to welcome you."

The faint roses in Dorothy's cheeks deepened in colour and she appeared confused for a few moments. "You know what you said about neighbours," she laughed. "Well, I came up to visit him as a neighbour."

"Come in, Dorothy," said Lucy, smiling, and led the girl up the steps. Before going in, however, she went to the end of the porch and called to the barnman to look after Dorothy's horse.

They went upstairs, and as Lucy ushered the girl into Ted's room Ted greeted her with a grin and sparkling eyes.

"You'll get skinned alive," he said cheerfully.

“What makes you think so?” said Dorothy, advancing to give him her hand.

“For coming up here,” Ted replied, giving the hand a hearty squeeze. “Your dad’ll just naturally kick out of the traces an’ run plumb wild.”

“Dad’s away up on the north range,” said Dorothy with something suspiciously like a giggle. “I waited till he was good and gone or I’d been up before.” She took a small glass jar from one of the deep pockets of her riding coat. “I brought you a jar of jelly,” she said shyly.

“Just what I need,” said Ted, nodding his head soberly. “I’ve been hankering for jelly for a week. That’s right good of you, Dorothy.”

Lucy, who brought up a chair for Dorothy, lifted her brows at this and looked at Ted quizzically. “He’s learning fast,” she thought to herself. And, inasmuch as the Lazy L root-cellar was half full of jellies, jams and preserves which she had been feeding to Ted daily, Lucy’s observation was not unwarranted.

Dorothy sat down in the chair. “I’m glad you’re getting well, Ted,” she said.

“If they’d let me out I bet I could take the humps out of a bronc right now,” Ted boasted.

Lucy Ware slipped out of the room and went downstairs smiling.

“How’s Balmer?” Ted asked.

Dorothy shrugged, as if mention of the S-S foreman was distasteful to her. “He’s out,” she answered. “Out and riding. I don’t believe he was hit so bad as he made out. I heard daddy tell him that they wouldn’t do anything to you for the—because of what happened. And then I had to put my fingers in my ears and hurry away from the door where I chanced to overhear them. Any man who would talk the way he did and swear so—well, I wouldn’t speak to him again if he was on the ranch for a million years.”

“There’s different kinds of swearing,” Ted observed philosophically. “It all depends on how you mean it, I reckon.”

“Do you swear, Ted?” Dorothy asked curiously.

“Not yet,” Ted answered. “But pa told me once that no man could hit his thumb with a hammer or live in the West without cussin’, so I suppose I’ll forget myself sometime. But not in front of *you,* Dorothy,” he added hastily with his old smile.

Dorothy’s roses bloomed again at his tone. “It’s awfully hot down in the basin,” she observed. “But it’s cooler up here.”

Ted laughed joyously. “You didn’t come up here to talk about the weather, did you, Dorothy?” he bantered.

“I thought maybe because you’re not outside you might be interested,” said Dorothy severely, covering her confusion.

“I’ll be out pretty soon,” said Ted, with a yearning glance out the window. “You know this was the first time I was sick in bed in my life.”

"Doctor Butler stopped at our ranch on the way back to Lamy and said it was a miracle you wasn't killed," said Dorothy.

Ted's eyes narrowed slightly. "Did your—your dad say anything about it?" he asked casually.

"No, but he looked serious when the doctor told us. I guess daddy didn't know you were hurt so bad. I came up to find out how you were and that made him angry, but he hasn't said anything since."

Lucy Ware came in with two glasses of an orange drink in which was cold water from the spring. It was as cool and refreshing as if it had been made with ice.

Dorothy stole many glances at her surreptitiously. She noted the kindly face that retained traces of a former beauty. And Lucy's voice was kindly, too; her manner frankly friendly. Dorothy decided that she liked her.

"You're taking awful good care of Ted, aren't you, Aunt Lucy?" said the girl.

"I'm trying to," said Lucy, with a quick look of interest. "He was cross as a bear when he first started to get well—which was a good sign—but he's his old young self again now. I guess he won't need any more medicine after your visit."

Dorothy stole a look at Ted and he winked openly.

"Dorothy an' I are just like that, Aunt Lucy,"

he said, crossing the first two fingers of his right hand.

Dorothy hurriedly finished her drink. “I’ll have to be going,” she said, without looking at Ted. “Daddy’s away, but he—he didn’t want me to ride far from the house—and they’ll miss me.”

Despite Ted’s protestations, she shook hands with him again and went downstairs with Lucy. The barnman brought her horse in response to Lucy’s call and soon she was riding down the road. Just as she reached the trees she turned and waved a hand toward the window where Ted was watching.

True to Lucy Ware’s prediction, the girl’s visit did Ted a world of good. Indeed, his progress now became so rapid that in less than a week he was walking a bit. Then Lucy and the coloured woman helped him down the stairs and he sat upon the porch. His strength came bubbling back hourly. He once more took his meals downstairs at the table. Then he was walking in the yard. At last the day came when he mounted his horse and took a short ride. From the time his feet touched the stirrups he was his former self. In a week he had ridden to the forest reserve range to see Buck, who shook his hand so hard he nearly shook him out of the saddle, and the cowpunchers waved their hats, cheered and rode wildly in circles about him.

August came and the range sweltered in heat.

The only relief came with the electric storms which broke suddenly and as quickly swept southward. Ted now was working with the outfit; but he always came in to the house on Saturdays and stayed over Sunday. He frequently rode down the lower meadows of a Saturday afternoon in hopes of catching sight of Dorothy, but he always was disappointed. In the first week in September, a week before they planned to take the cattle out of the higher hills, he saw her. He glimpsed her riding up the creek from afar and hastened to meet her.

Dorothy was sober to the point of solemnity this day. They dismounted and Ted looked at her anxiously after they had exchanged greetings and Ted had told her how he had ridden down many times in hope of seeing her.

"Daddy has been sticking close to the home ranch," she explained, "and I haven't had a chance to come out this way. I didn't want to make him angry again if I could help it. He is in town to-day making arrangements about me."

"About you?" Ted said with concern. "Why—what do you mean, Dorothy?"

"I'm going away," she said gravely.

"On a trip?" Ted asked.

She shook her head. "For all fall and winter—until next June. I'm going away to school."

Ted heard this news with falling spirits, and he couldn't think of anything to say.

"I didn't expect daddy to send me away until next year," Dorothy continued; "but he has changed his mind." She couldn't know that Nate Sinclair had decided that the best remedy for the girl's meetings with Ted was to send her away to school where he believed her new associations would cause her to forget the boy or to look at him as her inferior.

"Where are you going?" Ted asked dully.

"Somewhere in the East. I believe it's near Washington. But—I'll write to you, Ted."

"I reckon you will for a while," said Ted slowly, "an' then you'll sort of fall behind in letters. You'll be meeting a lot of fine people and fellows who—well, pa used to say that the West was a stone in the rough, but that in the East it was polished."

"Oh, Ted, I never would like those people better than my own kind of people out here," said Dorothy earnestly. "Don't you see? I *couldn't!* I was born here."

Ted shook his head. "I've been reading a lot, Dorothy. There's a thing they call environment. It's the place where you happen to be an' the people an' things around you. It changes folks. It'll change you. Just that one trip I took to Chicago with the cattle made some difference in me. They can't make a lady out of you because you're one already; but you'll—you'll get to look at things different. When are you going?"

"Next week," she replied. "Maybe I can come home for Christmas," she added hopefully.

"I hope you don't forget me, Dorothy," he said in the same slow voice. "I'll always be hoping that an' wishing you the best of luck. But—" He looked at her frankly. "I won't *have* you forget me!" he exclaimed. "I'm goin' to make sure that you don't!"

He stepped toward her and in a moment he had her in his arms. He raised her face to his and kissed her, and kissed her again. Then he released her and she stood with her breath coming fast, the roses in her cheeks fading.

"You shouldn't have done that!" she panted.

Then she ran for her horse and swung lightly into the saddle. There she looked at him again and Ted took off his hat. There was no smile on his lips.

"Good-bye," she said, and whirled her horse.

Ted Ryder stood, turning his hat in his hands by its big brim, until she was out of sight. Then he looked at the trees along the creek, at the sear, golden grasses of the far-flung plain, at the pink buttes swimming in a sea of purple haze, at the great, blue arch of sky, as if he had never seen them before. He took up his reins, climbed slowly into the saddle, and walked his horse up the long slope towards home.

Chapter XXIII

The White Spectre

They moved the cattle from the forest reserve range to the Lazy L the following week. The stock was in splendid condition. The hay had been cut, cured and stacked and a four-strand, barbed-wire fence built around the stacks. Lucy Ware figured the pay-roll with Buck's assistance, and Buck and Ted rode to the shipping point with Lucy's cheque and got the money for the pay-off. Armstrong, the banker, saw them outside the cage and came out to speak to Ted. He had heard of what had taken place, but he asked Ted about it nevertheless. Ted told him everything.

"An' if Levant hadn't nicked me I was goin' to send Aunt Lucy up to see you," he finished.

"Sinclair's going plumb daffy," was the banker's irrelevant expression. "How are the cattle?"

Ted let Buck answer this question. Armstrong looked at the Lazy L foreman keenly, appeared satisfied with what he saw and what he heard, and then turned back into the cage and passed into his little office in the rear.

Ted went to the post office, for it was here that mail for the ranch was received. There were some catalogues from mail order houses and one letter. Ted noted the postmark and his heart leaped. It was from Washington, D.C. He stowed the letter away and went out to join Buck for dinner. His mood had become so extraordinarily cheerful that Buck looked at him suspiciously.

"How long since you started hittin' the hard stuff?" Buck inquired. "I suppose you're turnin' from shootin' scrapes to likker."

Ted grinned at him amiably. "You're a nice sort, Buck," he said pleasantly. "You're a right good hand with cows an' you've got a fine head of hair. I reckon that's what your head's for, Buck—to grow hair on. You see, if you didn't have a good mop of hair your brains would freeze. Frozen brains is a very bad thing, Buck; *very* bad."

Buck stared at him. "Why, you danged yearling!" he exclaimed. "You get all shot up an' sit aroun' for a couple of months readin' books an' then you've got the gall to talk to me out of 'em. My brains are my own an' not somebody else's. I—"

The entrance of the red-haired waitress brought this banter to an end and Buck gave his attention to her.

They rode back that afternoon, arriving at the ranch just at dark, having made excellent time in both directions. Lucy proposed to pay the men off the next day and let the cowpunchers go for the winter, as was the custom. Buck said he and

Ted and the two old hands who were kept on the ranch could look after the cattle on the home range and attend to the feeding if it should be necessary. It was so arranged.

Ted waited until he was alone in his room that night before he took out the letter he had received. He opened it, sitting up in bed with the lamp on the small table at his side. There were two pages, written in a large, flowing hand. He looked at the signature at the bottom of the second page first, and smiled contentedly. Then he read:

> Dear Ted,
>
> I am in Miss Ayre's School for Girls on the outskirts of Washington and that is my address. It is very beautiful here, so many trees and flowers, although the flowers will soon be all gone. I ride every day although it's taking time to get used to the funny little saddles they have here. The girls are very nice to me and they ask me all kinds of questions about the West. They think our country is still swarming with Indians and that the men go around killing each other just as they please. I have to laugh at them. I bought heaps of new clothes and Miss Ayre herself went with me to see I got the right kind of things. There are no mountains here and I miss them. Sometimes at night I get

home-sick. I am taking piano lessons. Daddy brought me here and everybody was excited when they saw his hat and boots. They don't dress here like we do out there. I hope you and Aunt Lucy are well. I'm going to send you some books. I hope you will write soon.

Your friend,
Dorothy.

Ted put the letter on the table and stared straight ahead. New clothes and piano lessons. And they thought the men in the West went around killing each other just as they pleased! That was it. They would make Dorothy think that she came from a terrible place. Yes, Dorothy would change; she was *bound* to change. She wouldn't be able to help herself! But she had written, Ted exulted; and she hadn't written anything to show she was angry with him. He read the letter again twice before he blew out the light in the lamp and fell asleep.

The men were paid off the next morning and they drifted away, promising to show up in time for the horse round-up in the spring. Buck and Ted cut out such of the old stock which had been on the ranch when Sneed had bought the young cattle from Sinclair as was ready to ship. They drove this small herd down to the lower meadows. Ted went to his room early that evening and spent hours composing a letter to Dorothy. Next day, with the letter in his pocket for mailing, they started to drive the herd to the shipping point. There they sold the cattle to a stockman who was shipping to Chicago. Ted put the money to Lucy Ware's credit in the bank and they started home.

It was a cold morning, colder than usual for mid-September. There was no sun for the sky was overcast with a slate-grey sheet of cloud. In the north, this slate-grey darkened until ominous black clouds rolled along the horizon.

Buck threw a look over his shoulder and glanced at Ted. "Weather," he called laconically.

The black clouds mounted and then were hurled high in the sky. A grey veil crept down from the north. The wind freshened, came in gusts, and then blew with increasing violence, bringing the first of the snow. It became colder as the wind gained velocity, and then, when they were within fifteen miles of the Lazy L, the blizzard was upon them, howling, shrieking, spitting the stinging snow on their necks and faces, enveloping them in a blinding swirl of white. It was the first blizzard of the winter and Buck tried to remember one so early in the season that had shown so much ferocity.

They gained the ranch and Buck went out to inspect the cattle. The stock was on the south range and in a measure protected by the tall cottonwoods, pines and firs which broke the force of the wind to a considerable extent. No danger of the cattle straying down into the blizzard-filled basin. The snow covered the range and was drifting. But Buck went back to the house satisfied that the cattle were all right.

For five days the blizzard raged and when it finally abated the basin, hills and mountains were covered with snow—the peaks and high ranges never to lose their mantles of white until the following spring. It was very cold. Usually after the first storm, the warm, gentle Indian Summer of the semi-altitudes set in. But the north range waited for Indian Summer in vain. The sun shone for only a portion of each day; menacing clouds rode the skies; there were flurries of snow, biting winds, bitter cold mornings and nights. The old-timers on the ranch shook their heads and mouthed dire prophecies. The signs were all against a mild winter.

October came in with another storm which hurled its furies down from the north on Ted Ryder's birthday. But that didn't prevent Lucy Ware from arranging a big dinner, with a birthday cake bearing seventeen candles. All hands were invited. They made merry, showering Ted with congratulations, while the house rocked in the blast.

This second great storm was worse than the first. It lasted a week and brought zero weather.

It left a foot or more of snow on the range and the prediction of an early winter made by the old hands was confirmed. More snow fell and the cattle country began to wonder when the warm Chinook wind would begin to blow and clear the range. But no Chinook came.

To this day old-timers on the north range speak almost in whispers of that fearful winter when the white spectre stalked the range, bringing blizzard after blizzard in its wake; calling down the snows; beckoning to the icy winds; holding back the life-saving Chinook for which the stockmen prayed and looked for in vain.

The first week in December found the Lazy L beginning to feed. Before the month had ended the haystacks had dwindled to a point where it became necessary to arrange to buy baled hay. The snow was too deep for the cattle to get to the feed. The horses fared better for they would paw down to the grass. Then the weather moderated and the warm Chinook wind blew gently from the south-west. But the joy of the cattlemen was short-lived and the next change in the weather brought tragedy. When the snow had begun to melt the Storm King suddenly roused himself and the icy winds swept down out of the north vanquishing the south-west breezes and freezing the melting top-snow into a crust. This precluded the possibility of the cattle getting down to the grass. The losses began.

Buck and Ted drove into the shipping point and saw Armstrong. The banker was worried. He had big loans on cattle. Now, in order to protect his security for those loans, he had to keep the cattle alive. To keep the cattle alive meant that he had to loan money with which to buy hay. No stockman in that country raised enough hay to feed his herds through a hard winter when the feeding started as early as the first of December.

As Sneed had not pretended to go in for ranching on any considerable scale, there wasn't even a heavy wagon on the Lazy L. Armstrong arranged to finance the purchase of the wagon and the hay. Even then baled hay was bringing eighteen dollars the ton. Ted and Buck left the buckboard in town and drove back next day with a wagon-load of hay. Ted had another letter from Dorothy in his pocket, but in view of the emergency which confronted them it did not thrill him as had the first one.

Two weeks levelled the Lazy L stacks and they began to feed the hay purchased at the shipping point. January passed blizzard-ridden and February brought no better prospects. Again Ted and Buck drove to town.

"Have you had any losses?" Armstrong asked Buck in a worried voice.

"Near a hundred head of weaker stuff," Buck replied.

The banker shook his head and figured on a pad. "Every head of stock you lose increases the amount loaned on the others," he pointed out. "But there's no help for it. We can't control the weather."

So Ted and Buck drove back with another load of hay and another note for Lucy Ware to sign. After this the trips were made regularly through the balance of February and through March; and there were more losses.

Early in April came the tragedy that broke the heart of the stock country. The belated Chinook came suddenly, blowing cold at first, gradually becoming warmer until the icicles were running water and the snow was melting. In forty-eight hours the white carpet on the range had vanished and rivulets ran everywhere.

It seemed as though the grass turned green overnight. The sun shone warm and bright. Creeks and rivers swelled and flooded. There were bogs everywhere. The cattle were gaunt and weak. When a steer or cow got into a bog it lacked the strength with which to pull out, became hopelessly mired, and died there. Thousands upon thousands of head were lost this way. The other cattle, starved on scanty rations of hay that, in midwinter, cost as high as thirty dollars a ton, and which could not be procured at *any* price toward spring, fell eagerly to feeding on the green grass. This was worse than starvation; they sickened on the sudden effusion of green feed and died in more thousands.

It was the green grass which caused the Lazy L its greatest losses. There was no way to keep the cattle from it. Buck rode the range with Ted and all but wept at the sights which met their eyes. Everywhere the cattle were down—pathetic heaps of hide and bones. The bogs were few compared with those along the creeks and river in the basin; but those which did exist took their toll.

And in mockery of it all, the sun flooded the green land with golden light, the buds came out, soft breezes blew and the sky was flawless azure.

When, late in April, the remaining cattle showed sufficient strength to pull through, the count was taken. Only about a third of the splendid Lazy L herd remained.

Half of the men returned to the ranch but Buck kept only one of the men. He had no need for a full crew; nor was the money in prospect to pay them. The men understood and did not complain.

Lucy Ware alone remained cheerful. They had considerable stock left, she pointed out, even though they had lost two-thirds of the cattle. It was just as if they had started in on a smaller scale. She overlooked the business aspects of the situation, and Buck had not the heart to tell her. Trouble was no stranger to Lucy, but, since the shooting of Ted, her deadly fear that he might succumb to his wound, and his recovery, she no longer reckoned with dollars.

It was the second week in May when a visitor arrived in a buckboard. The barnman took charge of the horses, and Lucy went out on the porch to greet the man who walked slowly to the steps. It was Armstrong. The banker's face was haggard, his eyes seemed sunk in their sockets. He came up the steps slowly, as if he found climbing them a great effort, and nodded in response to Lucy's greeting.

In the living-room he put his hat carefully on the table and sank into a chair. Lucy looked at him anxiously. The man appeared positively ill.

"Miss Ware," he said in a halting voice, "if you have it, I'd like a drink of whisky."

Lucy remembered the scanty stock Jess Sneed had left, and hurried to comply with the banker's wish.

Chapter XXIV

Brands of News

Under the influence of the stimulant, Armstrong recovered himself somewhat, and the tired look in his eyes gave way to keen appraisal of Lucy Ware and the comfortable room in which he found himself. He poured another drink from the bottle Lucy had brought, but left the glass of liquor on the table.

"I rarely touch it," he explained, "but I've been driving about the country for days, and I'm pretty well spent. I'm going to ask you to give me some dinner before I start back this afternoon. Miss Ware, this range is ruined; or, most of it is. And I wouldn't be a bit surprised if I was ruined, too."

Lucy Ware regarded him with concern. "It was the winter, you mean?" she said.

The banker nodded. "I don't suppose it will do me any good to come up here," he said in a voice of resignation; "but I am visiting everybody whose paper I hold. You know, Miss Ware, I don't own that bank up there entirely. Some stock is held outside. And most of the money I've loaned has come from the East. Now these confounded Easterners are calling in their loans. I need money."

Lucy nodded dully. She hadn't given much

thought to the financial aspect of the situation.

"Just like them to jump on us at a time like this," Armstrong grumbled. "News of what we've gone through out here has been in the Eastern papers and scared 'em back there. They don't understand conditions here. I can call in my loans, but I can't get the money. If the cattle were here I'd be all right; but the biggest part of the cattle are gone. I had to feed the stock in an effort to protect my security, and the cost of hay put twenty or thirty dollars a head and more on top of my previous loans. Then the losses heaped a lot more on what cattle were left. If I had to take stock for the money I have out, I couldn't realise more than thirty cents on the dollar, I reckon. Most of the land is mortgaged, and you couldn't sell an acre in here now on a bet. I haven't had a sound night's sleep in weeks."

"I—I'm sorry," said Lucy hopelessly. The desperate nature of the situation was being brought home to her.

"Have you any idea how many cattle you lost?" the banker asked.

"Two-thirds of what I had," Lucy replied. "We couldn't help it. There was no way—"

"I know, I know," Armstrong interrupted with a wave of his hand. "And you haven't any money except the two thousand or more which remains on deposit with us."

"That's true," Lucy affirmed.

Armstrong looked at her thoughtfully. "I was thinking," he said slowly. "I was thinking that Sneed should have left some money. His—ah—operations were profitable, I believe. Of course, it's none of my business, and never was. It occurred to me—now you'll have to excuse my saying this, but you must remember this is a serious situation. I thought perhaps you—ah—might have some scruples about using any money Sneed left. But *lending* it would be a different matter."

Lucy Ware smiled wanly. "I don't doubt but that Jess left some money," she said. "In fact, I *know* he did, because he offered to pay Nate Sinclair cash for the cattle he bought from him. I wouldn't object to lending this money, an' I don't know as I'd have any scruples against using it. Jess gave his life for it in the end. But I don't know where it is!"

Armstrong was interested. "Do you think it's in a bank?" he asked. "He didn't have anything on deposit with me."

"No, I don't believe it's in a bank," Lucy replied. "It must have been around somewhere close or how would he have got all that cash for Sinclair? I think it is hidden somewhere on the ranch."

The banker took his drink from the table, downed it and pursed his lips. "I suppose you've searched the house," he ventured.

"From top to bottom," Lucy declared. "We

went over it soon after he was killed. Since then I've looked again in odd places, but I've never found anything. He never told me where it was, and he didn't leave any papers that would give me an idea. He was always more or less of a secretive man."

"Perhaps he buried it," Armstrong conjectured.

"Perhaps," said Lucy with a nod. "But what am I to do? Have the men dig up the whole place? I knew Jess well enough when he was alive to know now that he would put it somewhere where he could get hold of it in a hurry without having to use a spade or a pick an' shovel." Her face clouded. "Snark Levant thinks I know where the money is," she said bitterly. "I guess he thinks I've got it. He was here trying to tell me he was entitled to half of it. I think he got Ted out of the county jail and took him into the mountains thinking he'd be able to use him some way to get money out of me. Or he might have thought Ted knew. But *no* one knows, an' that's the truth."

Armstrong was thinking hard. Finally he shook his head and frowned. "I give it up," he said. "Much as I try, I can't think of a likely place where he would hide it. Sneed was a clever man. He wouldn't put it in any ordinary place. Such as the house or barn or root cellar or the like, I mean."

Lucy started slightly. She had overlooked the root cellar. There was a possibility that Sneed might have hidden his fortune there, but not enough of a possibility to warrant her giving the banker any hope by telling him that the root cellar hadn't been searched.

"He went to Morning Glory a great deal," said Armstrong. "They handle lots of hard cash in that bank up there. He might have some there. Have you made any inquiries?"

Lucy answered in the negative. "After I got the matter of the cattle payment fixed up with Sinclair I didn't think much about Jess Sneed's money," she confessed.

Armstrong leaned toward her. "There's another thing, Miss Ware," he said with more or less of an air of mystery. "What do you think! Nate Sinclair has never banked that cheque I gave you, nor has he presented it for payment."

Lucy was visibly surprised at this. "Why, I endorsed it an' gave it to him an' got the cancelled note."

"No doubt," said the banker. "I don't doubt that for a minute. I didn't think so much about it in the summer, knowing that he was busy on the range and one thing and another, but when it didn't show up all winter, I began to wonder. He has held that cheque for a reason. Did you tell him it was payable in cash?"

"He wasn't going to take the cheque at first," Lucy replied. "Said the agreement was that the note was payable in cash when presented. I told him what you told me to tell him—to present the cheque. An' I made him accept it." She smiled grimly at recollection of the interview in the S-S ranch-house.

"If he presents it now, he'll be out of luck," said the banker with a scowl. "An' so will I," he added gloomily. "Still, I don't believe he needs cash. He was hard hit last winter, and while he doesn't do any business with me, I happen to know he's the best off of any stockman in the basin. I believe he'd buy your ranch and take over your cattle to-morrow, if you wanted to sell—from what I've heard."

"Is that a hint, Mr. Armstrong?" Lucy asked. "Do you think I should sell? Do you want me to sell so I can pay off my notes?"

"I'm not advising you to," said the banker gruffly. "If you *did* it wouldn't help me so terribly much. There'd be time enough to think about it if Sinclair presented his cheque. At that, you might get help from one of the banks in Big Bend, although I wouldn't be sure of it. Suppose we have something to eat, and I'll start back to town. My trip up here was a sort of formality, anyway."

The weary look was again in his eyes, the tired note in his voice. Lucy hastened to see that he was served with a hearty dinner, for it was just after noon. When he had finished he took his departure.

No sooner was he gone than Lucy proceeded to the root cellar, which had been dug out of a knoll behind the house. She called to the coloured woman to help her, and between them they removed the vegetables from the bins and the jars from the shelves. Lucy searched every nook and corner of the place with the aid of a lighted lamp, but could find nothing. Next she dug in the walls and dirt floor, but her search remained futile. She knew now that she had no scruples about Jess Sneed's money. In the emergency which existed she only wanted to find it.

She had another idea as she entered the house. Sneed's room never had been occupied since his death. She took a sharp paring knife and went up to the room, carefully closing the door after her. She took the clothes from the bed and felt the mattress all over. Then she deliberately slit the covering of the mattress to pieces and explored the filling. Again her search was unrewarded. She sat down in a chair by a window and thought.

Her note at the bank was due in less than a month, as it was about a year since she had obtained the money with which to pay Sinclair. Armstrong would agree to renew it, she felt sure; but if the Eastern capitalists demanded a foreclosure she would be ruined, and she and Ted would be without a home. She shivered at the thought. There would remain but one thing to do—sell out to Sinclair. And she would have to do *that* before any proceedings were started; for if Sinclair knew a foreclosure was in prospect, he would refuse to buy in the realisation that his ends were to be accomplished anyway. Lucy hated the thought of surrender. Sinclair wanted them out of there. She could picture the satisfaction in his face if he succeeded in his designs. And yet, if she could save *some*thing— The old harassed look returned to her eyes. It was not her lot in life to enjoy any long period of happiness.

That night she wrote a note to the bank at Morning Glory making inquiry as to whether Sneed had an account there. Buck Andrews was sent forth at daybreak to deliver it, and return with an answer. During the rest of that day Lucy harboured her misgivings, obsessed with the conviction that the reply from the Morning Glory bank would be in the negative. The mining camp, she decided, would be the last place Jess Sneed would choose to bank money. If he *did* bank any, it would be in a place far removed from that locality.

Buck Andrews returned at dusk. He flung himself from the saddle, ran up the steps, across the porch and entered the open door as Lucy Ware came into the living-room.

"News!" he cried excitedly, tossing an envelope to the table with a shake of his head as if he knew its contents. “Morning Glory’s made! The experts have been there since the stain got thick three weeks ago. *They’ve run into copper, an’ the camp’s gone roaring mad!*”

Chapter XXV

Dame Fortune Smiles

Morning Glory was ablaze—afire with the wild enthusiasm, speculation and conjecture which follow a strike in a mining camp. Always this frenzy is intensified in a camp which has been revived, or in a ghost camp where the workings have lain idle for years. Originally a silver camp, Morning Glory had died when silver had "dropped into the sump"—to use a miner's expression. But some old-timers, working two or three of the mines on lease, had run into galena, a silver-lead ore, in paying quantities. Gradually the mines had been reopened, prospectors came back, and the camp once more thrived. That spring the Yellow Jacket shaft, which had been sinking through copper stain for some time, struck a vein of fine copper ore, and the boom was on.

Scouts from the great copper companies came, and down went the diamond drills. They disclosed an ore body that was not to be denied. Then the Consolidated Copper Mines and Smelting Company began to buy. A chief engineer came, and it was noised about that he brought a quarter of a million in cash. This figure, fed by rumour, swelled to proportions all out of reason. But the fact remains that the C. C. man, as he was known, *did* buy mines and claims for cash; and probably secured some bargains with the display of yellow-backed bills in lieu of a cheque.

Miners, prospectors, gamblers, and all the riff-raff that is drawn to a boom camp came by the scores. The head of the gulch and the sides of the hills were spotted with tents that gleamed like patches of snow in the sunlight.

"Another Butte!" went up the cry; and money flowed like water.

Ted and Buck arrived in Morning Glory about eleven o'clock the morning following Armstrong's visit to the Lazy L. They had started just before dawn. Ted had proposed to go alone, but Lucy had insisted upon Buck accompanying him. It was Ted's intention to learn what was going on in the camp, for, as the owner of a claim, he was interested in the strike. The note from the bank to Lucy had confirmed her fears. Sneed had nothing on deposit there. It occurred to her that he would not be likely to deposit any money anywhere in his own name—his right name—and she still believed that he had hidden his fortune, and had not entrusted it to a bank.

Ted was the recipient of many hearty greetings from citizens of Morning Glory who knew him by sight. He paid little attention to those whom he met, however. Having put up their horses in the hotel livery, they made their way up the hill to the house and office of Doctor Craven.

The doctor showed unmistakably that he was glad to see them. He had, in his own mind, taken the credit for having saved Ted's life—as he probably had—and he was proud of the big, strapping young fellow who gave his hand a squeeze that caused him to wince.

He looked at Ted reprovingly. "Remember, young man, that hand has to handle a surgical instrument now and then, and I want to keep the use of it."

Ted laughed. "I reckon I was glad to see you, doctor."

The physician could not conceal his pleasure. "I suppose you've come up to have dinner with me," he said, simulating a frown. "I don't know if my housekeeper has anything in the place to eat, or not. And you look like a pair that could clean out a kitchen in no time."

They all laughed at this. "No, doctor," said Ted; "we're not lookin' for free meals, although we'd be right proud to sit at your table. I came up because of what Buck heard yesterday. Have they made a strike up here?"

The doctor motioned them to chairs. "Yes," he said, "they have. They've struck copper. It looks good. The Yellow Jacket shaft is sitting on as pretty a vein of high-grade copper ore as ever slept in the ground."

"The Yellow Jacket!" Ted exclaimed. "Why,

that's just around the corner of the hill from pa's—from *my* claim."

"Quite true," the doctor nodded. "And I'm going to tell you something, and you mustn't get excited. You must keep your head, remember that every minute. The Yellow Jacket vein runs straight and true into your property. They've prospected up there, Consolidated Copper has, and I was about to send for you."

Ted looked wonderingly at Buck. It seemed too good to be true. He remembered having heard his father muttering about copper stain and other mineral indications, but he hadn't paid much attention to him. But there was *one* saying of his father's, repeated so often that it burned in his brain; and that was: "Some day, son, this is going to be a *camp!*"

"Now," the doctor continued, "I'm going to send for a man who wants to see you. I know this man, and I know he's all right. He's one of the most prominent mining engineers in the West, and an executive as well. But you must be careful to be calm and cool." He turned to his desk, wrote a note, enclosed it in an envelope, addressed it, and handed it to Buck.

"Take that down to the bank and hand it in at the teller's window," he instructed. "Then wait."

As Buck went out on his errand a man came into the office with his arm in a sling, and the doctor took him into his private office.

When Buck handed in the envelope the teller looked at the superscription, and took it into a rear room. Buck stood back against the wall, the teller returned to his cage, and in a short time a man came through a door at the rear of the space outside the cages and looked askance at Buck. There was no one else in the bank at the time.

"Did you bring this?" the man asked, waving a letter in his hand.

"From Doc Craven," Buck replied.

"All right," said the man, who was tall, bronzed, well-built, wearing riding breeches and boots, flannel shirt and a wide-brimmed hat. "Let's go."

They walked up the hill to Doctor Craven's place. The patient was leaving as they entered, and the doctor greeted the man cheerfully. Then he turned to Ted.

"Ted, this is Mr. Bronnell, representative of the Consolidated Copper Mines and Smelting Company. This is Ted Ryder, Bronnell."

The engineer shook hands heartily with Ted and turned to him again after he had been introduced to Buck, who took a seat by the window.

He looked Ted over critically. "Young man, you were built for an engineer if I ever saw one," he said admiringly. "But I understand you're in the stock business. I suppose I should be selfish and say I'm glad of it, because then you probably won't want to bother with that claim you have up north of here."

"I hadn't thought much about it," said Ted.

"Who's your guardian?" Bronnell asked.

"Guardian?" Ted looked puzzled.

"I don't think one has been appointed," Doctor Craven put in.

Bronnell pursed his lips. "Have to have a guardian," he said. "He's under age. Do you know someone you'd like to have as a guardian, Ryder?"

Ted looked at Doctor Craven.

"Not me," said the doctor, shaking his head. "I'm not enough of a business man."

Ted thought rapidly. His impulse was to name Lucy Ware, but, after all, she did not know so much about business. He would need sound advice. Then his problem solved itself quickly.

"I'd like to have Mr. Armstrong, the banker at the shipping point," he announced.

Bronnell looked questioningly at the doctor.

"Armstrong is absolutely square," said Doctor Craven.

"What's the name of this town and where is it?" Bronnell asked.

"The shipping point is Newton," Ted answered; "about forty miles from the foothills."

"All right," said Bronnell crisply; "we'll go down there in my two-lunger." He had reference to his small, battered car, the first that had been seen in Morning Glory.

Ted and Buck had dinner with the doctor,

and then Ted joined Bronnell at the hotel. Buck started for the ranch to tell Lucy Ware where Ted was going, that he was with Bronnell and might have to stay overnight at the doctor's or in Newton, and that he would come back to consult her as soon as the first part of his business was finished. Both Ted and Buck realised, before the doctor told them, that Bronnell was desirous of buying Ted's claim adjoining the now famous Yellow Jacket.

Ted and Bronnell arrived in Newton two hours after they left Morning Glory, and immediately went into conference with Armstrong, Ted introducing the Consolidated engineer. Armstrong listened to them and immediately agreed to become Ted's legal guardian. There were papers to be made out, and the court would have to appoint him.

"The court's in session now in Lamy," said Armstrong.

"Then we'll go down there," said Bronnell briskly. "And we'll get action to-morrow." He knew full well the magic of the Consolidated Copper Mines & Smelting Company's name. "I'll want to scout around a little down there to-night," he added, with a wink at Armstrong.

Thus Ted came to spend his second night in Lamy in the best hotel in the town.

Whatever Bronnell had done, and whoever he had seen, the result of his work was evident the next day, when the necessary papers had been made out and filed and Armstrong duly appointed Ted's guardian by one o'clock. The wheels of the law and the court had turned smoothly and quickly, greased by the magic of that name which stood for the greatest mining enterprises in the intermountain country.

They went to a room in the hotel after dinner, and Bronnell came to the point at once.

"The Consolidated wants to buy the Ryder claim," he said shortly.

"I knew that from the start," said Armstrong, "and I suppose Ted would sell if he could get the right price." He looked at Ted, who nodded eagerly.

"Of course the claim isn't developed to any extent," said Bronnell. "We should have to spend a lot of money on the property."

Ted caught Armstrong's eye. "It's hooked on to the Yellow Jacket where they've got the copper in sight," he said to the banker.

Bronnell favoured him with a keen look. "Do you know anything much about the property?" he asked.

Ted, of course, didn't know that the shaft had been examined, and that a diamond drill had been used down there without his permission.

"I heard the vein runs straight into my claim," he replied.

Bronnell turned his attention to the banker.

"Have you any idea as to the price you would ask?" he inquired.

"Oh, yes," Armstrong answered promptly. "But I don't know as we should hurry into this thing. It might be well to wait until we get a better line on the Yellow Jacket's ore body."

"We haven't bought the Yellow Jacket as yet," the engineer snapped out. "Of course we have an option, but unless we can get the properties we want we may decide not to purchase or develop. What price did you have in mind?"

"One hundred and fifty thousand dollars," Armstrong said slowly.

Bronnell raised his brows, while Ted gasped and stared at the banker.

"That's a price, all right and sure enough," said Bronnell with a wry smile. "But didn't you make a mistake by putting the hundred ahead of the fifty thousand?"

Armstrong smiled. "Nope. I'm a banker and I'm careful about figures. As a copper proposition, with a true vein in it—as there undoubtedly is—it's worth every cent of that and probably more. I'm not up as good on mining as I am on stock. And there's a proviso tied to the price."

"Let's hear it," said Bronnell shortly.

"We want the fifty thousand you mentioned in *cash;* and we'll want some of the other hundred thousand in cash from Butte. I suppose the Consolidated banks there."

"Yes," said Bronnell, "we bank there. Armstrong, I'll give you a hundred thousand."

Armstrong beamed. "It's all over but getting the approval of the court and signing the papers," he said. "You won't let fifty thousand stop you on a proposition you're ready to put a hundred thousand into. If you would, you'd not have the position you have with the Consolidated."

"It's my duty," said Bronnell, with a show of irritation, "to make as good a deal as possible for the Consolidated. I know my business, and I'll tell you frankly that the showing so far doesn't warrant paying a hundred and fifty thousand for the Ryder property. But I'll meet you halfway, split the difference with you, give you a hundred and twenty-five thousand, and you can *have* your fifty thousand in cash before your bank opens in the morning."

Armstrong sat looking out of the window. Twice he started to speak, but withheld his words. He looked at Ted, who nodded vigorously. But the banker knew his man. There was a chance that this would prove to be Bronnell's final offer. To refuse it might mean a wait of months before a sale was finally effected. And the banker did not doubt but that Ted would want to save the Lazy L if it came to a showdown. He owed it to Lucy Ware.

He turned on Bronnell suddenly. "All right," he agreed.

The sale was sanctioned by the court, the papers made out, signed and filed, a cheque for seventy-five thousand delivered to Armstrong, and the cash promised early in the morning.

They drove back, reaching Newton about half-past four. Ted went into Armstrong's office with the banker, while Bronnell waited.

"I want to pay our notes first off," said Ted stoutly.

"I had the right hunch!" exclaimed Armstrong, banging his fist on his desk. "Boy, you're a thoroughbred!"

So it was that when Ted left the bank he carried Lucy Ware's cancelled notes in his pocket. There was no mail. He rode off with Bronnell in his car to spend the night with Doctor Craven in Morning Glory and ride back to the Lazy L.

It was half-past five, a little more than half an hour after the departure of Ted and the engineer, when Armstrong looked up suddenly from his desk in his private office at the sound of a voice.

". . . and I'll take it in big bills!"

The cashier came into the office a few minutes later and put a cheque on Armstrong's desk before him. The cashier looked worried and waited anxiously while the banker looked at the slip of paper. It was the fifty-thousand-dollar cheque which Lucy Ware had given Nate Sinclair. It bore

Lucy's and Sinclair's endorsements, and it was Sinclair's voice Armstrong had heard.

"Tell him it's after hours," said Armstrong, handing the cheque back to the cashier.

A few moments later he heard Sinclair's voice again. It was high-pitched and angry. "What do you mean by after hours?" the rancher demanded harshly. "The bank's open, isn't it? Well, there's the cheque and I want the money. Where's Armstrong? Tell him I want to see him?"

When the cashier appeared in the doorway of the private office, Armstrong said quietly: "Show him in."

Sinclair came stamping into the office, frowning darkly. "What's the matter with that clerk of yours out there?" he asked in a loud voice. "I presented this cheque and asked for the money, and he said it was after hours. The bank's open and I'm here. That woman out on the Lazy L, as she calls the place, told me, when I demanded cash for those cattle, to present the cheque. Here it is." He held out the slip of paper.

Armstrong waved it aside. "I've seen it," he said. "In fact, if you'll look at it closely, you'll see that I *drew* it."

"All right," Sinclair snapped; "*cash* it."

"Didn't my cashier tell you it was after hours?" the banker asked mildly.

"Hours! What do you mean by hours?" Sinclair fumed. "The bank's open."

"There's a sign on the front window," said Armstrong in a slow, tantalising voice; "a gilt sign which says this bank's hours are nine to four except Saturdays, when the hours are nine to twelve."

Sinclair swore under his breath. "If your hours are nine to four, what're you doing open at half-past five?" he demanded.

"Oh, that's for the accommodation of our *customers,*" Armstrong explained with a cheerful smile.

"Customers, hell!" cried Sinclair. "Well, *I'm* a customer right this minute. I want this cheque cashed."

"You've held that cheque for nearly a year," said Armstrong softly. "How does it come that you need all this cash of a sudden at supper-time?"

"That's *my* business!" Sinclair barked. "Are you going to cash it?"

"We never cash cheques of any sizable amount after hours," Armstrong said cheerfully. "We stay open to receive *deposits*."

Sinclair looked about wildly and his gaze fastened on the window with such intentness that Armstrong wondered if he was going to jump through it. Then he turned on the banker.

"Look here, Armstrong," he said, striving to control his voice, "I'm a busy man and I can't be fooling around this way. I can't be running to this bank every few minutes trying to get this cheque cashed, understand? I need this money."

"And it took you 'most a year to find that out?" asked the banker.

"*I* know what's the matter," roared Sinclair. "You haven't *got* it! Your little tin-can bank is done, that's what."

"Then you must be out of luck," said Armstrong calmly.

"I'll get the State bank examiner up here!" Sinclair shouted.

"And if he doesn't know the way, get in touch with me and I'll tell him a short cut he can take," said Armstrong.

"Think you can bluff it out, eh?" Sinclair jeered. "Well, I'll tell you good an' plenty that *I'm* not bluffing."

Armstrong was looking at his watch. "Narin," he called.

The cashier appeared in the doorway, a joyful light in his eyes.

"We'll close now, Narin," said the banker. "Mr. Sinclair, here, will probably be in to-morrow."

Sinclair sputtered and swore. "I'll be in to-morrow in more ways than one," he promised hoarsely.

In the hotel he met Balmer, who had come to town with him as they were expecting a shipment of two carloads of stock the next day.

"I've *got* him," he told Balmer savagely. "He

couldn't cash the cheque. He hasn't got the money. I waited a year to catch him short. He put out the excuse that it was after hours and he only took deposits after hours. I'll be there *during* hours to-morrow and I'll bring him to terms. He'll foreclose on the Lazy L, that's what *he'll* do. I know that woman borrowed that money. Take it from me, Balmer, when I start, I finish. I gave her a chance an' she wouldn't take it. Now I'll see that she's thrown out an' that fresh kid with her, an' I'll get the ranch in the bargain!"

Balmer smiled contentedly as they went in to supper.

Early next morning a battered little car rattled and wheezed in and out of Newton. At nine o'clock sharp Nate Sinclair presented himself at the cashier's window in Armstrong's bank. He shoved in his cheque.

The cashier took up the cheque, examined its face closely, turned it over and studied the endorsements. Then he opened a drawer, put the cheque in it, and drew out four packages of bills. These he pushed across to the stupefied stockman.

"I think you'll find the amount correct," he said pleasantly. "Fine morning, isn't it?"

Sinclair gathered the packages of bills and gave the cashier a queer look. He walked out of the bank slowly, still holding the packages of bills in his hands. Balmer was waiting for him. He saw the strange look on Sinclair's face and noticed what he held.

"What's the matter?" he asked anxiously.

"Nothing," said Sinclair absently. "Nothing. I just—cashed a cheque." Then, recovering himself, he roared: "Say, you, go over and find out when those cattle are due before I fire you flat for meddling!"

Chapter XXVI

A Correction

Lucy Ware was dazed by the sudden turn in their fortunes. She, like Ted, had all but forgotten about the mining claim. That it should turn out to be the means of protecting them after the horrible experience of the preceding winter, with its financial entanglements, was hard to believe. She sat with the cancelled notes in her lap late into the night following Ted's return from Morning Glory with his stupendous news. Why, Ted was rich! Well, he would be richer some day; for Lucy had made a will leaving him everything in event of her death. As was the case with Ted, she had no relatives of whom she knew.

Wait until Nate Sinclair heard of Ted's good fortune! She wondered vaguely if it would change the stockman's attitude toward the boy. She did not know, of course, that Sinclair had learned the news in Newton that very afternoon before he had started back with the first shipment of his newly purchased cattle, with which he proposed to restock his range. The only effect the disclosure had had upon him was to make him more firm in his resolve to keep Dorothy and Ted apart. He had not permitted her to return home for Christmas, pleading the terrible winter and his trouble with the stock. But there would be no keeping her away from home during the summer vacation. He knew nothing of the letters that had passed between Ted and Dorothy.

Lucy finally burned the cancelled notes with a feeling of supreme relief. Once again the future was rosy-hued. They were clear of debt. She had told Ted he was a partner in the ranch. They had decided to play safe and not buy any more cattle that year. The next year they would be able to ship. Levant was gone and Lucy never expected to see him again; for his appearance in the locality would mean immediate action on the part of the authorities, as Sheriff Frost had declared. But Lucy was not a seer and could not foretell the future.

Early in June they had a visit from Armstrong, who looked a different man than he had looked on the occasion of his last visit. Ted's deposit in the bank had virtually saved it. Armstrong had been able to pay Sinclair and thus wipe that liability off the books. The increase in deposits for which Ted was responsible had impressed the Eastern capitalists, and when Armstrong had written them explaining the disastrous winter and the tragedy of the spring, and had directed their attention to the fact that foreclosures would mean a loss of seventy-five per cent, at least, they had granted extensions and agreed to give the stockmen a chance to recuperate.

Toward the middle of June Ted began to ride down to the lower meadows and even as far as the creek below the slope on S-S range. But it was the last week in that month before his eyes were greeted by the sight for which he had yearned—Dorothy Sinclair riding to the west range.

Now that the meeting was imminent he found himself suddenly beset with misgivings, almost afraid. What would Dorothy be like after her months in the East at the fashionable school to which she had been sent? For a wild moment he thought of taking flight, but he forgot his shyness when Dorothy reined in her horse beside him, smiling her old smile and holding out her hand.

"Dorothy," he said, taking the hand and holding it for a spell, "you look too good to be true."

"Thank you, Ted," she said with a light laugh. "I'm awfully glad to see you. Why, you've turned into a *man!*"

"Well, a fellow pretty near *has* to be a man in this country," he said with some embarrassment. "An' they've turned you out a—a young woman." He told himself that she was more beautiful than ever, and noted the smart riding habit and boots. Her manner had undergone a change, too. Yes, Dorothy was acquiring polish. She was a lady. "Do you—like the East, Dorothy?" he asked.

"It is very different there," she replied, "and it is very beautiful. Green grass and trees and flowers everywhere. But I was so glad to get home that I just cried. I read your letters over and over, Ted. They were good letters."

Ted flushed. He had spent much time and effort on those letters, and he was glad to know his endeavours were appreciated. And there was nothing in Dorothy's manner to indicate that she even remembered what had happened on the occasion of their last meeting, when he had kissed her. He wanted to think that since she had written to him first after going away, she had forgiven him and didn't resent his act.

"I wore yours plumb out reading 'em," he declared. "I couldn't always answer 'em as soon as I wanted because my trips up to town were irregular. I'll bet there wasn't any Eastern girl prettier than you!" His last statement came as an outspoken thought, and he was fearful as soon as he had said it as to how she would take it.

But Dorothy laughed merrily. "I'll tell you *one* thing, Ted," she said mischievously; "the Eastern boys are not the *only* ones who can spread the honey."

"I'm not spreading honey," said Ted, colouring through his tan. "I just happened to say what I was thinking. Are you coming up to see Aunt Lucy? She'll be tickled to death to see you. She likes you, Dorothy."

Dorothy's manner changed and her eyes became troubled. "I—I can't go up to see her, Ted. I'm—I'm sorry."

Ted appeared surprised and concerned. "Your dad told you to stay away?" he asked.

"No. That is—no, he hasn't." The troubled look deepened. "I'm no longer a little girl to be ordered about as I was, and daddy knows it. But, you see—well, there were some things I didn't know. But they've got nothing to do with *you,* Ted. I hear you've sold your mine and you're rich, Ted. I'm awfully glad."

But Ted wouldn't permit the subject to be changed. "If you haven't heard anything about me, except that mine business, then somebody—your dad, probably—has been telling you something about Aunt Lucy. Don't you think I'm entitled to know, Dorothy? You ought to play square with me and Aunt Lucy, so we can protect ourselves."

Dorothy had lowered her eyes and was twisting her bridle reins nervously. "It would only hurt you, Ted," she said in a low voice, "and it wouldn't help things."

"I don't see how anybody could say things about Aunt Lucy," said Ted soberly. "Why, Dorothy, she's pure gold, Aunt Lucy is. She never did a wrong turn to anybody in her life."

"But it might be that she did a wrong turn to herself," said Dorothy.

"To herself?" Ted's brow wrinkled in perplexity. "Tell me what you mean, Dorothy. Please." His tone was earnest; his look pleading.

“By—by living with Killer Sneed,” Dorothy said almost in a whisper. “It—of course it’s according to how one looks at it. But—” Her speech trailed off into silence—a silence which seemed to fall upon them like a dead weight.

Ted’s face slowly went white as he realised the import of her words. So *that* was what her father had told her. It was Nate Sinclair’s last weapon. And it was a lie. Suddenly Ted’s eyes blazed. Dorothy wasn’t looking at him. He started to speak, but the words would not come. He drove in his spurs and started at a mad gallop eastward toward the S-S ranch-house.

Nate Sinclair was just coming out on the porch when Ted rode up and flung himself from the saddle at the steps. The stockman’s face darkened as he saw him, but he had no opportunity to say what was on his lips. Ted bounded up the steps and confronted him.

“Inside,” said the boy crisply. “Inside—in your office. Do you hear me, Sinclair?”

Sinclair saw that the youth’s lips were trembling with anger and his eyes were blazing from between narrowed lids.

“Are you *going in?*” Ted’s words crackled on the still air. Sinclair was dumbfounded. Then Ted’s right hand moved fast as light and his gun was in his hand. He struck Sinclair in the face with the barrel and it flashed back to his hip, covering him.

Sinclair staggered back, more astounded than hurt, and backed through the door into the hall and his office.

Ted looked at him, his face white and working, his eyes fiery points of passion as the tempest surged within him.

"I've taught you to lay off of me," he said, standing close to the rancher, "an' you know it won't do any good to try any dirty work on me." He paused to gain control of his voice. "Now you'd knife a woman behind her back. I know what you told Dorothy. Lucy Ware is worth a million like you. She's square, do you hear me? *She's square!* She's pure gold. Now do you want to know the truth? *Do you want to know the truth?*"

He thrust the muzzle of his gun into Sinclair's ribs, and his eyes narrowed to slits.

The stockman instinctively raised his hands, his face going a shade paler.

"What—do you want to tell me?" he managed to get out.

"*I'll* tell you," rang Ted's voice. "I'll tell you an' you'll believe it, or I'll bore you as sure as the sun's shining. You lied to Dorothy! You lied about Lucy Ware behind her back to hurt her and to hurt me. It was plain dirt, Sinclair. You won't fight like a man. Do you know why Lucy Ware is up on that ranch? Do you know why she has lived there these years? I'll tell you. *Lucy Ware was Jess Sneed's wife!*"

Sinclair's eyes widened, clouded with doubt, came clear as he saw the truth blazing from Ted's orbs.

"Why didn't they tell anyone?" he asked.

Ted lowered his gun and stepped back. "They had their reasons. You ought to be able to figure it out. But anybody can know now, an' if you want proof she can give it to you."

There were footsteps on the porch, and a moment later Dorothy Sinclair stood in the office doorway. Ted's gun had flashed back to its holster.

"Tell her you lied," he commanded, facing Sinclair.

"It was natural I'd be mistaken since nobody knew," said the rancher.

"That's good enough," said Ted and, turning his back on Sinclair, he pushed past the girl.

As he reached the porch, Lute Balmer, who had seen Ted ride to the house with Dorothy following, came up the steps to see what was going on. Ted bounded across the porch and his right hand shot out. His fist caught the foreman flush on the jaw, and he went backward to the ground, where he rolled over and then began to crawl on his hands and knees, dazed.

Dorothy and Sinclair came out, and Dorothy started forward with a little cry. But her father held her back. He was staring queerly at Ted, who now ran down the steps and jerked Balmer to his feet. He held the foreman off, shaking him, and when the man had recovered he pushed him back three paces.

"You drew on a crippled man once," said Ted grimly, "an' you started all this trouble, I reckon. Tell 'em who drew first that day on the Lazy L when you got shot. Tell 'em, Balmer; tell 'em who went for his gun first. If you don't want to tell 'em—*draw!*"

Balmer's enraged gaze was tempered by a light which was not the cool light of bravery. He wet his lips and stood motionless.

"Tell 'em!"

"I drew," said Balmer through his teeth.

Ted's hand darted to his gun. He stepped forward and jerked the foreman's weapon from its holster. He broke it, strewing the cartridges about, and flung it to the ground. Then he turned to his horse, coolly took up his reins, mounted, and without a look back rode around the corner of the house and turned west.

Chapter XXVII

A Pact Is Broken

Ted did not tell Lucy Ware—by which name she was ever known in that country, even after the details of her marriage with Sneed became public property—anything about his wild visit to the S-S. He went out on the range late that afternoon and insisted upon remaining with the cattle, although Buck Andrews pointed out that one man, let alone three, could keep an eye on the depleted herd.

The boy's anger had cooled on the way back to the Lazy L; but not for so much as a single instant did he regret what he had done. Sinclair had been unfair. Ted could see, however, how the stockman could easily be mistaken, as many others were; and he realised that Sinclair lived for Dorothy. She was not only the apple of his eye; she was life itself to the grizzled rancher. But this did not shake Ted's determination to see the girl every chance he got. He wondered what she thought of what had happened. He certainly had not appeared at his best. He had been crazy with rage because of the attack on Lucy Ware. His greatest satisfaction came from the memory of his meeting with Lute Balmer. Well, both Sinclair and Dorothy now knew the truth.

But if Ted Ryder could have witnessed what happened on the S-S after his departure that day, his grave look would have melted into a glow of supreme content.

As he had ridden away around the house, Balmer's white lips parted to let out a string of oaths. He crouched and swore with a venom that made his black, distorted features the image of Satan himself.

Dorothy Sinclair shook off her father's hand on her arm and went quickly down the steps. She still held her riding-crop. Her face was the colour of white rose petals; her fine eyes were flashing.

"This is twice you have used the language of your breed in my presence," she said, and struck Balmer across the face with the riding-crop. "Now you can go!"

She went back up the steps and into the house.

Balmer, his tongue stilled, his face suddenly ashen, looked up at Nate Sinclair with a foolish grin. But he found no comfort in the stockman's steel-blue gaze. He mumbled something.

"You're through," said Sinclair sternly.

"Through?" Balmer blinked as though he failed to grasp the meaning of the rancher's words. "You mean I'm let out right in the middle of the season? After all I've done—"

"You've done enough," Sinclair interrupted. "You lied to me about that shooting up there. You showed the truth in your eyes and the white feather at one an' the same time this afternoon. An' no man on this ranch can curse before my daughter."

"But—" Balmer bit off his speech. He saw by the look in Sinclair's eyes that the rancher never had been more in earnest in all his life.

"You can pack up while I'm getting the money to pay you off," said Sinclair, turning on his heel. "I'll give you an extra month," he called back over his shoulder, entering the house.

Balmer, stunned by the rapid march of events, gathered up the scattered cartridges, retrieved his gun, loaded it absently and thrust it into his holster. He stared vaguely at the door. No use. No power on earth could move Nate Sinclair, once he had made up his mind. He was through. *Through!*

Nate Sinclair sat alone on the porch in the twilight after supper. Dorothy had gone for her evening ride. She loved to watch the sunset from the benchland. Sinclair's thoughts were of Lucy Ware. Not for a moment did he doubt what Ted had told him. She would tell the boy, of course. She had probably told him after Sneed had been killed. Well, it was like Sneed to marry Lucy. In many ways The Killer had been a man of principle. And Sinclair forgave Ted his actions of the day. He was young and impetuous. And he was absolutely unafraid. That impressed Sinclair more than anything else. "Gad!" he exclaimed to himself, slapping his knee. “He’s got it! The kid’s range stock, sure enough.”

Ted and Buck rode in to the ranch-house early on the third of July. Lucy regarded them suspiciously because of their beaming countenances and air of mystery. But when she surprised Ted in the act of getting out his finery—his best hat and boots and holiday clothes—she remembered the date and knew what it was all about.

“Buck an’ I are goin’ to Morning Glory for the Fourth,” Ted confessed. Then he had a sudden inspiration. “Why, Aunt Lucy, we’ll take you! We’ll go in the buckboard; that is, you an’ I’ll drive up in the buckboard behind the greys, an’ Buck can ride his horse an’ act as escort. That’s what we’ll do, Aunt Lucy,” he said with enthusiasm. Then he had recourse to his Chicago vocabulary. “Lay out your glad rags, Aunt Lucy,” he sang. “We’ll see the contests an’ the fireworks an’ you can stay at Doctor Craven’s place. He’s got an awful nice housekeeper. She’s a lady. I met her. You haven’t had a holiday in a month of Sundays, so get ready.”

Lucy demurred, hesitated, refused, wavered and finally gave way to Ted’s enthusiasm.

It was still dark when they were up in the morning, getting ready. Lucy had some good clothes, and she had jewellery that was the envy and despair of the prairie matrons. Never had she looked better than on this morning when, just before dawn, she drove away with Ted in the buckboard and Buck Andrews "breaking trail" ahead. They swung around the slope and by half-past nine had reached the Morning Glory road. The horses took the road at a smart trot, disregarding the gradual climb, and a few minutes before noon they were in the camp.

Morning Glory was bedecked with flags and bunting; crowded with merry throngs making carnival. Every old-timer who saw Ted saluted him and called a greeting. Ted was exceedingly popular because his sale of his mining claim had given the Consolidated the last property they had wanted, and now the development work had started in earnest. Although he was young in years, Ted found that he was regarded as one of the pioneers.

Doctor Craven gave them a great welcome, and his housekeeper, Mrs. Lawrence, took Lucy in charge. It was Ted who told the doctor that Lucy Ware was really Lucy Ware Sneed.

"My boy," said the doctor, "I guessed as much long ago."

During the celebration this news got about, and Lucy found herself treated in a friendly and sympathetic manner on every hand. She went to the drilling contests and other sports with Mrs. Lawrence, and enjoyed herself as she hadn't enjoyed herself since she first came to the hills.

Buck, who had ridden up on one of the best horses the Lazy L could boast, entered the horse race and finished first with three lengths to spare, while Ted bet every cent he and Buck had brought along, together with all Lucy had in her purse, and fifty dollars borrowed from Doctor Craven. He hadn't learned to write cheques, or he might have broken half of Morning Glory's sporting element flat and fair.

They watched the fireworks and went to the dance, where Ted, easily the handsomest youth in the hall, had no difficulty in procuring fair partners to teach him the steps. At two o'clock in the morning they finished with a sumptuous supper at Doctor Craven's house on the hill. Lucy was shown to her room, happily tired, by Mrs. Lawrence, and the doctor put Ted to bed on a couch in the little parlour, while Buck slept on the horsehair sofa in the doctor's office.

At three o'clock in the morning the dance was still in progress and high revelry was the order in the various resorts. Thus the arrival of a score or more of mysterious horsemen who rode into the space behind the Mother Lode resort was not noticed. They dismounted quickly and left their horses with reins dangling so they would stand, one man staying to watch the mounts. The others tied handkerchiefs just under their eyes, and then they moved, half to the front and half to the rear door, as by a prearranged plan.

The revellers in the "Mother Lode" were suddenly startled by the appearance of masked men, armed in each hand. Hoarse commands were shouted and charges of buckshot from shotguns shattered the lamps. Guns flashed flame in the darkness, but the light still burned in the little front office.

Three of the men had leaped over the bar. Two were taking the silver and bills from the cash boxes and stowing it in stout bags. The third, a slight man with beady, black eyes shot with a cruel light, drove the proprietor into the office. He pointed to the safe with the barrel of his gun.

"Open it!" he commanded. "Open it quick or you'll stop hot lead! *I'm in a hurry!*"

The proprietor had recognised Snark Levant despite the outlaw's mask. The old Sneed gang had come at last! He didn't hesitate. He opened the safe with trembling fingers. As he stood up, Levant knocked him aside with a blow of the heavy barrel of his gun. The man fell sprawling in a corner. Shots roared in the resort, cowing the revellers. Levant scooped package after package of bills into a sack, struck the lamp from its wall socket, and leaped outside. A shrill whistle, and the outlaws were out of the place, firing a final volley. Sneed himself could not have done better than Levant on this last, desperate attempt to gain a fortune on the north range.

Men ran out of the resort shouting as the

echoes of flying hoofs died away down the road. Sheriff Frost, who had come up to be on hand in event of disturbance during the celebration, was on the scene in less than two minutes, running from the dance hall. His deputy arrived just as he turned from the frightened, wailing proprietor of the "Mother Lode." In another two minutes the formation of a posse was in speedy progress.

Frost hurried up the hill to Doctor Craven's house. He knew Ted was there; had seen him and spoken to him during the day before. He pounded on the door and roused Buck.

"Where's Ryder?" the sheriff demanded.

At that moment Ted, also awakened by the sheriff's arrival, came out of the parlour with a lighted candle.

"Listen," said the sheriff sharply. "Levant's been here with his crowd. They cleaned out the 'Mother Lode,' and I guess there's some men shot down there. He got clear away. He won't hit for Canada. They're looking for him up there. He'll try to cross the big range. You know the trail, Ryder; you know his hang-out up there. I want you to come with us, and we're starting *now*."

Ted's eyes flamed. Levant had raided a place in Morning Glory. He had broken Jess Sneed's solemn pact with the authorities not to molest the north counties.

"I'll go," he said. Then, turning to Buck: "You take Aunt Lucy home an' tell her not to worry."

Fifteen minutes later Sheriff Frost and Ted rode at the head of a posse which thundered down the road on the trail of the man who had betrayed Killer Sneed's trust.

Chapter XXVIII

A Round-up

At the point where the broad trail leading to the Ryder mine joined the Morning Glory road the posse turned north. Ted led them past the mine, across the meadow where his father was buried—a spot which Bronnell had promised would never be disturbed—and along the foothill trail. As he had travelled the trail many times, he had no difficulty in finding its junction with the trail leading to Smoky Lake pass.

Here he called a halt and dismounted. It required the light of but one match to show him the tell-tale imprints of the hoofs of many horses, freshly made, all indicating that a body of horsemen had recently ridden up that trail.

"You were right, sheriff," he said cheerily as he swung back into the saddle. "They're making for the pass and no doubt intend to go on over the Divide. We'll give 'em a run for their plunder."

He swung into the lead and they proceeded at the fastest pace with which their mounts could negotiate the slopes and ridges.

Ted wondered if Levant had known that he was in Morning Glory for the celebration. He could easily understand the outlaw's reason for selecting the early morning of the day after the Fourth for his raid. He would know that the "Mother Lode" had done a tremendous business, not only on the Fourth, but on the night before and during the night and early morning after. There would be a large sum in the safe and cash boxes. Moreover, it was generally known that the "Mother Lode" *always* carried a large sum of cash to protect its games, and especially the private games which were held in the rooms in the rear of the place, and in which the stakes often ran into four figures. But if Levant had had a spy in town; if he knew that Ted was there; would he not suspect that Ted might be induced to lead a posse to the rendezvous near Smoky Lake? There was the chance, of course, that he didn't know, or hadn't taken Ted into consideration. In this event he was liable to stop at the rendezvous to change horses, get something to eat, or even to get two or three hours of rest. Then Ted experienced a thrill. With the Divide to cross, Levant and his men would *have* to change horses if they were intending to make any sort of time.

Dawn flickered and glowed in the east and the light of day spread swiftly over the hills. Ted and the sheriff looked down at the trail with grim smiles. The fleeing outlaws had left their signals in the dust and on the hard dirt stretches as plainly as would have been the case if they had stuck red flags along the path of their flight.

And there were two thoughts in the minds of both Sheriff Frost and Ted: Flush with the success of his first big raid, Levant, in his exultation, might become careless; and he undoubtedly lacked the natural ability and wily cunning which had been Sneed's.

The sun was up and well started on its climb in the eastern sky when they entered the forest. They rode single file, nearly forty of them—men who did not propose that Morning Glory should be taken as an easy mark at the birth of its new prosperity. Many of the men had carbines in the scabbards on their saddles. All were grim-faced, and a majority were men of the saddle, cowpunchers from the basin and north prairie country, who would welcome a fight with shooting irons as a fitting climax to their brief holiday.

Back in Morning Glory the Craven household was astir. Lucy had not awakened when the sheriff had come for Ted, nor had Mrs. Lawrence. The doctor had got up and had found Buck holding the candle, after closing the door on Ted and Frost. Buck had explained, and in the morning they had fold Lucy. She had not exhibited any particular tear, knowing that Ted was with the sheriff and the posse as a guide. And in her heart she didn't believe they would find Levant and the other outlaws. It was the climax of Levant's operations thereabouts. Surely they were rid of him for ever, whether he was captured or killed or not. She started back to the Lazy L with Buck in the buckboard. Ted had taken Buck's horse.

Higher and higher into the mountains rode the posse, and now that ugly gash in the high range below the Divide known as Smoky Lake pass could be seen from the summits of the climbing ridges. It was some time before noon when they reached it. They approached it warily, thinking there might possibly be a look-out there; but there wasn't. They clattered through the defile and started down the steep trail on the western side of the range. Ted had been talking over his shoulder, telling the sheriff about the location of the rendezvous. As he had been unconscious when the sheriff had visited the ranch after Levant had shot him, Ted had been unable at that time to describe its location. By the time he was able to talk, Frost knew practically for certain that Levant was in Canada and so had lost interest in the mountain retreat.

The word had been passed back that they were nearing the place where they might find the outlaws, and members of the posse were holding guns and carbines in their hands. Finally they rounded a turn where the trail flattened out. Ted raised his hand and signalled. Then he spurred his horse, the sheriff and another beside him, and galloped for the entrance to the rendezvous.

They dashed into the defile between the rock

walls with one of the posse who had drawn somewhat ahead in the lead. A shot rang out, and this man slumped in his saddle, his horse plunging on. Both Ted and the sheriff fired at the man who was running for the meadow, and he went down on his face.

The horse ahead turned off in the meadow, its rider slipping from the saddle, and then the remainder of the posse swept into the rendezvous. They divided, half going on each side of the creek, and rode madly up the long meadow. Their first glimpse of the cabins showed men running and staggering about. Horses, saddled and bridled, were standing with their reins down. A man came lurching out of a cabin firing blindly in the air. And then Ted knew! When in the Mother Lode resort the outlaws had helped themselves to bottles of the fiery brand of liquor served there. In their enthusiasm over their success they had started drinking. They had doubtless stayed in the rendezvous longer than they intended. Now half the band were drunk!

The two divisions of the posse closed in; carbines roared and pistols barked. Some of the posse slipped or toppled from their saddles. Riderless horses dashed about wildly. The outlaws tried to take refuge in the rear of the cabins. Many went down before the deadly fire which the posse poured into them. Others stood unsteadily in the doorways of the cabins, holding up their hands in token of surrender. The fight seemed likely to last less than three minutes.

Ted gasped with surprise as he saw a well-known figure running wildly toward a horse. It was Lute Balmer! The former S-S foreman had in some way got in touch with the band and had joined up with Levant. Possibly he thought that in that way he might secure revenge on Ted; perhaps on Sinclair, too. Even as these thoughts raced through his brain, Ted saw Balmer go down, first on his knees, then backward on the sward, to lie still.

A shadow streaked along the north side of the meadow. Ted whirled his horse and dashed in pursuit. Through the trees he glimpsed a rider speeding like mad for the opening to the rendezvous. His heart came into his throat with a bound as he recognised the familiar figure of Snark Levant in the saddle ahead.

When he came out of the trees at the lower end of the meadow Levant had disappeared. He raked his horse with the steel and fairly flew through the rocky defile. One look beyond the entrance showed the open country to the west by Smoky Lake to be free of any visible human. Ted started up the trail to the pass. He looked down as he rode and soon saw the fresh tracks left by Levant's horse. He pushed his own mount as he had never called upon a horse on an up-trail before. As he reached the pass a gun roared in the defile and a bullet sang past his ear. Then he saw Levant in the centre of the pass.

The outlaw's gun came up and spoke as Ted reined his mount sharply to the left and answered Levant's fire. He missed. And now, as Levant fired again without effect, the outlaw's horse showed that same unreliability under fire it had exhibited at the Lazy L the day Ted had been shot. It reared as Levant once more fired, causing the bullet to go wild. The animal came down stiff-legged and spoiled the aim of Levant's fifth shot. Then, instead of saving his sixth and last cartridge for a more favourable opportunity, Levant, whose face showed that he was in a frenzy of rage, uncertainty, and acute disappointment, fired again and saw Ted, who had rested his gun in the expectation of a capture, ride up to him and cover him with his weapon, smiling unpleasantly.

The shooting over, Levant's horse quieted down, champing at the bit. The outlaw held his empty gun at his side, his breath coming hard.

"I reckon you forgot something early this morning when you pulled that raid in Morning Glory," said Ted quietly.

Levant didn't answer. His eyes appeared dull, as if it was hard for him to realise the suddenness of the catastrophe which had fallen.

"You forgot your trust with Jess Sneed," Ted went on. "You broke the pact with the sheriffs of the north counties. That was my main reason for taking your trail with the posse."

Levant found his tongue, the cruel look returning to his eyes. "*I* had no pact with *any*body," he shot through his teeth. "Whatever arrangement Sneed had was ended when he died. An' he threw us out before that. So you're doin' this on Sneed's account? An' him dead an' gone? We didn't do any worse than *he* did time after time. Who do you suppose taught me this game? Do you think he would have let you lead those hell-hounds after me if he'd been alive? Tell me that!"

Ted frowned. "You were warned out of this part of the country," he said. "An' you tried to kill me. That's enough reason for me helping to round you up."

"But you brought Sneed an' his agreement into it at the start," Levant snarled. "Now I'm goin' to tell you what kind of a man you're stickin' up for. You remember the morning your dad was killed?" He leaned on his saddle-horn and fixed Ted with a steady gaze almost hypnotic in its intensity.

"Your dad spoke to this fellow Buck at the livery barn that morning," Levant continued in his hissing voice. "Told him he was too good or something like that to travel with us. This Buck, who's on the Lazy L now, told Sneed. Then Sneed led us up to your place. He wanted to get even with your dad. He got off his horse and went up where your dad was. *Then* what?" Levant's lips curled. "Why do you suppose Sneed took you in hand; took you back to his ranch an' looked after you? Because he wanted to hand out charity?" The outlaw's eyes glowed with black cunning as he saw he had Ted vitally interested. He laughed scornfully.

"He took you under his wing because he didn't feel none too good over what he'd done that morning," Levant declared in a loud voice. "He thought maybe he owed it to you to look after you. Why? Because when your dad sassed him back *he threw him down the shaft!*"

Ted sat his horse as if turned to stone.

"*That's* why your great god Sneed and his woman took you in," Levant jeered. "An' now you'd turn me in on account of the man who murdered your father!"

"I don't believe it," Ted said in a low voice.

"No?" sneered Levant. "Well, ask your side-kick, Buck, what took us up there that morning. He'll tell you every word your dad said to him. He'll tell you that he told Sneed. He'll tell you, unless he lies, that that's what sent us up there that morning. Ask *him* if he believes your dad *fell* down the shaft. Do you reckon an old miner like your dad is goin' to fall down any shafts? Sneed got mad an' *threw* him down, I tell you. I got off my horse and crawled up there to find out what was goin' on, an' *I saw it!*"

Ted's brain was in a turmoil. Was this true? And did Lucy Ware know about it? Was it really the reason why Sneed had taken him in.

He came to himself with a start. "Take off your gun-belt an' throw it on the ground," he ordered; "an' hand over that saddle-bag you're packing."

Levant looked straight into Ted's eyes for a space of several seconds. Then he unbuckled his cartridge-filled gun-belt and tossed it down.

"The gun, too," Ted commanded.

The outlaw's weapon dropped. He held out the saddle-bag, and as Ted grasped it he suddenly kicked Ted's horse with all the force he could muster. Ted's mount shied and turned. By time Ted had the animal in hand, Levant was galloping out the east end of the pass.

Ted spurred his horse through the defile and saw Levant riding down the trail at a perilous pace, his horse slipping and sliding on the rocks. Levant was risking his neck to gain his liberty.

The boy could not bring himself to fire at the unarmed outlaw. He was strangely averse to going in pursuit. His thoughts kept reverting to what Levant had told him. While he waited in indecision, Levant gained the shelter of the trees below and disappeared. Ted turned back through the pass.

Chapter XXIX

End of the Tether

Ted returned to the rendezvous, where he learned that nine of the outlaws had been killed, five wounded and seven taken prisoners. Three of the posse had been killed in the fight and five were wounded. Balmer was dead, he ascertained. It was the most serious clash between outlaws and a posse in the history of the north range.

It was some little time before Ted could draw the sheriff aside and tell him of Levant's escape. He told him exactly what had happened, but he made no mention of what Levant had told him about the death of his father. He handed over the saddle-bag which Levant had carried and, as he had expected, it was found to contain a good share of the loot taken from the "Mother Lode." The other outlaws had been searched and a large sum taken from them. The sheriff believed they had recovered all the plunder. He looked after Ted curiously as the youth turned away and walked to the cabin where some of the posse were cooking a meal. Had Ted permitted Levant to escape? The sheriff shrugged. In any event, Ted had guided them to the rendezvous, the band was broken up, and Levant could hardly expect to raise another following in that country.

Ted allowed his horse three hours of rest before he informed the sheriff of his intention to start back to Morning Glory.

"We'll be along some time to-night," the sheriff said, consenting to his departure.

Ted was a prey to his tortured thoughts on the way back. There had been much logic in what Levant had told him. Why, indeed, now that he looked back upon it, had Sneed taken him home? Was it because of remorse for having murdered his father—if he *had* murdered him? And did Lucy Ware know; had she known from the beginning and befriended him for that reason? It altered his position in the Lazy L household, in his mind. He felt that he would never be able to ask Lucy Ware for the truth. If Levant's story were true, he would never feel at home on the ranch in the future as he had since the death of his father. And did others know about this thing? Why hadn't Levant told him when he was a prisoner in the rendezvous? Perhaps the outlaw had thought that it would turn him more than ever against the band. Ted resolved to have a talk with Buck Andrews when he got back to the ranch. He could talk to Buck about this thing, for, if what Levant had said had been the truth, Buck was the one man who could substantiate the outlaw's story.

Ted arrived in Morning Glory about ten that night. He put up his horse and went directly to

Doctor Craven's house. He told the doctor what had happened in the rendezvous, but gave no details of Levant's escape. Then he went to bed for a well-earned rest. In the morning he got his horse and started for the ranch without taking the trouble to inquire about the arrival of the sheriff with the wounded and prisoners. He reached the Lazy L shortly after noon and told Lucy Ware in laconic sentences what had taken place. Lucy noted the sober change in his manner and ascribed it to what he had seen in the rendezvous of the outlaws. After dinner he changed his clothes and went out on the range to see Buck Andrews. Buck, too, had to be told of the events of the day before, and then Ted drew him to the shade of a cottonwood, persuaded him to dismount and sit down beside him on the grass.

Slowly, and with infinite detail, Ted recited the story told him by Snark Levant. Buck listened closely, and when he had finished he brought his right fist smashing into his left palm.

"Levant's a liar!" he exclaimed. "*I* was the one who got off my horse and climbed up to see what was doing. I don't know what the talk was about, but just as I got up there I saw your dad make a jump for a rifle that was there, stumble, an' fall into the shaft. That's gospel truth, Ted, an' I reckon you know me well enough so you could tell if I was lying."

The light came back into Ted's eyes as Buck

described that night in the Mother Lode resort when Ted's father had defied Snark Levant and Sneed had saved him from Levant's fury. He made clear what Ted's father had told him next morning—that he seemed too clean-cut a chap to be in such a business.

"I told Sneed, yes," Buck confessed readily. "But you've got to remember, Ted, that Sneed got me out of a heap of trouble an' I was running with the bunch, although I hadn't been in any raid. I suppose I was the cause of it all, but I told Sneed because I thought it was sort of a joke—me supposed to be lookin' so clean-cut an' all that. Sneed took you home because, whatever else they say about him, he was generous and he had a good heart in a lot of ways. An' you bet he told Lucy Ware exactly how it happened. You don't want to let this worry you *now*."

Ted looked at him with a smile. "Buck, I don't blame you a bit for *any*thing," he said earnestly; "an' I believe every word you've said. I should have known that Levant was lying."

"No, you shouldn't," said Buck, shaking his head. "It all sounded reasonable enough. He told you that thinking you might let him go, or that he could get you sort of bewildered with thinking about what he said an' catch you off your guard; which he did, in a way. But I can tell you that nobody believes Sneed killed your dad. He had notches in his gun, all right, but he always let the other man start for his smoke wagon first. A stunt like this wasn't his style."

Ted put out his hand and Buck grasped it warmly. Then they rode out on the range.

In the hills behind the Lazy L ranch-house a rider sat his horse on a ridge commanding a view below. He had a thick stubble of black beard, this rider; his eyes were sunk in caverns, but they gleamed fiercely. It was Snark Levant. He had started north the day before, but as he rode the anger had swelled within him. At first his chief thought had been of escape; but he nursed a grievance against Lucy Ware and Ted Ryder that rapidly became a passion of intense hatred. He was without a gun and with only a modest sum of money in his pockets. His band was gone. He told himself he had been betrayed; and his warped mind soon placed the blame on Lucy Ware. He had turned in the night and crept back to the Lazy L. From his point of vantage he had glimpsed Ted and Buck on the range to southward. Now he started down the ridge, an evil smile on his thin, drooping lips.

It was nearly sunset when Lucy heard a light step upon the porch and looked up from her needlework in the living-room, expecting to greet Ted on his return from the range. But the smile on her face froze as Levant glided across the porch, opened the screen door swiftly and entered.

Lucy's right hand went into her work-bag as Levant spoke.

"Didn't ever expect to see me again, did you?" he sneered. "Well, you're seein' me for the last time. For all I know now, it's maybe the last time you're seein' *any*body. This isn't any social call. An' I haven't got much time." His eyes gleamed menacingly.

"If you'd had any sense you'd have cleared well and away from here when you had the chance," said Lucy calmly. "For all *I* know, Ted let you go thinking you'd do just that." She looked in vain for sign of a gun on the outlaw.

"That double-crossin' kid let me go?" Levant snarled. "He brought those hounds into the mountains. An' it's a fifty-fifty bet you told him to do it." His face was black with rage.

"I didn't," said Lucy. "But I'd have told him to do it if I'd known. Levant, what do you want?"

"You know what I want," he said through his teeth, "an' I'm entitled to it. Sneed left plenty of it. Money! That's what I want an' what I'm goin' to have. The gang's busted up an' I've got to slope a long ways. You've got to come through, girl, or—" He paused, his features working convulsively.

"Or what?" Lucy asked sharply.

"Or I'll choke it out of you!" Levant exclaimed, striding towards her.

Lucy Ware's right hand came out of the work-bag. There was a glint of the barrel of the little gun as it came up on a level with Levant's heart. Then a dull click and Levant leaped upon her, wrenching the gun from her hand, knocking her against the back of the chair. The gun had missed fire!

Lucy's face went white while Levant, breathing hard, his lips drawn back against his teeth, stood over her.

"You'd—kill me yourself!" he panted in a frenzy of rage. "That makes it easy. You'll hand me a stake to leave on, or I'll kill you with your own gun!"

He drew back with the look of a maniac in his eyes. Then he remembered something, and, keeping watch on Lucy, he turned to the top drawer of a cupboard across the room. Sneed always had kept a gun in that drawer. He jerked it open, and a weird cry like that of some wild animal gurgled in his throat. His hand went into the drawer and came out grasping a forty-five. He looked at Lucy in triumph, and the little, pearl-handled weapon went crashing through a window.

"I told you I was in a hurry," he said, fondling the big pistol in his hand. "I'm goin' to get money or I'm goin' to get even. How'll you have it?"

The horror of the situation made Lucy dumb. Levant was desperate—crazed with rage. He would never believe that she didn't have Sneed's lost fortune. It would do her no good to protest that there was no money in the house. She would have to resort to a ruse. But her brain seemed numb before the menace in Levant's blazing eyes. He might shoot. He probably *would* shoot. He had forgotten everything except her and the money he thought she possessed.

"How'll you have it?" Levant repeated in an uncanny voice.

"I'm—I'm thinking how to get the—the money," Lucy said, sparring for time. "It isn't right handy. Let me think. I—" She broke off her speech as the clatter of hoofs came from the courtyard.

Levant tensed. Then he ran to the door with the light-footedness of a cat. As he opened the screen door and stole out on the porch, Lucy regained the power to move. She left the chair and ran to a window opening on the courtyard, a choking sensation in her throat. She screamed hysterically. She had never touched the gun Sneed had left in the drawer since his death; and she knew it was loaded.

Ted Ryder, who had dismounted, whirled as he heard that scream and saw Levant leaping from the porch. Even as he landed on the ground the pistol in Levant's hand shattered the silence. But Ted had leaped to one side and down on his left knee, his gun whipping into his hand. He fired twice with such rapidity that the shots seemed to come almost as one.

Levant stumbled and turned clear around, his gun spurting wild bullets. Ted deliberately shot again, true to the mark. Levant crumpled in a heap with a bullet in his heart.

In the living-room, Lucy Ware slipped to the floor by the window in a dead faint.

Chapter XXX

A Barbecue and—

The news of the manner of Snark Levant's going spread like wildfire through the basin, on the north range, and in the hills. Ted Ryder was marked for a hero. But Ted had ceased to wear his gun, except when he was on the range, where he might have occasion to use it in an emergency.

Lucy Ware once again was happy. With the passing of Levant, the menace that had long hung over the Lazy L was removed; the thread of the old life was broken. She put all thoughts of the money Sneed was supposed to have left behind aside, and, as a matter of fact, it never was found. Two weeks after the death of Levant, an incident occurred which filled her cup of happiness to the brim.

She was sitting on the porch in the early afternoon when a horseman came riding up the road in a cloud of dust. It proved to be Nate Sinclair. He dismounted by the steps and came up on the porch, taking off his hat and wiping his brow with his handkerchief.

"Getting mighty hot," he observed; and a stranger would not have known from his tone but that he and Lucy were old, old friends.

"Yes," said Lucy, at a loss to account for this unexpected visit. "It's very warm. But, then, it's July."

"That's right—it's July," Sinclair nodded. "You know, Miss Ware—that's what everybody calls you—I sort of did you an injustice awhile back an' it has rankled lately. You see, I didn't know—I—well, I didn't know you an' Sneed had been married, an' I made a remark that got to young Ryder's ears through Dorothy. But that young devil soon set me right! Dast me if he didn't come down to the ranch so fast that the dust couldn't keep up with him, tap me on the nose with the barrel of his six-shooter, stick it in my ribs with the hammer back ready for business, an' make me chew an' swaller that remark. An' I had to tell Dorothy I was plumb mistaken in the bargain. I suppose he told you about it."

"No," said Lucy, her eyes shining brightly. "He didn't tell me."

"Well," said Sinclair, "you might tell him I came up here to-day an' told you I didn't feel any too good over my—mistake. There's been a lot of misunderstanding on this range of late, but I've always aimed to be square. I got foul of my own rope for a while, but I reckon it's all straightened out now."

"This is—good of you, Sinclair," said Lucy, looking straight ahead with a mist in her eyes. "I'll tell Ted, and I know it'll make him happy."

For a long time after the stockman had gone, Lucy sat with her hands in her lap enjoying the sensation of having received an apology from the most powerful rancher in the basin, and one who had been an enemy.

Ted winked at her across the table when she told him that night. "It's a good sign," he said.

Lucy suspected a hidden meaning in his remark, but she made no comment and asked no questions.

Dorothy rode up to visit them after that, and came again before she left for the East in August to visit a schoolmate. She did not return before her school opened.

Fall came with a long Indian Summer, and the winter which followed was normal. Ted and Dorothy corresponded regularly, and she came up to see them as soon as she returned home in the spring. Ted noted more changes in her manner, for Dorothy was taking on the polish he had predicted. But there was no artificiality, no affectation about her. They saw each other often during that summer and Ted soon forgot there was a matter of education between them. Dorothy went East early, as she had the year before.

The Lazy L shipped beef cattle that fall and went into the market and bought; for Ted, now as good a cowman as Buck Andrews, decided to restock their range to its limit. Armstrong agreed to this. The cattlemen were getting on their feet.

They had an open winter and the stock thrived wonderfully. The next summer Dorothy did not return to the S-S. She spent the summer with friends in the Adirondacks and the Thousand Islands. Sinclair had sanctioned it, but he finally went East to see her in August. He found it lonesome on the big ranch.

Another good winter favoured them. Ted and Dorothy continued to correspond. She was to graduate that next spring. She didn't return home for Christmas. Ted was hungry for a sight of her, yet he harboured his misgivings as to their next meeting. What would she be like? Not his sort, of course. Gradually he became obsessed with the conviction that he had hitched his wagon to a star. But he forgot everything except that he was writing to Dorothy when he composed his letters. And long letters they were, with bits of range philosophy and much wit, and a subtle hint now and then which conveyed a message of his regard for her. He never failed to receive an answer promptly, and this fanned the flame of the hope in his heart.

Morning Glory's boom became solid prosperity. The Consolidated was pouring millions into the development of its big property and shipping copper ore. A branch railway line to run from Newton to the camp was under construction. Armstrong's bank was thriving as it had never thrived before. The stock country had come into its own again and land values had increased. Lucy Ware had insisted that Ted accept a half-interest in the ranch, and he was regarded as a rich young man.

On a day in June Ted learned that Dorothy Sinclair had returned to the S-S. He took to riding down to the lower meadows, looking forward to their first meeting, yet also shrinking from it. "What will she be like?" was the question he kept asking himself. It was never answered. And then one day Dorothy came riding up the slope and met him just as he emerged from the trees on the way down.

Ted caught his breath. Dorothy had blossomed into womanhood, ravishingly beautiful.

"Hallo, Ted," she greeted.

"Hallo, Dorothy," he said.

And then they looked at each other. Dorothy saw a tall, handsome, splendidly-formed youth who sat his saddle with a bewitching natural grace. And Ted saw, in his mind—an angel.

"How—how long are you going to stay, Dorothy?" he asked, rather foolishly.

"From now on," was her reply.

Ted's eyes widened. "You're not going back East?" he asked incredulously.

"Nope," she said with a toss of her head. "I'm going to stay out in this country where there's 'nothing and yet everything,' as you said in one of your letters. Anyway, I've graduated, so *there*." She favoured him with her old smile.

Ted's heart skipped a number of beats and made up for them all at once. He swallowed hard. "I thought you liked the East better than this country," he said. "You stayed there all last summer."

Dorothy laughed softly. "Oh, Ted," she said, sobering. "You're a frazzled goose. Do you know why I stayed away from home last summer, and why I didn't come back for Christmas vacations? Of course you don't. You wouldn't guess it in a million years. I stayed away on purpose so that when I *did* come back, father would never want me to go away again."

Ted's heart did a flip-flop. "You'd rather be here?" he said.

"Of course, silly. Let's get down and sit on the grass. But since you've become a real stockman, as dad says you are, I don't suppose you have time to bother with wandering females who have little else."

"I'd take time to sit down with *you,* Dorothy, if my whole range was afire," declared Ted.

"Well said!" Dorothy exclaimed, clapping her hands. "In the East, Mr. Ryder, a gentleman usually assists a lady to dismount."

In a twinkling Ted was out of his saddle and handing her down. A thrill shot through him at the touch of her. When the thrill was gone he found it had taken along much of his shyness. He was ready for another.

"I can't tell you how glad I am to see you again," he said as he dropped upon the clean grass beside her. "About the only real pleasure I've had while you've been gone was reading your letters an' answering them."

"You write wonderful letters, Ted," she said dreamily.

"Now don't start stringing me," he protested.

"You're one man I wouldn't think of stringing, Ted Ryder," she said softly, looking him full in the eyes for a few moments. "Your letters have made me know you better than you know yourself." She put a hand on his arm and the thrill was back, tingling in every fibre of his body. "Why, I know what you're thinking about this very minute!"

He looked at her aghast. "Then you must think I'm an awful chump," he said, colouring through his tan.

"Maybe I don't, Ted," she murmured.

He looked at her quickly, but she lowered her gaze. "Why, say, Dorothy," he said, his voice growing bolder; "if you knew what I was thinking about, you know how much I think of *you.*"

"Is 'think' the word, Ted?" she asked softly.

He took her hands, his eyes shining. "No, I'll be doggoned if it *is,* Dorothy," he said with great earnestness. "I reckon I'm brave enough to tell you that you've got my heart and soul roped and tied. I'm dead an' gone in love with you!"

Dorothy put her mouth to his ear. "That's one of the reasons why I'm so glad to get back, Ted, dear," she whispered.

In a moment his arms were about her and he was kissing her, holding her close as if he never intended to let her go. And as Dorothy's arms crept about his neck she didn't seem to care whether he ever let her go or not.

They went up to see Lucy Ware and told her. Lucy clasped the girl to her breast and kissed her cheeks and hair. She never could remember what she said to them. She watched them ride away with happy tears in her eyes.

It so happened that Nate Sinclair was in his office when Ted and Dorothy reached the S-S ranch-house. They crossed the porch, entered the house, and went into the office, Ted going ahead. Sinclair looked up and started as he saw Ted. He looked from one to the other of them and leaned back in his chair. Dorothy's cheeks were glowing with colour, her eyes mysteriously bright. Ted stood straight; his hair, the colour of a ripe chestnut, was ruffled; his face serious.

"You haven't been here in a long time," said the stockman smoothly. "Seems to me I *remember* the last time you were here. Did you want to see me about anything in particular?"

Ted had flushed slightly. "I was—sort of

excited the last time I was here," he said. "An' I'm more excited *this* time, although I'm trying not to show it. I want to marry Dorothy, Mr. Sinclair."

The rancher sat up with a jerk. "Why, you young bandit!" he roared. "You come here an' rap me on the nose with your six-shooter, an' poke it in my midriff an' threaten to blow me out of my skin, an' try to get my foreman into a shootin' match so you can kill him, an' now you've got the nerve to try an' steal my only daughter!"

"I'd rather not have to steal her, Mr. Sinclair," said Ted, holding his own. "I'd rather take her with your permission."

"Oh, you *would,* would you?" said Sinclair with a terrific scowl. "An' you're using the 'mister' as a handle to my name to-day. Don't you know my daughter wouldn't marry you if you were the last man on earth?"

Dorothy's eyes sparkled as she waited for Ted's answer.

"If I was the last man on earth I'd pick Dorothy out of all the women in the world," he said quietly.

Sinclair's fist came down on the desk with a bang. "Slick!" he exclaimed. "Native cunning! Dorothy, would you marry this cowhand, who just missed being a train-robber or something worse?"

"Yes, daddy," said Dorothy sweetly.

Sinclair rose, a twinkle in his eyes. "Well, Ted, I reckon you're too dangerous to have running loose outside the family, so I guess I'll take you in." He smiled as he held out his hand.

Another June came with its radiant skies, its flowing green of plain, its golden sun, its flowers, and its sweet scent of growing things. The Sinclair ranch-house was a well of blossoms and the front porch was nearly smothered in them. There were crowds in the courtyard and on the lawns. Far and wide the news had been sent that Ted Ryder was marrying Dorothy Sinclair and that Nate Sinclair wanted every man, woman and child on the north range who could walk, ride, or be carried at the S-S for the ceremony and the monster barbecue. And they had come. Cattle barons, their wives and families, cowpunchers, mule skinners, miners, prospectors, gamblers and preachers, school teachers and section hands—and all were made welcome.

Lucy Ware was there in magnificent new finery, and with the only genuine rope of pearls in Northern Montana about her neck; Doctor Craven and Mrs. Lawrence were there; Armstrong, the banker, was there; Sheriff Frost was there with all his staff, including the county jail turnkey; Bronnell of the Consolidated had come clear from Butte; Buck Andrews was there, all smiles and importance in his capacity of best man; every

Lazy L cowpuncher was there, as well as the barnman and the coloured housekeeper; scores were there from Morning Glory. The front lawn looked like a cattleman's convention, for the popularity of Nate Sinclair and his reputation for "doing a thing up right" when he *did* do it, was a tradition of the range.

Dorothy had never looked so beautiful as she did this day in her bridal dress and veil. Ted was worth a second look from any man, a third from any woman. Nate Sinclair was the soul of hospitality and good cheer.

"By gad, she picked a stockman," he boomed whenever the opportunity offered.

It was noised about that the bridal pair would take a wedding trip to New York; and it was known they would make their home on the Lazy L.

Dorothy and Ted were married on the porch before the big throng at noon. Then came the barbecue and the wedding "breakfast," and within an hour the newly-wedded pair were driving away in a buckboard behind the two highest steppers the S-S could boast, bound for Newton and the railway. Scores of cowpunchers circled about the buckboard, and scores of handkerchiefs fluttered on the lawn about the house.

Nate Sinclair and Lucy Ware stood on the porch and watched until the buckboard bearing Dorothy and Ted was out of sight.

"By George!" Sinclair boomed. "I'll have to send a man to town to bring that team back. I plumb forgot about that."

Lucy Ware's happy laugh rippled like the music of a waterfall.

"An', by Jupiter!" Sinclair exclaimed. "There's a bottle of wine down cellar that's been there since the last white man was scalped. I plumb forgot about that, too. Come on in, Lucy, an' we'll drink Mr. an' Mrs. Ryder's health."

He led her smiling into the house.

Center Point Large Print
600 Brooks Road / PO Box 1
Thorndike, ME 04986-0001 USA

(207) 568-3717

US & Canada:
1 800 929-9108
www.centerpointlargeprint.com